"I've got one!" Elizabeth shouted

"Don't give him any slack!" Matt shouted back.

Right, no slack, Elizabeth thought, let the fish run. No, reel him in. No, wait. What *was* she supposed to do?

In an instant, Matt was behind her. Holding the rod with one hand and steadying her hand on the reel with the other, he held her in a tight embrace as he guided her movements. "Let him run," he directed her. "Steady now. Okay, the line's going slack. Reel him in. Now, let him run again. That's right. Good. That's the way...."

As the fish began to tire, Elizabeth noticed that Matt's hips were pressed tightly against hers. She could feel his involuntary reaction to the pressure. She also noticed that the fish was no longer really fighting and that Matt could have released her if he wanted to. But he didn't.

She twisted her head so that she could see his face, and her heart began to race. He was looking at her, too, and he was not smiling. Their eyes locked. Elizabeth swallowed convulsively, and her tongue darted out to moisten her lips for the kiss she knew was coming....

ABOUT THE AUTHOR

"I've lived in twelve states and had twenty different jobs," says Patricia Chandler. It was in Oregon, though, where she was the director of an art gallery, that she first began to write. "We lived in a small town," Patricia recalls, "and it was dead all winter. Not a single person came into the gallery. So I just sat there, working away at my typewriter. That's when I realized I could do it—become an author."

Currently, Patricia lives with her husband in Arizona, where she plans to stay put for a while. She has two grown daughters and four stepsons.

Deception Bay

PATRICIA CHANDLER

Harlequin Books

TORONTO • NEW YORK • LONDON
AMSTERDAM • PARIS • SYDNEY • HAMBURG
STOCKHOLM • ATHENS • TOKYO • MILAN
MADRID • WARSAW • BUDAPEST • AUCKLAND

Published February 1992

ISBN 0-373-70489-5

DECEPTION BAY

To Peter,
who helped me write this story,
and to Ron,
who told it to me

PROLOGUE

A MAN AND A BOY stood on the edge of a rocky bluff overlooking the Old Coast Highway. Below, an ancient station wagon lumbered protestingly up the narrow, winding road.

The boy glanced anxiously upward. "Do you think that's her?"

"Could be. She's supposed to arrive today." The man's eyes remained fixed on the struggling automobile.

The two were a study in contrasts. One was tall and blond, with a close-cropped beard that was several shades darker than his yellow hair. The other, much younger, was short and dark, his obviously Oriental features subtly muted by the light brown of his hair and eyes. Alike were the expressions on their faces—apprehensive and wary—as they watched the highway from the seclusion of the wind-sheared pines that covered the bluff.

The station wagon lurched to a stop at the junction of two gravel roads, then made a sharp left turn toward the ocean.

"That's her, all right," the boy announced. "Look, she's going up to the old caretaker's quarters. And the license plate says—" he sounded the words out with painstaking accuracy "—La-nd of Lin-coln. Land of Lincoln?"

"Pretty good, Tran." The man rested his hand on the boy's shoulder as together they looked down at the struggling automobile. "Land of Lincoln. That's Illinois. And what I can't figure out is why anyone would come all the way from Chicago, Illinois, to disrupt the lives of people she doesn't even know."

"It's far away, Chicago, Illinois?"

"It's halfway across the continent. And in a lot of ways it's even farther than that. The people—" he searched for the right words "—they live different lives."

"Different? How?"

"Well, for one thing, they do different kinds of work there."

The boy looked incredulous. "They don't fish?"

"Oh, they fish, all right—some of them. On weekends, when the weather's good, in yachting caps and brass buttons. No, they conduct the business of the world in cities like Chicago, Tran. But they don't fish much."

"Cities? Like Ho Chi Minh City? I remember..."

The older man, too, remembered Ho Chi Minh City, the rubble that had once been Saigon. "No," he said briefly. "Nothing like that."

"Why is she coming here, anyway?" The boy returned to the subject at hand. "Doesn't she know she is not welcome?"

The man smiled ironically. "I'm very much afraid, Tran, that she's coming to drag us kicking and screaming into the twentieth century!"

CHAPTER ONE

NOT ALL THE LIGHTHOUSES along the rugged Oregon coast were tall and imposing. Some were squat and unassuming, their beacons cheerful and friendly, their foghorns shrill and piping. Deception Head wasn't like that. It stood exactly as it had stood for over a hundred years, in solitary and decaying majesty, its pyramidal white tower rising full-blown out of solid rock.

There was something gallant about a lighthouse, Elizabeth La Salle, lately of Lakeshore Drive in Chicago and currently of an ancient, overloaded station wagon, thought as she pulled the station wagon to a creaking halt in the patchy sea grass of the cape. Something indomitable. This one had stood on this windswept headland for over one hundred years, unsung but faithful, warning a century of anonymous sailors on nameless ships of the dangers of this treacherous coast.

Elizabeth got out of the car and walked to the edge of the cliff. The gale force of the wind whipped her hair across her face and plastered her clothes against her body like a damp second skin.

A hundred feet below, the surf pounded restlessly against the base of the cape. Far out to sea she could see a few fishing boats, mere dots on the shimmering surface of the water, and farther out, the fog bank that perpetually spanned the horizon.

The lighthouse itself was surrounded by a tall hurricane fence and No Trespassing signs. Through the fence Elizabeth noted the white paint streaked with rust, the brambles climbing the frame of the heavy iron storm door, and the wild, thorny roses that clustered around the foundation. The windows had been sealed with concrete when the Light was decommissioned, giving it a blind, brooding look.

A few hundred feet to the left, the intermittent sun glanced off a slanted gray roof almost hidden among the wind-sheared pines. That would be the caretaker's cottage, her home for the summer.

She turned and walked back to her car—her parent's car, actually, which she had borrowed because her own sporty little convertible was too small to carry everything she needed for this journey. The station wagon was idling fitfully.

Time enough later to enjoy the solitude of Deception Head Light. Just now, she had driven two hundred miles on a highway meant for mountain goats, her car was overheating, and she could use some lunch.

She coaxed the station wagon into gear, then lurched off to find the Coast Guard station in the town of Deception Bay.

"I WISH YOU'D RECONSIDER, Matt." Behind the desk, the man in uniform put on his most persuasive tone. "It's only for the summer. What've you got to lose? Hell, she'll pay you as much as you make hauling fishermen around—and it'll be a whole lot easier."

"Sorry, Milt." Matt McCullough was cheerfully adamant. "Why not try someone else? Maybe Jory at the icehouse?"

"Jory!" Captain Milton dismissed him with a contemptuous gesture. "I told the lighthouse people I'd give her a hand, not get her drowned! Besides—" his voice fell sheepishly "—I already asked Jory. And everyone else I could think of. They all feel the same way you do. They don't want her here and they're not going to make it any easier for her to stay."

"Can't help you, Milt. Wish I could."

"No, you don't." Captain Milton slouched down in his swivel chair and shoved his hands into the pockets of his summer whites. He eyed Matt darkly. "She's not going to go away, you know, just because you all refuse to help her. She's got the Lighthouse Society behind her, and the U.S. government to boot. She'll just find some out-of-towner, from California, no doubt. C'mon, Matt, as a friend."

The reference to California wasn't lost on Matt. The rivalry between Oregon fishermen and those from California was well known. Milt was bringing out the big guns!

"You're a good friend, Milt. But you're not from around here—"

"And it's damn glad I am of that, too! You people are the most provincial, the most *uncompromising* bunch I've ever had the misfortune to work with! I sometimes wonder if you even realize you're part of the United States!"

"And you'll be transferred to another duty station in a few years," Matt continued doggedly. "But those of us who live on this coast will still be here, and we'll be stuck with the results of what this woman is trying to do."

"What's so terrible about what she's trying to do? Paint a few pictures, sell a few books—what's the harm?"

"It'll advertise us," Matt stated tersely. "That's what's so terrible. You know what that kind of publicity will do to the way of life here. More people will come, and more will stay...."

"You know, Matt, the whole world isn't massing on Oregon's borders, waiting to sneak in the minute your back is turned!" The captain's smile took the sting out of the gibe. "But speaking strictly as a non-Oregonian, I must admit I can't see why that would be so bad. It's going to happen sooner or later. *You* must know that, even if the old-timers don't."

"Of course I know it. I just rather it were...later."

The rattle of the doorknob interrupted Captain Milton's brusque reply. The woman who stood framed in the doorway was a stranger, and because there were no strangers in Deception Bay, Captain Milton knew immediately who she was. He moved quickly to his feet and straightened his rumpled tie. "You must be Mrs. La Salle," he said, extending his hand. "Welcome to Deception Bay."

Early thirties maybe, Milton thought, sizing her up. Ivory skin that made him think of his wife's heirloom porcelain, the underlying bone structure as fine as one of Melanie Milton's fragile china cups. Hair an exotic contrast—night-black, cut in a sleek, boyish style that barely cleared her collar.

It was the only thing boyish about her. Superbly made—round in all the right places and long, show-girl legs, set off to perfection by a slim skirt and high-heeled sandals.

Her flawless skin had a glow from the brisk wind that blew in off the ocean, and when she pulled her huge sunglasses away from her face, he saw that her eyes were a light and luminous gray, the almost translucent color of rain. An incredibly striking woman, if you liked the type. Milton himself preferred petite blondes.

"Captain Milton." She took his proffered hand. Her voice was a husky contralto, with the broad, flat *a*'s characteristic of the Midwest. "I've been looking forward to meeting you."

"The people at the Lighthouse Society told us to expect you. We're prepared to be of assistance in any way we can. I hope you'll find the accommodations adequate."

"I'm sure they will be. I stopped there on my way into town. The view is magnificent. And what have you been able to arrange about a guide for me?"

Gets right to the point, Captain Milton thought with grudging admiration. He cleared his throat. "Well, as a matter of fact, Mrs. La Salle...it gets pretty rough out there beyond the headlands. Most of our guides...that is, they're not willing to take the responsibility..."

"You *haven't* been able to locate a guide for me?"

"Well, yes and no." Milton hadn't risen to the rank of captain without acquiring a modicum of diplomacy. "It's just that the Oregon coast can get pretty rough, as I said. You might want to reconsider..."

Elizabeth drew herself up to her full height. In the heels she wore, her eyes were almost level with Milton's. "Perhaps the Lighthouse Society didn't make clear to you my purpose in coming here." Her voice took on a frosty edge. "I will need to paint the lighthouse from every angle. It is imperative that I be able to view it from the sea. That is, after all, the way it was meant to be seen."

"I realize that, Mrs. La Salle, but the fact is...that is, I wish I could help you but..."

"I can arrange for a guide myself, I'm sure, but as I'm completely unfamiliar with this area, it would be so much more efficient to deal with someone who already understands my requirements." She tacked a smile onto the end of her words, but her determination was unmistakable.

"I'll do it."

The voice startled Elizabeth, who hadn't been aware that anyone else was in the room. She whirled around to see a long blond giant rising from the depths of a cracked leather chair behind the door.

Captain Milton was equally surprised, but he quickly recovered and broke into a broad grin. "Mrs. La Salle, may I present Matthew McCullough? Matthew, Mrs. La Salle."

"Elizabeth," she said automatically. It was the beard she noticed first. You didn't see beards in Chicago anymore. More was the pity.

He looked like a modern-day Paul Bunyan in jeans and a plaid Pendleton shirt, the sleeves rolled up past his elbows to reveal the muscular contours of a workingman's arms. *This is the way clothes should look on a man,* she thought. *Basic. Functional. Unequivocally male.* It suddenly occurred to Elizabeth that the three-piece business suits that surrounded her on a daily basis were nothing more than a foppish and foolish affectation.

Belatedly she offered her hand and watched it disappear into his rough brown one. His lips curved into something that might have been a smile, except that it turned down at the corners, looking as if he yielded to amusement unwillingly.

He inclined his head politely, as any man would upon meeting a stranger for the first time. But his startling green eyes—sea-green, like the turbulent waters off Deception Head—held hers a moment longer than was strictly necessary, and Elizabeth saw their expression quicken from simple courtesy to a frank appraisal that she found extremely unsettling.

His callused, laborer's hand tightened on hers. "Matt," he said.

Elizabeth wasn't an inexperienced woman. She recognized the expression in his eyes for exactly what it was—desire. Immediate and unmistakable. In the next instant the eyes cleared, becoming the gentle, innocent green of sunlit meadow grass. The reluctance vanished from the corners of his mouth, leaving behind only the strange, down-turned smile.

She blinked uncertainly. It was as though he'd slipped a mask into place, so quickly and so completely that she wasn't sure of what she had seen. All she was sure of was that her own body was vibrating like a wire stretched taut and then plucked by talented finger—and this from the simple touch of a hand and the flash of chameleon eyes!

Captain Milton clapped Matt jovially on the back. Relief made him voluble. "Well, that's just great! Yes, sir, that'll work out just fine! Matt's one of the best. No, he is the best, the *very* best guide we've got! I'm sure you'll be very satisfied with his services. Perfect for everyone, yes, sir!"

"When will you expect to get started?" Matt asked. He spoke slowly, as if the words were being pronounced against his will. The slight, down-turned smile still played around his lips.

"In a day or two, after I get settled in." She forced herself to shift her attention back to the Coast Guard captain. It took her a moment to collect her thoughts. "If you'll give the keys...?"

"Yes, yes, certainly." Captain Milton rummaged through the top drawer of his desk and came up with a handful of tarnished keys on an old brass ring. "They're all marked, see?" He displayed the keys one at a time. "House. Back door. The gate. And this skeleton key is for the lighthouse." He handed the key ring to Elizabeth, who dropped it into the leather bag slung over her shoulder.

"We'll have to talk," she said brightly, turning again toward Matt. She had recovered sufficiently to interject a brisk and businesslike tone into her voice. "I'm staying at the old caretaker's quarters. You could come by or... I mean, I could meet you somewhere, or..." *Stop!* she ordered herself firmly.

"Have you had lunch?" Matt interrupted.

"Yes. No. I mean, not lately. Not today." More flustered by the minute, Elizabeth turned again to Captain Milton. "Thank you," she said, pumping his hand enthusiastically. "I'm sure I'll be seeing you around, won't I? Of course I will. It's not that big a town, is it? No, of course it isn't." She was grateful when Matt opened the door and she could exit with as much grace as she was able to muster.

"Matt, wait." Captain Milton touched his elbow as Matt prepared to follow Elizabeth outside. "What made you change your—? Oh... I see."

"No, Milt, I don't think you do see. I figure someone's going to have to tell her the situation around here. It might as well be me. As you said, it's not like she's going to get discouraged and leave."

Captain Milton watched Matt walk down the steps of the Quonset hut that served as a Coast Guard station. He saw him point Elizabeth in the direction of a battered old pickup truck, and then he got a quick glimpse of smooth, bare thigh as she hiked up her skirt and disappeared into the passenger seat.

Well, well, well, he thought as he saw Matt walk around the truck and climb into the driver's side. *So the iceman has a melting point, after all. Who'd have figured?* He watched the truck pull away in a flurry of small stones. *Well, well, well.*

CHAPTER TWO

THE TOWN OF DECEPTION BAY spread itself thinly along both sides of the Old Coast Highway. It rose on one side into the tall pines of the Cascade Mountains and fell on the other into the wind-sheared pines of the spectacular Pacific coast. As the truck rumbled down the road to town, Elizabeth kept one eye on the landscape and the other on the man who sat beside her. Both were magnificent.

Live oak spread their boughs like a canopy over the curves of the road, and only dappled sunlight reached the ground. Far behind the oak and the pines lofty redwoods filled the sky. Ancient. Ageless. Centuries older than the lighthouse at Deception Head, and almost as old as the cliffs on which the lighthouse was built.

And the man. They grow them big up here in the Northwest, Elizabeth thought, studying him with interest. It had been years since she had experienced such a physical response to a man. Not since Jonathan.

The pain of Jonathan had long since subsided to a dull ache, but she was still determined not to let herself in for that dreadful feeling of failure again—not from the high-powered management types who inhabited her professional world, and certainly not from the noble savage who sat beside her now.

Still, he was intriguing. His profile, framed by the open window, was rough-hewn and deeply tanned, seasoned by years of exposure to the elements. Sun-bleached, straw-colored hair blew straight in the wind over deep-set eyes that had already startled her with their greenness. And his neck, she was willing to bet as her eyes fell to his open collar, had only a passing acquaintance with a tie.

"Matthew McCullough." The name had a pleasing cadence as it slipped off her tongue.

He turned toward her and grinned engagingly. The grin involved his entire face. His flaxen brows arched upward, his eyes narrowed to crinkled slits and his tanned face fell into deeply etched laugh lines.

"Matt," he reminded her. He pronounced it *May-yut,* his easy western drawl drawing out even one-syllable words until they sounded as though they had two. "And you? What do they call you back home?"

"Elizabeth."

"That's all? Just Elizabeth? No Lizzie? No Liz? No Beth?"

It *had* been Lizzie once, when she was a child roller-skating on the sidewalk in front of the old brownstone on Chicago's near north side where she'd grown up. It had been Liz to Jonathan, when they'd struggled together to build their small advertising agency into one of the most respected and successful in the city.

But between brownstone and boardroom she had learned something about winning through intimidation. Now it was Elizabeth, when it wasn't Ms. La Salle. She had learned to establish the ground rules right from the beginning. The formality did away with a lot of the jockeying for position that went on between men and women in the business world. There wasn't much Lizzie left in her these days, and since Jonathan, very little Liz.

"That's it" was all she said. "Just Elizabeth."

"I guess people are more formal in Chicago." He kept his eyes fixed on her, the same small smile playing around his mouth, and suddenly Elizabeth realized that the hairpin turns of the highway were streaking beneath the truck with harrowing speed. She gripped the door handle with white knuckles.

"People also keep their eyes on the road in Chicago," she quavered uneasily. "Might I suggest you do the same?"

Matt laughed. "I'd rather look at you. Besides, I could drive this road blindfolded. Sometimes I do." But in deference to her wishes he slowed the truck imperceptibly.

"Blindfolded?"

"Sure. When the fog rolls in, sometimes you can't see six inches in front of your face. It comes in real handy to know the road by heart."

"When the fog is as thick as that, wouldn't it be more sensible just to stay indoors?"

"Well—" he pronounced it *way-ell* "—if you did that around here, you'd spend most of your life indoors!"

The Old Coast Highway changed its name to Main Street as it entered Deception Bay, which looked very much like the old western town that it was. Both sides of the street were lined by rustic clapboard storefronts and wooden boardwalks. In front of the parking meters pickup trucks stood waiting for their owners. Elizabeth could easily imagine the horses that would have occupied the same positions in the previous century.

Matt swerved to the curb in front of a storefront café. A neon sign flashed above it, proclaiming simply Diner.

"It's nothing fancy," he warned under his breath as an insouciant, frizzy-haired blond waitress showed them to a corner booth. In other parts of the country, Elizabeth thought, she might have been wearing pink polyester or white nylon; here she wore tight blue jeans and a tighter T-shirt that assured her customers that Loggers Do It in the Woods.

The waitress bestowed a brilliant smile on Matt as she handed him a menu. "Celebration," he said, "this is Elizabeth La Salle. She's going to be spending the summer with us."

Giving Elizabeth the once-over without comment, Celebration upturned two cups and filled them with coffee.

"Celebration?" Elizabeth asked as the girl sauntered away. Several pair of eyes followed her nonchalant progress across the diner, drawn like magnets to the acid-washed jeans that showed not the slightest trace of a panty line.

"We have a lot of names like that up here. Moonflower. Star. The waitress on the evening shift is named Earthling."

"Indian?"

"No. Their parents were the flower children of the sixties." He smiled the slight, wry smile that appeared to be his principal facial expression. "You didn't know? This is where the hippies came when they grew up."

"Oh? And what do they do here?"

"A few became professional marijuana farmers, but aside from that, basically the same things everyone else does. Cut the grass, paint the house, go to PTA meetings. Celebration's mother is a psychic and her father weaves baskets for the tourists."

His smile broadened reassuringly. "Celebration's all right. She'll warm up to you."

Elizabeth didn't say what she had already observed—that Celebration's warmth was obviously reserved for

Matt McCullough. She did, however, recognize the twinge she felt as jealousy and was surprised.

Matt withdrew a slightly bent cigarette from a crumpled pack in his pocket and stuck it in the corner of his mouth. "So," he began pleasantly, "you're going to put Deception Bay on the map."

"Yes, if I'm any good."

"Are you any good?"

"I think so. But I'm not sure. That's what I'm here to find out."

"Why lighthouses? And why us?"

"Pure coincidence. My agency in Chicago does the layouts for a number of small magazines. One of our clients is the United States Lighthouse Society. We've done some graphics for their journal. Maybe you know it— *The Keeper's Log?*"

Matt nodded.

"Yes, well, I heard that they were planning to produce a pictorial on lighthouses of the Pacific Rim, and I convinced them to give me first crack at it."

"What do you know about lighthouses?"

"Nothing," Elizabeth confessed candidly. "Nor anything about Oregon. This project was simply something that came along exactly when I needed it. I wanted to get away for a while, and Oregon seemed about as far from civilization as I could get without needing a passport."

"We do eat with knives and forks up here, you know," Matt said dryly.

"Oh, I'm sorry! I didn't mean that the way it sounded. I only meant that, well, Oregon is rather a private place, isn't it? I mean, no one knows much about you, do they? Just lots of trees, lots of rain, rugged individualism—that sort of thing?"

"Certainly that's part of us . . ."

"Well," she hurried on, feeling at best tactless and at worst, ignorant. "I'd always wanted to be an artist. People used to say I was good. But I got sidetracked. I sold out, you might say. Now I want to see if I really do have talent." She shrugged. "It may be that I don't. It may be that I never did. But I thought I owed myself this one last chance to find out, or I'd spend the rest of my life wondering."

"What if you discover that you *don't* have talent?"

"Then I'll go back to Chicago with my tail between my legs and consider myself lucky that I didn't waste any more time on a pipe dream."

"And if you do? What then?"

"I'm not sure. If the Lighthouse Society likes my work, possibly they'll give me a contract to do the other lighthouses of the Pacific."

"And you'd stay out here on the coast?"

"Oh, no!" She looked startled, as if the thought had never before occurred to her. "La Salle and La Salle needs me. But I would come back during the summers. And I could paint in the park on weekends at home—when the weather permits, of course! And maybe some-day...well, who knows?"

She uttered an ironic little laugh. "I can't work for-ever, after all! *If* I decide that I have some talent, maybe someday when I retire I'll have the time to devote myself full-time to painting." She gave another wry laugh, wondering vaguely why the idea sounded so bleak.

"Sounds to me like you're wishing a lot of years away," Matt observed mildly.

"Not at all!" she retorted much too quickly. "They'll be busy years. Productive years!"

"Happy years?"

"Of course! That goes without saying."

"Of course," Matt repeated in a neutral voice that nevertheless managed to suggest otherwise. "Will Mr. La Salle be joining you later?"

"I'm not married," Elizabeth said briefly. "There is no Mr. La Salle."

The unlighted cigarette dangled loosely between Matt's lips. "There must have been once," he suggested. "Milt did call you *Mrs.* La Salle."

"Oh, there was, of course. The divorce was very civilized. Very painless."

He smiled slightly. "I think civilized divorce is a contradiction in terms."

"We don't feel that way in the business world. Divorce is actually very good for your career—all that sublimated energy, you know. In Chicago you act as though it didn't really matter very much, anyway, and you put in longer hours and work more weekends. And then, just to prove how little it did matter, you go down to Rush Street on Friday night as soon as possible to look for someone new."

"Sounds barbaric."

"It's considered quite civilized." There was a bitterness in her voice that had remained long after the divorce was history. The divorce itself had been civilized, even painless. Elizabeth had stopped caring for Jonathan years earlier.

The pain had come sometime later when Jonathan remarried a much younger woman, simple and unsophisticated, who wouldn't have been able to hold her own five minutes in Elizabeth's fast-paced world.

Really, it hadn't been the remarriage that brought the pain home to her like a fist to the stomach, nor even the birth of the new Mrs. La Salle's first baby. It was the birth of the second child, a rosy and cheerful little girl to whom Elizabeth had sent a very expensive silver toilet set.

One child could be a fluke, an accident. It was the second that indicated a pattern. Jonathan—sharp, caustic, ambitious Jonathan—had become a husband and father, a family man, harassed and happy.

He never wanted to have children with me, Elizabeth had thought bleakly, and the pain of that knowledge had taken a long time to heal. It hadn't healed yet. Her throat constricted, and her voice rose an octave—tiny fragments of body language that weren't lost on Matt.

"I'm the creative end of an advertising agency that my ex-husband and I built up from a one-room print shop on the skids. He's the business end. He and I worked well together. We still do. But when it came to playing, he . . . well, he played elsewhere. Still, I'm proud of what we accomplished. I have a career that I love..." Her voice trailed off.

"Do I hear a 'but' in there somewhere?"

Elizabeth hesitated. "I'm thirty-two years old," she blurted unexpectedly. "And I have no emotional attachments in my life."

It wasn't what she had intended to say. She stopped, astonished at her own mortifying lack of reticence. What, after all, did this total stranger care about her private life? "It's just that this isn't . . . where I expected to be," she finished lamely, "at this point in my life."

"Emotional attachments or the lack of them—they complicate life, don't they?"

The quiet intensity of his voice surprised Elizabeth. "I would have thought that life would be basically *un*complicated in a small town like this."

Matt cocked one eyebrow quizzically. "What makes you think I've spent all my life in Deception Bay?"

Blue-jeaned Celebration ambled back, setting before them the special of the day, a rich seafood gumbo and delicately flavored salmon fillet. Elizabeth remembered that she was famished. She nudged aside the sprig of parsley that decorated the plate and, with gusto, attacked the fish.

Matt took the still unlighted cigarette from the corner of his mouth, slipped it back into the crumpled pack in his pocket and did the same.

By the time Celebration came back with refills of coffee and the check, the diner had begun to empty, the locals going back to work and the tourists back onto the road. Elizabeth could see Celebration leaning against the cash register, chin resting in her palm as she gazed desultorily out the diner's plate glass window. Country music whined nasally from a radio in the kitchen, accompanied by the clatter of pots and pans and the off-key tenor of the busboy.

Elizabeth smiled at Matt over the rim of her second cup of coffee. "I'm afraid I've been doing all the talking. Tell me something about yourself."

"What would you like to know?"

"Everything." The word sounded unduly eager. She backpedaled furiously. "I mean, that is, everything I *should* know about someone I'm going to be working closely with for the summer."

"Well, let's see, I own my own boat, the *Chinook Wind,* and I operate a guide service. When the season's slow, I do some commercial fishing. If you get a nice piece of fresh salmon in the middle of winter back in Chicago, it might very well have come from the *Chinook Wind.*"

Of course, Elizabeth mused, *your basic, uncomplicated life. What you see is what you get.*

"You were expecting something a little more...
romantic maybe?" he asked. "This is a small town.
Nothing much happens here."

"You said you haven't always lived in Deception Bay."

"True. I moved down here from Portland. I guess I
should tell you that I'm a veteran of the divorce wars,
too. And I have a son. That's about it."

"Why did you come here?"

"For the same reason you did, I think. Originally at
least. I needed some time out, to lick my wounds for a
while."

"That isn't why I'm here," Elizabeth retorted much
too quickly. "I'm simply taking a few months to...
to...reexamine my options."

Matt withdrew the same disreputable cigarette from the
pack in his pocket and inserted it between his lips. "I
guess they call it something different in Chicago."

Elizabeth thought he sounded impudent. Piqued, she
waited for him to ask her permission to smoke. She was
going to make some arch remark about not caring about
his health if *he* didn't. Finally she grew exasperated.
"Aren't you going to light that thing?" she demanded
impatiently.

He looked surprised. "Oh, you mean this!" He removed the cigarette and looked at it as if he had never
seen it before. "I really don't smoke. Only when I'm
nervous, like when I've got a charter out and no one's
catching anything."

Sheepishly he slipped the unlighted cigarette back into
the pack in his pocket. "This is just sort of a...security
blanket, I guess you'd say. Gives me something to do
with my hands."

Security blanket? Elizabeth thought. Licking his
wounds? It must have been *some* divorce! Funny, but he

didn't look like a man hiding out. He looked as though he could handle just about anything without even breathing hard and without ever disturbing that off-center, down-turned smile.

Matt reached into the pocket of his jeans and came up with several wadded bills, which he tossed onto the table as he slid out of the booth. As if on cue, a boy came loping across the street. He was short and slight, and his distinctively Oriental features were drawn into a frown. He approached the diner window where Matt stood and held up his wrist, running backward a few steps so that Matt could see the wristwatch he was wearing. He pointed to it emphatically several times.

"Tran," Matt explained, turning to Elizabeth. "He's reminding me that I have a charter at two o'clock."

He nodded to the boy and gestured in the direction of the pickup truck, and the boy trotted away. When Matt and Elizabeth returned to the truck a few minutes later, Tran was already there, sitting in the bed of the pickup, propped against the back of the cab. He acknowledged Elizabeth's greeting with a noncommittal grunt.

The wind rushed in the windows as Matt drove back through Deception Bay. There seemed to be no one on the streets. At the corner by the one and only traffic light a man in an apron was energetically sweeping the sidewalk in front of a drugstore. Farther down the block several cars waited at the drive-through window of an ice-cream parlor. The sun broke through the clouds for the first time that day, shining down on the sweeping man and the cars at the ice-cream parlor and the clean, quiet streets of the town.

I bet they even have a volunteer fire department here, Elizabeth speculated to herself. *How quaint!* The thought began derisively, but ended in a surprising wave of nostalgia for a way of life she'd never known. *And everyone goes to church on Sunday. And all the kids go to the city as soon as they get out of high school, but they always come back to raise their own children, like the salmon swimming upstream to their own birthplace to spawn.*

"You know, there's more to lighthouses than meets the eye." Matt spoke loudly over the rushing wind. "I don't suppose the lighthouse people told you about the ghosts."

Elizabeth's eyes narrowed skeptically.

Matt laughed. "Of course they wouldn't. But every lighthouse has one. They lend themselves very well to that sort of thing."

Elizabeth gave an inelegant snort calculated to express her precise opinion of ghosts.

"Don't scoff!" The corners of Matt's mouth twitched wickedly. "Some folks say it's only the creaking of an old house, or the wind rattling in the shutters. But wait till you've been up there when the fog's as thick as pea soup and it's as quiet as a tomb, and all of a sudden you hear footsteps on the stairs. Or the wind's howling like a witch, and all of a sudden it's *your* name she's howling. Oh, yes, there are ghosts all right! Ask Tran. Tell her, pardner," he shouted through the open back window. "Tell her about the lady at Heceta Head."

"Ol' Rue?" Tran spoke up sullenly. "Sure, I seen her. She lives in the old caretaker's house, but I seen her on the road, too. She's got no feet and she just kinda floats, but I ain't scared of her. She wouldn't hurt no one. She just wants to make sure the light's bein' tended." He paused. "Some of the others, though, like the wanderin' ghost of Evan McClure—folks see him out drifting in a lifeboat whenever there's a storm comin'. They ain't so nice...." The boy's sullen voice trailed off.

"Tran knows all the ghosts," Matt told her with a grin. "You want to know anything about ghosts for your book, you just ask Tran."

"I'll do that," Elizabeth said, silently vowing to have as little as possible to do with the ghosts *or* with this petulant boy who was on such familiar terms with them.

When they arrived back at the Coast Guard station, Matt pulled in beside Elizabeth's vintage station wagon. "Thank you for lunch—" she began formally.

"Two o'clock," Tran warned through the window.

"We still haven't gotten down to business," Matt said. "Let me come by in a day or two. You'll have a better idea by then about how you want to work this thing."

A day or two. It sounded like an impossibly long time. If this were Chicago, her turf, she would have known how to handle the situation. She would simply have asked for his telephone number. But she was a stranger in a strange land. Who knew what the customs were here? So she set her feminist principles aside for the moment and demurely extended her hand.

"I'll be looking forward to it," she said.

IT WAS A FAR CRY from the sleek efficiency town house she leased on Lakeshore Drive, Elizabeth thought as she surveyed the cottage that was to be her home for the summer.

True, it was every bit as charming and picturesque as the Lighthouse Society had said it was—or it *would* be, if the porch didn't sag so dangerously and the steps weren't so rickety that she was half-afraid to climb them, and if the floorboards didn't creak with every step she took.

It was also musty and damp. An enormous fieldstone fireplace extended the full length of one wall, and its gray

stone was blackened from uncounted years of use. After
searching in vain for a thermostat, Elizabeth regretfully
had to conclude that the fireplace was the only source of
heat in the drafty old house.

Scattered around the living room were several large
pieces of furniture that would have fetched hefty prices
in any antique shop in Chicago. In the drawer of an old
oak armoire she found a patchwork quilt, which she
hugged around herself against the damp chill that permeated the air.

Outside, the house was pure Cape Cod. Inside it was
an eclectic blend of the past. Tenants long vanished had,
at different times, remodeled, adding whatever modern
conveniences they thought they couldn't live without.

That was why the scarred floor in the kitchen was made
of pegged hardwood, while the countertops gleamed with
bright Formica; why the range was a modern gas stove,
while the refrigerator was an old-fashioned icebox; why
the hand-carved spool bed in the bedroom had a state-of-
the-art mattress, while the blankets were old, tattered afghans.

There was an early American sofa directly in front of
the fireplace, flanked on either side by high-backed
rocking chairs. The red chintz pattern on the sofa was
faded, but the cushions were plump and comfortable,
and there Elizabeth sat, looking over her domain with a
doubtful eye.

Matt had spoken of ghosts. She was very much aware
of ghosts in this house—ghosts of the people who had
spent their lives here, the keepers of the light.

Who had knitted those afghans? Who had spent their
lives in this lonely place, tending the light night after
night, year in and year out, so that unknown sailors on
unknown ships might be safe? How many ships had been

wrecked on this rugged and beautiful coast, and how many drowning men had the keepers saved from the sea in their shallow, broad-beamed surfboats?

Restlessly Elizabeth stood. Still wrapped in the quilt, she went into the kitchen where she put on the kettle for tea. She thought she'd rather have a good stiff martini, but not having realized until too late that the house had only an icebox, she had no ice.

Luckily, she thought wryly, this summer night was cold enough that she could put her perishables on the porch and they would stay adequately refrigerated.

While she waited for the water to heat, remembering some vague admonition from her grandmother about watched pots never boiling, she gazed instead out the window. Odd. She hadn't thought about Gran for such a long time—it must be something about this old house. It was only evening, but the fog had rolled in early, blocking out the daylight. The glow from the kitchen window reflected in the fog as a pale yellow smear.

Fog. What had Matt said? *Pea soup.* Beyond the weak light from her window, the world was shrouded in gray vapor. It silenced everything but imagination. It was frightening, this silence, especially to someone whose tenth-floor bedroom window reverberated all night with reassuring traffic noises from Lakeshore Drive.

The haunting fog was thick and choking. Elizabeth felt suffocated. The mist that drifted up from Lake Michigan was never like this. With a pang that astonished her with its sharpness, she longed for something familiar—for home, for a place to be that held no memories except her own.

She shivered, feeling every bit as isolated as the old lighthouse. *What am I doing here in this godforsaken part of the world,* she thought uneasily, *with dangers and demons I know nothing about?*

The kettle shrieked and she jumped. With trembling hands she poured hot water into a mug on the counter. Her pulse had just begun to return to normal when another unexpected sound, an abrupt knock on the front door, sent it racing again. Her hand shook and the cup tipped, scalding her fingers with a splash of hot water.

This is ridiculous, she told herself firmly. *Come on, you've faced worse things than a few ghosts and goblins in your life—you've ridden the Chicago subway after dark!*

Resolutely she walked to the door and pulled back the curtain. "Matt!" She was weak with relief as she undid the dead bolt and opened the door.

The first thing he noticed was the pallor of her skin. "Fog getting to you?"

"Oh, no, not at all," Elizabeth lied. Self-consciously she dragged the quilt from around her shoulders.

"Jory at the icehouse told me you hadn't been by to pick up any ice. I figured you didn't know you needed it."

On the porch beside him was a block of ice as big as a small child. He hoisted it to his shoulder with a pair of lethal-looking tongs and carried it into the kitchen, where he poked the icebox door open with one booted foot and deposited the ice inside. Then he stood in the middle of the kitchen, hands on his hips, and surveyed the tiny room with a critical eye. "Finding everything you need?"

"Oh, yes."

If he noticed a demon or two still in her eyes, he was discreet enough not to mention it. He glanced at the cold hearth. "Haven't had time to lay a fire, I see."

"I haven't gotten around to it yet. I've been so busy moving in." With a wide sweep of her arm she gestured to the chaos around her.

The contents of the station wagon now cluttered the house. Suitcases were half-unpacked on the floor. Her entire summer's inventory of art supplies was piled on every available surface. She hoped he wouldn't suspect that she didn't have a clue in the world how to start a fire.

"You've moved in, all right. I can see that."

He crossed to the fireplace and began placing crumpled newspaper and small sticks of kindling on the andirons. Then he added several smaller logs from the hod and laid one large log on top of the rest. Finally he applied a long fireplace match to the newspaper at the bottom of the pile, and in a minute or two the kindling flared.

He stepped back from the hearth with a satisfied expression, brushing his hands together briskly. "Bank it when you go to bed and it'll be all set for you to fire up in the morning."

"Bank it?"

"Cover it with ashes so that it'll burn low. In the morning you'll just have to add a small log or two to get it going again." He leaned one shoulder against the mantel and crossed his arms. "Weren't you ever a Girl Scout?"

"There wasn't much necessity for starting fires in the middle of a city," Elizabeth countered. "Can I offer you a cup of tea? Or some instant coffee maybe?"

"Thanks, no. I'd better be on my way." He pushed himself away from the mantel. "If you need anything—" he produced a pencil stub and a scrap of paper from his pocket and scribbled on it "—here's my number." His hand brushed Elizabeth's as he handed her the scrap—a big hand, with strong, square fingers and blunt-trimmed nails.

Elizabeth thought that she'd never looked at a man's hand before. *Really* looked. Or maybe it was simply that she had never seen one like this—a hardworking hand, sinews standing out on the back like ropes, a bruise on the thumb, calluses on the palm, blond hair on the wrist looking gold in the flickering firelight.

Did he have the same crisp golden hair everywhere, this blond bear of a man? A muscle coiled somewhere in the vicinity of her stomach.

Rattled, she forced herself to concentrate on his hands again—surely hands were safer! But it didn't help. They were hard and the skin was rough, but some instinct told her that he would keep them very gentle.

She let out the breath she hadn't realized she was holding. "I appreciate your coming over," she said in a voice that sounded only a trifle huskier than normal. "I think the fog may have given me the heebie-jeebies."

"It happens to a lot of people at first," he said with a reassuring smile. "You'll get over it." He turned and walked to the door. "If you need anything," he repeated, opening it, "anything at all, you give me a ring, okay?"

Then, too quickly, he stepped out onto the porch and pulled the door shut behind him. She heard his footsteps descend the rickety stairs. Suddenly the fog seemed thicker than before, and she shivered as she threw the dead bolt.

SOMETIME DURING THE NIGHT, Elizabeth woke with a start. She sat bolt upright in the dark, uncertain for a moment where she was. Her heart was pounding furiously.

At first she didn't know what had awakened her. Then she heard it again—scrabbling, scraping, bumping noises that sounded as though someone were trying to claw their way through the front door. She listened carefully, and over the pounding of her heart she heard footsteps on the boards of the porch!

Her urban survival techniques came back to her. Quietly she crept out of bed and made a dash for the kitchen, where she seized the long-handled butcher knife she had seen earlier in the cutlery drawer. Clutching it in front of her face, she slid noiselessly along the kitchen walls and into the living room.

She flattened herself behind the door and pressed her ear to the wall, scarcely moving, scarcely even breathing. The sounds continued unabated. Whoever was out there hadn't even noticed her approach.

Suddenly it dawned on her what the scrabbling noises were—someone was breaking into her food supply, which she had forgotten to move into the icebox! In the same instant she realized that it wasn't some*one*, but some*thing*, and she leaped for the relative safety of the sofa.

She burrowed into the plump cushions and huddled there, knees tucked under her chin, pulling the old quilt around her body and keeping a rigid hand clenched on the wooden-handled butcher knife.

She knew she wouldn't sleep again.

CHAPTER THREE

THE MORNING SUN PIERCED the tattered window shades with several separate beams. One struck the moisture-pitted mirror that hung over the fireplace, creating a weak reflection. Another made a pool of light on the blackened hearth. And one shone directly into Elizabeth's eyes where she lay curled up in a corner of the couch.

She woke with a start. Instinctively she reached for the butcher knife, then realized that it was no longer necessary. She pulled the old afghan up to her chin and burrowed deeper into the cozy sofa, peering out at the room with some trepidation.

The sun flowed into the farthest corners, illuminating nothing more malevolent than dust balls and a few mouse droppings. Elizabeth shuddered, then turned over to look at her watch. Ten o'clock! She couldn't remember the last time she had slept so late! Pulling the afghan around her shoulders, she rose and walked to the door, where she pulled aside the curtain and looked out.

Her eyes widened. Appalled, she stared at the remnants of what had been her small supply of perishables. Cellophane wrappers that had contained cheese and cold cuts were torn into shreds, every last bit of their contents gone. Milk was puddled in the sagging boards of the porch. The only thing left undamaged was a bottle of white wine, which had rolled from the porch and now lay unceremoniously in a clump of sea grass.

Elizabeth surveyed the damage with dismay. Animals! Why hadn't she considered the possibility of wild animals in this remote part of the world? The answer was painfully obvious: never before in her life had she *had* to consider animals, except perhaps yappy little dogs being walked on leashes by bored doormen.

She scrutinized the dark recesses of the woods that surrounded the house. She half expected to see savage yellow eyes glittering back at her, but the wolves, or bears, or whatever they were, seemed to have gone. She slammed the door quickly, throwing the dead bolt with hands that shook.

Despite the sun streaming through the windows, the house was cold. Recalling Matt's instructions, she poked up the warm ashes in the fireplace, added a log and was gratified to see small flames begin licking upward.

When the fire had taken the chill out of the room, she went into the tiny bathroom, where she twisted the hot water faucet. The pipes shuddered protestingly, and a halting stream of rusty water trickled down from the shower. She glared resentfully at the dripping shower head.

Becoming more irritated by the minute, she climbed into a pair of designer jeans and a silk-screened T-shirt with padded shoulders, laced a brand-new pair of running shoes onto her feet and went outside to clean up the porch.

AN HOUR LATER Elizabeth was on her way to town. Because it was nearly noon, anyway, she wisely decided to skip breakfast and go directly to lunch, and she was headed for the one place in town where she knew she could get food without having to cook it. She was suddenly eager for hot coffee and warm food, and the sound of human voices. Even Celebration's scowling face seemed appealingly familiar.

Another face, more familiar and more appealing, flashed across her mind. She wondered if Matt Mc-Cullough might be at the diner. At least half a dozen times last night she had considered telephoning him, but the distance between her perch on the sofa and the old-fashioned wall phone in the kitchen might as well have been an uncharted wilderness for all the inclination she had to cross it.

This morning, of course, she was glad. It had been her first real test of survival in this inhospitable part of the world, and she had conquered it on her own. It was a good feeling.

With the window rolled down Elizabeth smelled the acrid, salty sea air and the woodsy scent of the pines. There was also a pungent, smoky aroma that she couldn't identify but which smelled a little like barbecue. After she had passed several fish houses and seen smoke billowing up behind them, she realized what it must be—the locals were smoking their morning catches of salmon and selling it from the roadside stands that dotted the highway.

Smoked salmon. Twelve dollars a pound at the best delicatessens in Chicago. Suddenly she was ravenous, and she pulled into the next fish stand. A familiar brown face confronted her.

"Tran! Good morning!"

Tran muttered something unintelligible that might be construed as a greeting, then regarded her with hostile eyes. "What d'you want?"

"Well, I was thinking about some of your smoked salmon," she said, forcing a friendly smile. "Is it fresh?"

"Caught it myself, smoked it myself," Tran grunted, obviously torn between hostility toward her and pride in his product. "They don't come no fresher'n that."

"Good. I'll take that piece in the corner." As Tran wrapped the piece she had chosen, Elizabeth studied him curiously. *What a hostile child!* she thought.

She recognized him as Amerasian. She had seen faces like his for many years on the evening news—a bitter war's bitter legacy, children smiling hopefully into the television cameras with their fathers' eyes. But now they were no longer children. Now they were becoming adults, and their eyes were hard and angry. Like this one.

He was distinguished by the distinctive combination that characterized so many Amerasians—his features were Vietnamese, but his coloring Caucasian. His upswept eyes were shaped like almonds and of the same color, and his hair was russet brown.

To Elizabeth he looked rather like an old-fashioned tintype—shades of brown and beige instead of black and white. And like those old photographs, his face was grim and unsmiling. He would be a good-looking young man, she realized, if he ever decided to drop that chip he carried on his shoulder.

"Where are you from, Tran?"

He glared at her resentfully. "Deception Bay," he muttered.

"Of course." So much for small talk.

"That's two dollars even."

Elizabeth counted out the money and pushed it across the counter. "Do you know where I might find Matt?"

"He's got a charter out."

"Do you know what time he'll be in?"

"Beats me." Tran shifted his eyes to a spot somewhere over her left shoulder, and Elizabeth felt that the conversation, such as it was, had been terminated.

"Where does he keep his boat?"

"He has a slip behind the icehouse. Jory's."

"One more thing..."

With a pained expression Tran rolled his eyes back to her.

"Are there... wolves, or bears maybe, around here?"

For the first time since she'd met him, Tran almost smiled. "Yeah," he said.

CELEBRATION LOOKED at Elizabeth as though she had never set eyes on her before. To all Elizabeth's attempts at conversation she made peevish, monosyllabic grunts until Elizabeth, chagrined, finished her second cup of coffee and left.

Jory, when she located him at the icehouse, was no more communicative. She found him behind a display case, arranging and rearranging dusty fishing tackle under an even dustier glass counter.

He was a wizened old man with a squint and grizzled gray hair that tufted from beneath his cap like quills. There was a gold plug in one ear, and Elizabeth knew without a doubt that it wasn't a concession to fashion; the earring had probably been there forever. Jory did, in fact, look rather like a pirate as he squinted up at her suspiciously.

"Ye must be the lady what's gonna draw the Light," he rapped between missing front teeth.

"Yes," Elizabeth replied pleasantly, prepared for some warm words of welcome.

The old man shook his head. "Damn shame, that's what it is. A bloody damn shame. That old Light's been standing there fer nigh on to a hun'ert 'n fifty years, and it ain't never needed no one to paint its pit'cher before.'' Muttering darkly to himself, Jory turned his back and shuffled away.

"Wait!" she called. "I'm looking for Matt Mc-Cullough."

The old man squinted at her over one shoulder. "What fer ye want Matt?"

Elizabeth bit back her first impulse, which was to tell him it was none of his business. "He's going to be my guide. If you'll just tell me where I can find him . . ."

Jory looked at her as if she were a lunatic. "Never Matt," he chortled confidently. "Never Matt!" Still snickering under his breath, he shuffled out the sagging screen door at the back of the shop. Its hinges squeaked as it banged shut behind him.

Elizabeth pushed open the door and followed him outside. *What is it with these people?* she fumed. Every person she met was more surly and disagreeable than the one before. And why "never Matt?"

As she stepped from the dim interior of the shop, the sun's reflection off the cobalt-blue ocean blinded her, and for a moment she could discern nothing but shadows and light. Then she caught sight of Jory, scurrying across the sand like a crab. Looking ahead to his destination, she felt a surge of pleasure as she recognized the tall, spare silhouette of Matt McCullough standing near the water's edge. He wore jeans and a rough-knit black turtle-neck and a navy pea jacket with the collar turned up, unbuttoned and flapping open in the wind. He bent his ear to the fiercely gesticulating Jory, then looked up and smiled. His smile was like sunshine, warm and welcoming.

Relief flooded her face. For reasons she didn't understand, her welcome seemed to have quickly worn thin in this town, and it was gratifying to know that Matt, at least, appeared glad to see her.

Not that it mattered, of course. She had come here to do a job, that was all. And in September, when the job was finished, she'd be well on her way to fame and fortune or else back behind her desk at La Salle and La Salle, Incorporated. In either case Deception Bay and its antagonistic inhabitants—even this splendid specimen of masculinity whose lazy smile broadened as he watched her stumbling progress across the rocky beach—would be only memories. "Hi," she said a little breathlessly. "Beautiful day."

"Yep." His head moved imperceptibly down and then up again, and Elizabeth knew he was scanning her closely from behind his sunglasses. In the jeans that hugged every womanly curve and the T-shirt that boldly proved the bra she wore to be no more than a wisp of lace, she felt nearly naked. The secret muscle coiled in the pit of her stomach.

"Do I pass?" she asked. The best defense is a good offense—one of the first rules she had learned about winning through intimidation.

"Sorry!" He pulled the dark glasses off his face, and she was pleased to note that at least he had the grace to look embarrassed. His green eyes squinted engagingly, and he smiled his strange, down-turned smile. "I didn't mean to be rude. It's just that you're a little... overdressed ... for a fishing boat."

"What overdressed?" she protested, laughing. "This is just jeans and a T-shirt!"

He glanced at the designer label in her waistband and shrugged. "Well, maybe it's just the way they look on you."

As good as Celebration's looked on her? Elizabeth wanted to ask, but didn't. "I didn't plan on sailing today," she said. "I just want to discuss my needs—that is, my *requirements,* with you." She wondered what she would wear when she was sailing. One of her several *other* pair of designer jeans? Furtively she scuffed her stark white, unmistakably new running shoes in the sand.

Matt turned and began walking toward the pier, and Elizabeth fell into step beside him. They climbed over clumps of sea grass and long ropes of seaweed washed up by the tide, dodging the fringe of surf that lapped the rocky shore. Elizabeth smiled at the tiny sandpipers that skittered across the sand and peeped contentedly among the kelp. Overhead, gulls shrieked and circled low, searching, like the sandpipers, for bits of edible flotsam washed up by the tide.

The brisk ocean breeze became a steady westerly as they mounted the steps to the pier and walked past the fishing boats toward the T-head. Elizabeth shivered.

"You must be freezing," Matt said. He stopped walking and took off his pea jacket, which he then draped around Elizabeth's shoulders. The coat was warm with the heat of his body, and she hugged it around herself gratefully. "I guess I should have warned you about summer on the Oregon coast."

"What about it?"

"It's seldom warm. And usually overcast. Winter's when you want to come here—sunny, and the sky's blue."

"Well, summer is all I have. I'll have to make the best of it."

"I've got jackets and rain gear aboard the boat. I reckon we can find something to fit you."

The *Chinook Wind,* tied up at the end of the T-head, was a thirty-eight-foot cabin cruiser. Bare, worn, utilitarian—a real working boat. Elizabeth balanced herself against Matt's outstretched arm as she stepped onto the gunwale and jumped deftly to the deck.

"Big," she commented, twirling around to give the boat a once-over. Her cursory glance took in the tarnished brass railing, the painted white deck, the huge downriggers secured to the gunwales.

It smelled strongly of fish and diesel fuel. Elizabeth could feel the waves lapping against the hull as they rolled the boat in a gentle, circular motion.

Matt was looking at her expectantly. Obviously there was something more she should say about his boat. It wasn't one of the excursion boats that cruised Lake Michigan, serving a candlelight banquet at sunset with a five-piece band and dancing on the promenade deck after dark, but it seemed serviceable.

"A person shouldn't get too seasick on this," she ventured hopefully.

Matt leaned against the gunwale and slid his hand across the railing. "She's just an old Chris-Craft, but she suits me just fine." His fingers moved over the smooth brass with the unconscious sensuality of a lover.

Elizabeth crossed the deck and joined him, propping her elbows on the rail and clasping her hands over the water. "What does *Chinook Wind* mean?"

"Chinook is a kind of salmon. The big silvers. A chinook wind is a wind that blows in from the ocean in the spring. It's a restless wind, the Indians say, and it starts the salmon running."

She tilted her head to look up at him curiously. "That doesn't sound like an appropriate name for a boat of yours. It doesn't fit. At least you don't seem a bit restless to me."

"I'm not anymore. But I used to get that way sometimes when I first came to live here. And whenever I got to feeling tied down, I'd just go to sea for a while."

"You don't do that anymore?"

"Not often. That was a long time ago. Now I have... other responsibilities." He gave her his engaging grin. "Making a living—that sort of thing."

The wind at Deception Head was high, and the sea was choppy. Breakers crashed against the stone jetties that protected the natural harbor on the north and south. The tide was out, and crags as big as houses jutted up from the ocean floor. To the south, Deception Head Lighthouse was almost invisible in the mist.

"How lonely the Light looks," Elizabeth murmured. Her tone was unexpectedly wistful.

The foghorn that had bleated at regular intervals for over a hundred years had long since been replaced by an automatic radio beacon on North Jetty.

The beautiful prism lens, three hundred and fifty thousand candlepower, once visible twenty miles out to sea, was darkened forever. Now it stood blind and mute, an anachronism, an outdated remnant of another era. "It's as though it's just... fading into the mist. I wonder if it knows that its time has passed?" She looked up at Matt. "Why do they call this place Deception Bay?"

"The Spanish named it. They called the promontory Puenta Decepción because of the hidden killer reef just offshore. Even after they charted it, it was a mariner's nightmare. Actually, Oregon has four hundred miles of the most beautiful and most treacherous seacoast in the world.

"In the old sailing days it was even worse," Matt continued. "Shipwrecks littered this coast—everything from Indian dugouts to ocean liners. The last big wreck was the Japanese freighter *Blue Magpie,* off North Jetty at Yaquina Head in 1983. You can still see what's left of her on Yaquina Bay Bar at low tide."

"What happened?"

"It was November, one of those freak winter storms that blow up with no warning. Winds at forty-five knots with swells at eighteen, twenty feet. Graybeards—waterspouts—everywhere. The *Blue Magpie* was working her way north from Cleft of the Rock Light at Cape Perpetua when the storm hit. She tried to make Yaquina Bay, but she didn't get past the bar. She reached her 'port of no return,' as folks around here say."

"What happened to the crew?"

"Nineteen men on board. Saved them all." Matt sounded as proud as if he himself had done the saving. "So you see, even with our most modern technology, sometimes the sea still gets the best of us."

"That's where the legends about the ghosts come from?"

"Partly. Also, pirates terrorized the Pacific coast clear down to Baja, and then they ran for cover up here. There's supposed to be a king's ransom in buried treasure somewhere, along with the obligatory corpses buried alive to guard them."

Matt withdrew a cigarette from the pack in his shirt pocket and tapped it thoughtfully on his thumbnail. Finally he turned to Elizabeth and cocked a quizzical eyebrow. "How are you liking Deception Bay so far?"

"Well, I haven't run into any ghosts yet, but nothing would surprise me at this point. What with the wild animals and—"

"*Wild animals?*"

"The wolves or the bears or whatever it is that you have up here."

"What makes you think we have wild animals?"

"Because they came up on my porch last night and tore my food apart! I was so afraid they were going to break in that I hardly slept all night!"

Matt threw back his head and laughed. "Wild animals!" he exclaimed. "Those weren't bears or wolves or anything of the sort! Those were raccoons!"

"*Raccoons?*"

"That old house has been vacant for so long they probably think of it as their own. They would have been as frightened as you were if they'd known you were there." He gave her a reassuring smile. "We have no wild animals around here, except maybe a few brown bears, and they're as timid as the raccoons."

"That's not what your friend Tran said."

He looked at her sharply. "When did you see Tran?"

"This morning on my way into town. I asked him if there were wild animals around here and he said there were."

"Sometimes Tran's English trips him up. Maybe you didn't understand—"

"No, that's what he said." Elizabeth's voice was cool. "But you're partially right. I *don't* understand what's going on around here. Tran. Jory. Celebration. Even the cashier at the grocery store. They treat me like a pariah! You're the only one who's been even civil to me since I got here. Why? What have I done to make the entire town dislike me so?"

"It's not what you've done," Matt said carefully. "It's what you're going to do."

Elizabeth frowned. "What do you mean?"

"Paint the Light."

"Paint the Light? Why on earth wouldn't they want me to paint the Light?" She was bewildered. "It'll be nothing but good for the whole town. Lighthouses fascinate people. When my paintings are published, tourists will swarm to Deception Bay just to *see* the Light. It'll be a real boost for the whole economy—and I don't mind telling you that this town looks as if it could use a shot in the arm!"

"Folks around here don't see it that way." He stuck the cigarette he'd been holding between his lips and began patting his pockets, looking for a light. When he located his lighter, he lit the cigarette slowly, carefully cupping his hands around the flame to protect it from the wind, then blew smoke and watched it spiral upward.

His security blanket, Elizabeth recalled impatiently. It was obvious he was playing for time.

"Folks around here…" he began, still not meeting her eyes. "Folks around here like things the way they are. They don't want sightseers coming to Deception Bay, spoiling things. Most folks who live here think they've found a little bit of heaven right here on earth, and they'd like to keep the rest of the world from ever finding out about it."

"But that makes no sense at all! What about progress? What about growth? You can't stop people from coming here just because you don't want them!"

"Maybe not." The cigarette dangled loosely in the corner of his mouth. His profile, chiseled out of the sunny blue of the sky, looked unhappy. "I'm just telling you how it is. You aren't going to get much cooperation from folks around here. They'd much rather see you pack up your duds and go back to Chicago."

She looked at him sharply. "And you? What about you? Why are you willing to help me when no one else is?"

"I'm not sure," he said. Then his half smile widened. "No, that's not true. I like you. From the minute you walked in the door at the Coast Guard station, telling a Coast Guard captain how to do his job, I liked you. I didn't want to see you . . . hurt."

"It's going to be worse for you than for me. I'll be gone in September, but you'll still have to live here."

"I can handle it, if you're convinced it's what you want to do. Are you?"

"Yes," she said with a confidence she was suddenly far from feeling. Did she really have the assertiveness to fly in the face of a town full of people who wanted her gone?

It had been very lonely last night, feeling the haunting fog close her off from the rest of the world. It could get a whole lot lonelier by the end of the summer. She set her chin firmly. "Yes," she said again. "And I'd like to get started soon. Is that all right with you?"

"You're the boss. When?"

"How about tomorrow? Early?"

"Early can be pretty foggy."

"Good. Fog suits a lighthouse, don't you think?"

"It's one of the reasons for their existence."

Elizabeth turned away from the rail and started to take off the coat Matt had given her.

"No, keep it," he said, reaching with his big hands to anchor it more firmly on her shoulders. "I have others. No sense your catching cold before you even get started, is there?"

"Thanks, Matt." She smiled and slipped her arms into the long sleeves and buttoned the lapels up under her chin. The pea jacket swallowed her completely from neck to knees. Then, gripping Matt's outstretched hand for support, she boosted herself up onto the gunwale and stepped out onto the wooden pier.

She looked across at him standing on the painted deck, looking very much in his element with the black turtleneck reaching up to his ears, the wind ruffling his shaggy hair and a cigarette in the corner of his mouth.

"Look, Matt," she began hesitantly, "I'm glad you . . . like me. But I think you should know that I came here to do a job. That's all." She didn't know where the words had come from, but some barely articulated instinct told her it was important that they be said—for her own sake as well as for his.

He took one last drag on the cigarette and then flicked the butt overboard. The whimsical half smile on his face remained unchanged. "And I'm here to see you get it done." Immediately he inserted another security blanket between his lips and lit up.

CHAPTER FOUR

RUSTY HINGES SQUEAKED protestingly as Elizabeth forced open the heavy iron storm door. A shaft of weak sunlight streamed in as she held the door open with one hand and shone the flashlight around with the other.

Inside, the lighthouse was very dim. There was no electricity—hadn't been for years, Captain Milton had told her—and the windows had been sealed with concrete long ago. She moved her flashlight around the small circular foyer in which she found herself.

The plaster had crumbled away from the walls, revealing the old red brick behind. Generations of mice had scribbled their footprints in the thick dust that covered the granite floor, recording in jagged hieroglyphics their long history in this place.

The rank, musty odor also spoke of the generations of furry, scurrying creatures that had lived and died here. Even now she felt their eyes peering at her from the darkened corners of the room—wary, watchful, waiting for her to leave.

A few sticks of broken furniture were all that remained of the human inhabitants of the Light. A round mess table balanced on three legs in the middle of the room, surrounded by several straight-backed wooden chairs that were also thick with dust and the scribbling of the mice.

Elizabeth could almost see men sitting around the table—the ghosts of the keepers and their lifesaving crews, men with hard bodies, muscular arms, tattoos, telling stories, perhaps, that grew more elaborate with each telling, or playing interminable games of poker, holding their cards close to their chests, flicking them down with cool precision.

Through the open door an unseen current of air drifted in, shifting the dust on the floor, dispelling the ghosts and erasing the genealogy of the mice.

Feeling rather like an intruder, Elizabeth shone her flashlight up the spiral staircase at the opposite end of the foyer. The beam of light threw long shadows on the stained walls and then disappeared into darkness.

Three hundred steps, Captain Milton had told her. She released the door, which slowly creaked almost to a close behind her. Then, clutching the brass key ring and the flashlight in one hand and the wooden banister in the other, she began to climb.

The staircase was steep. When she reached a landing about halfway up, she stopped to catch her breath and shone the flashlight down the distance she had just come. The door at the bottom admitted only a thin crack of daylight, and when she continued her climb, it disappeared altogether beneath the landing.

The top of the spiral opened into another room. Her flashlight found an iron door, identical to the one below, which she guessed led to the lantern gallery. With some difficulty she pulled back on the corroded old dead bolt and yanked the handle of the door. Hinges made stubborn by rust and time wouldn't allow it to budge.

One hand was obviously not sufficient for the job, so she set the flashlight down next to the doorjamb and pulled the handle with both. The hinges grated as they resisted momentarily, then haltingly the door gave way, opening just enough so that she could squeeze through.

The cold sea air was bracing after the musty odor inside. The wind caught her hair and whipped it wildly around her head. It was steady from the west, blowing in off the sea, and it buffeted her with nearly gale force as she made her way to the railing of the gallery and looked out.

This must be what it's like to be a bird, she thought in delight. Nothing beneath her but empty space falling into the pounding sea; nothing around her but the few insignificant bits of iron and stone that made up the balcony. Gulls circled the tower, shrieking harshly, soaring on downward drafts to examine the unknown creature who had invaded their roost. The walls of the tower and the lantern balcony were white with over a century of their droppings.

Gripping the railing to keep from being blown back against the wall, Elizabeth walked around the circular balcony. On either side she could see the stark cliffs of the headland, honeycombed with dozens of caves the sea had carved into the basalt. Behind the cliffs she saw the wooded hills and the slanted roofs of the town. It was a long way off. She couldn't even see the highway, only a few miles away, through the thick live oak and the misshapen, wind-sheared pines.

Returning to the front of the balcony, she gazed out to sea. Beyond the treacherous reef that had given Deception Bay its name, numerous fishing boats trolled, dragging their huge downriggers behind them. Elizabeth wondered if one of them might be Matt.

It was late afternoon, and the fog bank that waited over the horizon was rolling back in, blending its gray with the darkening gray of the sea and the sky.

Elizabeth shivered. The dampness in the wind made her clothes sticky and uncomfortable. She felt the wet tendrils of her hair becoming an uncontrollable mop. When she came up here to sketch, she would have to remember to bring warmer clothing. Matt had certainly been right about summer on the Oregon coast!

Turning, she made her way back to the door and slipped inside. Due to the clammy sweating of the old walls, it was nearly as chilly as on the lantern gallery, but at least it was marginally warmer beyond the reach of the wind.

Elizabeth pushed the protesting door shut behind her while she reached for the flashlight. Her fingers closed on empty space.

Baffled at first and then frantic, she groped around the floor. Her frenzied fingers disturbed the thick carpet of dust, and it drifted around her like smoke, filling her nostrils with its rank, fetid odor.

Her hand touched something warm and furry, and her throat constricted in sudden panic. Quickly she jerked open the heavy door and in the weak light that streamed in, scrutinized the room. Impossibly the flashlight was gone!

Fear, primitive and raw, hit her like a fist to the stomach. She was alone in the dark, stranded three hundred terrifying steps above the warmth and light and safety of the world below.

She listened with pounding heart to the scratchy, scrabbling noises she had hardly noticed before. They suddenly seemed closer, more menacing, and the wind was picking up. It rattled the lantern gallery like the dry winter branches of a denuded tree. A chill went down her spine as the wind suddenly began to howl.

Her breath came in shallow gasps. Her heart pounded in her ears, drowning out even the distant rumble of the crashing surf.

With trembling hands she closed the door to the lantern balcony and threw the dead bolt—the fading light brightened only the circular lantern room, anyway. Then, cautiously, clutching the banister with one icy hand and feeling her way along the dank wall with the other, she began the long descent.

The spiral steps were narrow at one end and widened at the other, like spokes on a wheel. She crept very slowly, feeling for each stair with the toe of her foot before leaving the security of the previous one. It seemed as if she were moving in slow motion, and her whole body was taut, half prepared for something unknown to come flying at her in the dark.

The banister was smooth to the touch—worn smooth, she guessed, by the hands of all the keepers of the light, hauling themselves up these three hundred steps night after night, day after day, year after year, for over a century. The stone steps were worn smooth, too, from the feet of those same bygone keepers.

When she passed the landing and saw the thin crack of light from the door below, she sobbed with relief. Hurriedly she covered the last few steps, taking them two at a time, and when she reached the bottom, ran to the door and dragged it open with frenzied hands.

Her knees gave way beneath her. She sagged weakly against the doorjamb, heart pounding wildly, and breathed in the fresh outdoor air with great gulps.

Gradually her panic subsided. Scraping her tangled hair back from her forehead and pressing cool palms against her pale cheeks, she pushed herself away from the door and let her glance travel over the dim foyer.

It was just a forsaken, deserted dwelling, where people had once lived and now they didn't. That was all. How could she have permitted the dark and a few ghost stories to overwhelm her like that?

Squaring her shoulders, she tugged at the heavy door, finding it much more difficult to move now that the adrenaline was no longer coursing through her veins. Suddenly her eyes fell on an object lying in the dust at the foot of the stairs.

The flashlight. She approached and picked it up, brushing off the dust on the side of her jeans. She turned it over in her hands, examining it doubtfully. It must have rolled down the stairs, propelled by a gust of wind from the gallery door or by a nudge from an inquisitive mouse.

But how odd, she thought uneasily, three-hundred steps and not even the lens was cracked. Almost simultaneously another possibility popped into her head. Someone else was in the lighthouse!

Panic threatened her again. Her body stiffened with fear, and for the length of a heartbeat she felt the helpless vulnerability of being watched against her will.

Flicking the flashlight on, she moved it rapidly up and down the walls and into the shadows beneath the stairs. Nothing. The footprints in the dust were smudged, but showed no sign of someone else's footsteps. The lighthouse was like a tomb, with no trace of any life but her own and the resident mice. A chill ran down her spine.

She began to back warily toward the door, her eyes darting around the room like those of a cornered animal. When she felt the door handle at her back, she turned and jerked it open. Sunlight filtered in, heavy with the scent of the wild, thorny roses that grew around the foundation of the lighthouse. The crashing of the surf below broke the unnatural stillness.

Taking herself firmly in hand, Elizabeth stepped out into the thin yellow of the afternoon sun and wrenched the iron door shut behind her.

Everything was exactly as she had left it. The gate in the hurricane fence was still ajar, with its combination lock still hanging open from one of the chain links. The keys were still in the ignition of her station wagon. A quick check of the front seat proved that her handbag was untouched, her money and credit cards intact.

She shook her head ruefully at her own imagination. A few mice, a little dust and a howling wind, and she was as bad as that sulky kid Tran!

It was absurd. Deception Head Light was so isolated that the closest inhabitants were more than five miles away in the town of Deception Bay. There was no way anyone would have known she'd gone up in the lighthouse. Even if someone had, why on earth would they follow her into the tower just to remove her flashlight and deposit it at the bottom of the stairs?

And the other explanation, the bizarre, supernatural one that had flashed unbidden into her mind during her mad flight down the stairs, was even more absurd.

Of course the flashlight had fallen! There was simply no other plausible way it could have gotten down the stairs. And rather than making herself crazy about it, she should just be glad that it hadn't broken and she didn't have to buy a new one!

CURLED UP on the sofa in front of the fireplace, Elizabeth decided that the little cottage was beginning to feel like home.

She had gathered wildflowers—daisies and a bouquet of the roses that grew around the lighthouse—and now they bloomed in a jar of water on the mantel. She suspected that it wasn't the first time, either. The keepers' wives must have gathered bouquets, too, the ancestors of the same flowers she had picked today.

Women did things like that; they always had. They left the record of their lives in things like flowers and quilts and scrubbed floors. And children.

Odd, the way it always came back to children lately. Jonathan's little girl would be walking now. And Matt— he said he had a son. Where was the boy? In Portland with his mother, where Matt had lived before he'd come to Deception Bay? She hoped he looked like Matt. She found herself picturing a small towheaded boy with grass-green eyes and an infectious grin.

Her biological clock ticked like a time bomb in her chest. It was a cliché, she knew, but like so many clichés, there was truth behind it. She had always expected that in her future would be a husband and children—a family. But the future was hard upon her now, and there seemed to be no sign of it.

Restless, as such thoughts always made her, she stood to poke up the fire, and her eye fell on several old photographs that were framed on the mantel. One was of a dour-looking old man with a corncob pipe in his mouth, and a notation across the bottom that said Deception Head, 1943. In another a group of men stood around a surfboat, squinting into the sun, men in mackinaws, thick frieze-cloth trousers and long rubber boots with the tops folded down, dated 1901. A third showed a laughing young woman in a long dress with leg-of-mutton sleeves and a lace ruche at her neck, with several children gathered close to her skirts and the inscription Jenny, 1895.

Who were they, she wondered as she examined their blurred, bland faces, those old keepers of the Light, and their women and their children? She would have to ask Matt; he seemed to know so much about the lighthouse.

It was important that she know, too, so that somehow she could include them in her paintings. She must find a way to let them, those dauntless men and their heroic families, speak through her. Their souls and their bones and their legends were part and parcel of the Light, as much a part of it as the tower itself or the wind-sheared trees that surrounded it.

She would ask him tomorrow.

Tomorrow. Anticipation tingled through her body, but she found that she was thinking more about her guide than about the job she had come here to do.

Under the circumstances that was a mistake. This summer was only a sabbatical, a brief departure from the career that had occupied all her time and energy for the past ten years. She had to see that she used it well, used it to renew her drive and youthful enthusiasm, or in September she would find herself back on the same sterile, barren treadmill that had precipitated this desperate flight into the wilds of Oregon in the first place.

She had to discipline herself to employ her recreational time as efficiently as she did her work time. It simply wouldn't do to let herself be distracted.

She sighed despondently. Lately it had begun to seem as though both working and playing required the same stringency, the same careful planning, the same rigid self-control. She sighed again, but the minute she left her mind to its own devices, her perverse imagination once more assumed a life of its own.

An entire day with this fascinating man, whose sensual appearance was so at odds with his diffident, almost shy, manner. She suspected that it was going to be difficult to concentrate on Deception Head Light with Matt McCullough in such close quarters.

Yawning, she glanced at the clock on the kitchen wall. Nine o'clock! In Chicago the nightlife didn't even *start* until after Johnny Carson!

There was just one more thing she had to do before she set the windup alarm clock for two hours before dawn. She walked into the kitchen and took a package of hot dogs from the icebox, then opened the front door and tossed it out onto the porch for the raccoons.

CHAPTER FIVE

THE *CHINOOK WIND* wasn't the only fishing boat getting under way before dawn. From inside the icehouse Elizabeth could see the running lights of a dozen small craft move silently over the dark waters of Deception Bay, looking like red and green fireflies.

Although it was the middle of June, the temperature was wintery. Even inside the heated icehouse, even through the several layers of clothing she wore, the dampness chilled Elizabeth to the bone. The steam from the foam plastic cup she held in her hands condensed on the cold window.

She was grateful that Jory had invited her, albeit grudgingly, to wait for Matt inside. "No sense freezin' yer arse off," he had growled, fixing her with a baleful eye, "even if ye got no business here." Then he had poured a cup of coffee from the pot that was perking cheerily on the counter and thrust it at her.

"How much do I owe you?" Elizabeth asked, extending a dollar bill across the counter.

Jory glared and shoved the money back at her. "Keep it, keep it, keep it," he snapped. "It's on the house." Then he shuffled off, muttering darkly to himself a litany of imprecations concerning the state of the world in general, women in particular and women who poked their noses where they weren't wanted most particularly of all.

Smiling to herself, Elizabeth turned back to the window. Her own face looked back at her from the darkened glass.

Outside, a string of bulbs along the wooden pilings spotlighted groups of fishermen standing in the shadows. Most had their hands wrapped around cups of coffee. Most were unshaven. At this hour of the morning they all looked tired and washed-out, their faces pale oval smudges under the stark lights.

Might be something to include in a painting, Elizabeth mused. Very minimalist—just the bulky silhouettes of the men under the stark white lights, the shroud of fog thick over the water, the tiny points of red and green . . .

"Been waiting long?"

Elizabeth glanced up. The whole of Jory's dusty little shop was duplicated transparently in the window, and in the reflection she saw the figure of a man sauntering across the room.

A navy pea jacket, unbuttoned, flapped open as he walked, and a flat Basque fisherman's cap was tipped over his forehead at a rakish angle. A black turtleneck sweater reached nearly to his ears, and unruly yellow hair curled over the collar.

His eyes met hers in the glass and she smiled. "Matt. No, I've just been watching the boats putting out to sea. How do they manage it in this fog?"

"Compasses. Lorans. But mostly a gut instinct that comes to you after you've spent enough time on the water." His reflection vanished as he poured himself a cup of coffee, then reappeared to stand beside Elizabeth's in the window. As he sipped his coffee, he dropped his free hand to her shoulder in a friendly, companionable way that made her feel almost, but not quite, like one of the boys.

A third face materialized in the window. "Goin' out to draw the Light?" Jory rasped as he shuffled up behind them.

"Yes," Elizabeth replied, although his question was directed to Matt's reflection.

"Well, long as she's gonna do it," he continued, talking about Elizabeth as though she weren't even there, "she may's well do it right. Take her out to Whale Cove. Ain't nuthin' purtier'n that old Light from Whale Cove."

"Good idea, Jory. I'll do that."

Grunting ungraciously, Jory shuffled away.

"I think Jory may have the soul of a poet," Elizabeth said under her breath as her laughing eyes met Matt's in the window.

Matt grinned. "We all have our moments."

THE DISEMBODIED white lights at the end of the pier retreated to tiny pinpoints as the *Chinook Wind* marked her course between the jetties and headed for the open sea. Her bow cut through the water with a steady splash. The blackness of the water changed ever so slightly, taking on a charcoal tinge now that the dawn was trying to burn through the fog.

Once past the reef, Matt cut the engines and lowered the anchor, then joined Elizabeth at the rail. "You might as well come inside and keep warm. It'll be half an hour before you'll be able to see anything."

"I just want to be sure to be here when the fog starts to lift," she replied through chattering teeth. But because it was dark and because it was cold, she allowed herself to be escorted into the tiny main cabin.

The odor of coffee permeated the air, smelling thick and black. Elizabeth inspected the cabin curiously. These quarters *might* sleep four, she thought, but only if they were very, very friendly!

Like the rest of the boat, the main cabin was strictly utilitarian, without ornament except for a calendar on one bulkhead. In garish colors, the only splash of color in the bare, masculine room, it advertised Jory's Icehouse and Bait Shop—For All Your Fishing Needs.

The ceiling was low. She noticed that Matt had to duck whenever he passed under the light. Beyond the gleaming windows that wrapped the cabin on three sides there was only the salt spray and the drifting mist and a faint smear of light in the eastern sky; the west was still swathed in darkness.

Perched on the shoulders of the sea, the *Chinook Wind* lurched precariously, dipping and swaying on swells that ran the full length of the reef. One especially hostile bounce sent Elizabeth staggering unceremoniously across the cabin and sat her down abruptly on one of the wooden benches that served as seats during the day and beds at night.

Her face blanched and her gray eyes darkened anxiously. "Does this thing have seat belts?" she asked, her voice quavering.

Matt grinned. "No, but it does have life jackets." He lifted the seat of the other bench to reveal bright orange life jackets heaped inside. "But we don't need to worry about that. We're going to have fair weather today. I guarantee it, and so does the Coast Guard weather station."

He poured two mugs of coffee and handed one to Elizabeth, bracing himself with a hand against the ceiling as the roll of the boat threatened to send him sprawling.

The coffee was as thick and black as she suspected it would be. Real witch's brew. She shuddered, but she found that its warmth dissolved the queasy knot of sea-sickness and fright that had congealed in her stomach.

"Why did you want to get started so early?" Matt asked. From across the cabin he leaned forward and propped one foot on the seat beside Elizabeth. He rested his elbow on the upraised knee as he held the steaming mug in both hands.

The angle between his long legs spanned the entire width of the cabin. It was a very provocative stance, and she wondered if he knew it.

"I have an idea how the lighthouse should look just as it's emerging from the fog. It should look as though...it's not quite there, as though maybe it's only a dream, and if you...look too hard, look too close..."

"Yes?"

"It'll just vanish into the mist."

"Yes," he agreed thoughtfully. "I've seen it look like that."

His body filled the cramped quarters as he hovered over her like a genial blond giant. The atmosphere suddenly seemed very close. It overwhelmed her. *He* overwhelmed her.

Above the strong odor of coffee she became aware of other odors. He smelled of fresh sea air and diesel fuel, and faintly of fish. Other, more intimate scents enveloped her—the frank man scents of soap and toothpaste and tobacco, and just the merest suggestion of aftershave.

His pea jacket hung open, revealing a broad expanse of chest beneath the black sweater, jeans low-slung on narrow hips, a lean flank that angled into the powerful thigh where he rested his elbow, and banished all thought from her mind except one—that she wanted him.

It came to her without words, with feelings alone, and with an onslaught of raw physical desire that shocked her. This bore no resemblance to the charming, inconsequential games played with such sophisticated skill on Rush Street. This was no game. This was something violent and urgent, not civilized. And not to be denied.

She wanted him—wanted him in all the wild, primitive ways that a woman wants a man. She shifted uncomfortably on the hard wooden bench.

His head, bent slightly to avoid bumping the ceiling, was very near, so near that she could see herself in his eyes. Golden flecks, like glints of sunshine on the deep green of the sea, danced across the reflection of her face in his dark pupils. She wondered if he could read himself as completely in her eyes.

Then she saw that he wasn't looking at her eyes at all, but at her lips. A vein throbbed in his temple. His lips, still curved into their habitual down-turned smile, suddenly seemed less innocent.

He wants it, too, she realized with another stab of desire, so sharp and so unexpected that her breath caught in her throat. That made it much more complicated, much more dangerous. She shifted again. "Why do you always smile like that?" she asked abruptly.

"Like what?"

"Like that." She almost reached up to touch his lips with inquisitive fingertips, then drew back. Instinct warned her that she was perilously close to some port of no return of her own. Just like the *Blue Magpie*. Just like every incautious traveller who ventured too close to a dangerous shoreline. "As though you know some secret joke that no one else knows."

He grinned. "Maybe I do." He glanced past Elizabeth's shoulder to the brightening world beyond the porthole. "Look, the sun's coming up."

She turned and saw that the fog was indeed going to burn off early today. Grateful for the distraction, she seized her sketchbook and chalks, and hurried out the hatch as if the devil himself were behind her.

Elizabeth's artistic instincts proved correct. The fog was being sucked out to sea along with the tide, and it revealed the headland and its lighthouse a few tantalizing inches at a time. The peaked red cupola came first, the sun glinting off its brass tip in a golden starburst, then the black parapet that ringed the massive masonry tower. Finally the fog slid down the white monolith itself, exposing the long sheath of masonry foot by enticing foot.

Elizabeth was totally absorbed in her work, sketching with broad swaths of color the landscapes and seascapes she would later execute in oils on canvas. She was conscious of nothing else, only of capturing each magical moment, each new angle of light, as the fog receded from the cape. She even forgot Matt, who stood watching her from the bridge, eyes narrowed to mere slits and his face kept prudently blank while a cigarette burned, forgotten, between his fingers.

The fog had retreated altogether from the cape itself but still swirled thickly at the base of Deception Head. Chiaroscuro. Light and dark. The lighthouse looked as though it were suspended in space, supported on nothing more substantial than clouds. Once on the wane, the fog withdrew rapidly, and soon the distance between the *Chinook Wind* and the shore glistened in morning sun. Huge basalt crags, only partially submerged by the ebbing tide, gleamed wetly. The turquoise swells were tipped with silver.

The frosted waves were the last of Elizabeth's sketches, then she closed her sketchbook and slumped tiredly against the gunwale. Only then did she notice that her hands were red and chapped, her fingers frozen and that her legs ached from balancing on the deck that heaved beneath her feet. A rainbow of chalk dust was streaked through the damp tendrils of her windblown hair, and a patch of charcoal adorned one cheek.

She made her way aft and collapsed in a heap on the fish-fighting chair bolted there.

Tension flowed from her body. She leaned back in the chair and propped her feet on the gunwale, letting her glance wander aimlessly over the few clouds that dotted the sky, and the soaring, shrieking gulls. The huge downriggers creaked softly in the wind.

She sighed contentedly as she settled farther into the chair and rested her head against its back. The sun felt delightfully warm on her face.

Idly her glance traveled up to the flying bridge where Matt sat behind the wheel. The man, the sea and the sky—it made a picturesque arrangement when viewed from below and against the sun.

He leaned backward against the sky as if his body needed no other means of support, and except for his wind-ruffled hair, he was as motionless as if he had been carved out of stone. A cigarette hung immobile in the corner of his mouth.

His gaze was turned toward a trawler steaming across the horizon. His hands on the wheel seemed to exert almost no pressure as he kept the *Chinook Wind* quartered into the wind.

Elizabeth studied him curiously. He looked different somehow. It was so subtle that she was unable to put her finger on it. Apparently thinking himself unobserved, he had allowed his features to fall into an expression very different from the one he usually wore.

Against the clear blue of the sky his profile looked bleak. But it was more than that. The lines etched in his skin were somehow more pronounced, giving his face a brooding quality Elizabeth had never noticed before. It made him look gaunter somehow. It made him look older.

Fascinated, she picked up her sketchbook and began to draw. She filled several sheets and turned them under, trying to get the planes exactly right—the slope of his forehead, the angle of his chin, the rise of his cheekbones and the dark hollows beneath them, the flesh tones and the copper-colored slashes of cheek and lips.

Her hands flew across the paper of their own volition, shading here, highlighting there, until she thought she had caught what she was aiming for. She looked at the portrait, puzzled. It was Matt, and yet it wasn't.

Just then he turned and caught her eye. "What are you doing?" he called.

"Taking a break." She was embarrassed, almost as though she'd been caught spying on him.

"C'mon up."

She tucked her sketchbook under her arm and mounted the ladder that led to the bridge. The wind nearly swept her off her feet. Despite the sunny sky she was glad for the bulky sweater she wore, although she felt like an awkward, clumsy bundle as she sat down next to Matt.

"Can I see what you've done, or is it top secret until publication?"

Silently she handed him the sketchbook. He leafed through the pages one at a time, making no comment.

"You can't tell much from these rough sketches," Elizabeth offered hesitantly.

"Yes, you can," he replied, not looking up from the drawings. "I think you've got something here. I know that lighthouse inside and out—and these say something to me." He glanced at her obliquely and grinned. "I'm no expert ... but I like them."

Elizabeth was inordinately pleased by the compliment.

Shuffling through the sheets, he came to the last few, and he glanced at her again. "Your subject matter is open to question," he said. "But the technique is pretty good."

"The subject matter is pretty good, too, I think." Now that she saw the sketch and the man together, she realized what the difference was: the smile, the slight, wry smile that always played around his lips, wasn't on the face in the picture.

That face wasn't amused. It had a look of sadness that Elizabeth hadn't recognized until she saw it on paper. A puzzled frown creased her forehead. It was almost as though when he'd let down his guard an entirely different personality had emerged.

Her eyes moved from one to the other, studying first Matt and then his portrait. It was something about the eyes, fixed on the horizon yet somehow turned inward, something about the small, taut muscles around the mouth that pulled it into a stern line.

The sadness, if that was indeed what it was, looked chronic. It looked as though it had been there for a very long time, lurking just beneath the smile, and was so familiar that Matt no longer even noticed it.

What did it mean? she wondered uneasily as her eyes moved from one to the other. And which was the real Matt McCullough—the relentlessly cheerful expression he put on in public, or the one he wore when he thought he was alone?

Matt closed the cover on the sketchbook and handed it back to her. When he felt her icy fingers, he tsk-tsked reprovingly, then pulled off his gloves and slipped them over her hands, where they protruded from her sleeves like the absurd, oversize hands of a puppet. They were warm from the heat of his body.

He extended one arm along the back of the bench, and in comfortable silence they gazed landward at the lighthouse on Deception Head. The rough wool of his pea jacket felt scratchy where it brushed the back of Elizabeth's neck.

"There's so much I'd like to know about lighthouses," she said, trying to brake the sensations that were threatening to run away with her. "What's going to happen to them now that everything's automated?"

"Oh, lots of different things." Matt squeezed her shoulder companionably and pulled her imperceptibly closer to his warmth. "Some of them are turned into museums. Some become national parks and historical landmarks. Sometimes private citizens buy them and turn them into bed-and-breakfasts.

"Tillamook Rock Lighthouse," Matt continued, "better known as Terrible Tilly, up by Garibaldi, is probably the most unique. She stands a mile and a quarter offshore on a crag that rises straight up from the ocean floor. The sea's ferocious up there. Her light shone for nearly ninety years, went from whale oil to coal oil to a Fresnel prism lens.

"More than once, when storms knocked out the panes of the lantern and threw rocks and fish and seaweed into the lantern room, the keepers worked up to their necks in water to keep her going. She was a legend, one of the world's best known sea sentinels in her day. Now she's a mausoleum.''

"A *mausoleum?*"

He nodded. "The world's first lighthouse mausoleum. People can have their cremated remains stored there. Presumably for eternity.''

"It seems such an incongruous end, somehow, for a legend...."

"It's not the worst way to go. At least she made it to a ripe and respected old age. It isn't that way for all of them. Scotch Cap Light, for example.''

"What happened there?''

"Scotch Cap Lighthouse, up on Unimak Island, probably one of the loneliest lighthouses in the world— it was destroyed by a tidal wave in 1946. The top of the wave just broke over the cliff back of Scotch Cap and tore the reinforced concrete tower from its foundation.

"Coastguardsmen from the mainland tried to raise her all night. At daybreak they dispatched a message to headquarters—'Scotch Cap Light believed lost. Light extinguished and horn silent.' But it was the next day before they could get close enough to see what had happened, and then they sent another message—'Scotch Cap Light Station lost, all hands.' All that was left of her were a few twisted steel rods.''

"'All hands.''' Elizabeth shuddered. "How terrible. Did they ever find the men?''

"It was over a week until the sea began washing up the bodies.''

Valiant, bold men, Elizabeth thought with something resembling awe. A special breed. Where did they find such men, willing to take such risks and live such lives? And where were such men today?

"You want to know about lighthouses, there's a fellow I think you'd enjoy talking to. Guillaume Aubergine's his name. He was the last keeper at Deception Head Light before it was decommissioned. Lives in the old caretaker's quarters up at Heceta Head. Are you game for a cruise up the coast?"

"Oh, yes. I'd love it! And I'd love to meet him!"

"It'll have to be an overnighter," he warned. "Heceta Head's about five hours north. Can you get away for that long?"

Could she—? Elizabeth didn't hesitate. "Of course. That's why I came here."

"Well, let me make a few telephone calls and I'll see what I can do." The enthusiasm in her eyes made him smile. "You're a very lovely woman, Elizabeth La Salle. But I suppose a lot of men tell you that." He looked down at her, still smiling, but with eyes turning a dark and inscrutable green. "*Do* a lot of men tell you that?"

"Some," Elizabeth admitted. "But it doesn't matter. Everyone says it. It's just a line...." She lost her train of thought completely as his hand reached up to smooth her damp hair back from her face.

"Not to me." His hand moved down the side of her face, where it paused to outline the shape of her ear with a gentle forefinger before coming to rest on the curve of her cheek. "Very lovely, even with that streak of charcoal across your face."

With tentative fingers he reached up and brushed the charcoal dust away. Then, just as tentatively, he tilted up her chin with thumb and forefinger and kissed her.

He lifted his head to look down at her with a smile as tentative as the chaste, diffident kiss. "What are you doing here, Elizabeth?" he whispered huskily. "Why have you come to Deception Bay?"

His words brushed across her lips as soft as feathers, and his beard tickled her skin. "Why...why, to paint the lighthouse, of course," she faltered, confused as much by the kiss as by the question.

Her eyes flickered down to his lips. Just for a moment she allowed herself to forget the lighthouse and the U.S. Lighthouse Society, and the reason she had come to Deception Bay in the first place.

She melted into the curve of his arm and wondered if he would kiss her again. The tip of her tongue darted out and unconsciously moistened her lips, then she felt the warmth again, and the heat, and the gentle, tentative pressure.

"No, I mean why did you *really* come?" The words were light and teasing, and there was an unmistakable gleam of amusement in his green eyes as he sat back and regarded her with his customary calm smile.

This wasn't the way it was supposed to be. When they had the advantage, they took it. Everyone knew that. Those were the rules. But he seemed to be playing by a different set of rules, and they obviously included caution. Maybe that was how things were done in this part of the world, she thought almost regretfully.

She sat back, too. She was disappointed and vaguely dissatisfied and more than a little shaken by her immediate and instinctive response.

"I think the real reason you came," Matt continued in the same teasing voice, "is to disrupt the safe little world I've created for myself here."

"I...I don't even know you," she demurred faintly.

"Ah, but I know you."

Unexpectedly she recalled the look in his eyes the first time she had met him—the inexplicable recognition, even though she knew they had never set eyes on each other before.

"I was afraid you'd come eventually." The down-turned corners of his smile deepened. "Don't you believe in fate?"

The question caught Elizabeth off guard. "I never thought about it." She folded her hands in their ludicrous gloves in her lap and looked up at him, puzzled. "What are you afraid of?"

"A number of things. Afraid you'd come. Afraid you'll leave—"

"But of course I'll leave! I've only come for the summer."

"Yes, I know." His voice was low, and if it hadn't been for his smile, Elizabeth would have thought it sounded unhappy. "You're like some beautiful, exotic bird, stopping here for a little while on your way to somewhere else. You don't belong here. I know that. And me—I've been hiding out in this little backwater so long that I know I'll never leave."

"What do you mean, hiding out? You're happy," she paused. "Aren't you?"

"Yes. At least, I've never regretted coming here, never missed the world outside. Before. Now..."

"Now?"

"Now I'm a little sorry. Not a lot, just a little. But I've been here too long. My options have narrowed considerably."

"But...do you mean that you *want* to leave? Where would you go? What would you do?"

"Well, I can navigate by the stars. I can read the sky and predict the weather. I know the best holes for steelhead and where the spring run of chinook begins. I guess that should qualify me for just about anything." He chuckled as if it were some great joke on himself.

Elizabeth tried to picture him in some other world, in the world of advertising, for example. She couldn't. "I would have thought you were quite content. You seem so... natural here." And he did, as though the setting— the breathtaking coast, the majestic mountains and the tall, proud pines—were nothing more than a background for him.

"Basically I am content. Just sometimes... well, I wonder, that's all." He gave her an ironic smile and let his arm fall from the back of the bench, then returned both hands to the wheel. "Want to work some more?"

"I think I've done enough sketching for one day."

"Well, then, how would you like to get a bite to eat? If Tran were here, he could rustle us up some lunch, but—"

"Tran? He goes out with you?"

"Sometimes, whenever I need him. He's kind of my odd-jobber when he's not in school. Bait boy, cook—that sort of thing."

"I'm surprised."

"Why?"

"Oh, it's just that Tran... well..." She hesitated, and the boy's image flashed across her mind—hands thrust in the pockets of the ratty army surplus jacket he wore, the hostile, combative expression that was always on his face. "He just isn't the most personable kid in the world, is he? I can't imagine he'd be very good for business."

Matt chuckled again. "Tran's all right. He's a hard worker. Most of my regulars like him just fine."

"Well, I'm sure they see an entirely different side of him," Elizabeth replied in a conciliatory voice. They'd *have* to! she added sourly to herself.

"Are we on for lunch then?" Matt asked. "It's included in the price."

"Oh, well, in that case, by all means!"

He took hold of the wheel and brought the boat about.

SEEING ELIZABETH and Matt together a second time did nothing to sweeten Celebration's disposition. Her face was a mask of teenage angst as she showed them to a booth and offered them coffee. Behind the wide, artificial smile and the unnaturally bright voice, Elizabeth could sense the girl's desperate unhappiness, and she could see that Matt's kindly teasing only made matters worse.

"You aren't very nice to her, you know," she said, leaning over the table confidentially after Celebration had taken their orders and wriggled away.

"Who?"

Elizabeth nodded in Celebration's direction.

"Celebration?" Matt sounded surprised. "What do you mean?"

"She's in love with you."

Matt smiled. "Oh, that. It's just puppy love. She's had a crush on me since she was no taller than my knee."

"Well, she's not a puppy now!" Elizabeth retorted tartly. "I can't believe you don't see that."

"I do see it," Matt said comfortably, "but she'll get over it. Celebration's all—"

"Yes, I know! Celebration's all right! Jory's all right! Tran's all right!" Elizabeth shook her head with mock exasperation. "I don't think you see things as they really are, Matt! Jory—well, *maybe* Jory's all right. He didn't act as though he'd like to stick a knife between my ribs this morning, at any rate. But Celebration! She's miserable because of you, and you don't even see it! And

Tran—well, from what I can see, Tran is the local juvenile delinquent, and you talk about him as if he's just a high-spirited kid!''

"What would you have me do?''

She shrugged, a little ashamed of her outburst. "It doesn't concern me, of course,'' she said in a calmer tone, "but I think you could be a little more...involved. They're important to you, after all. They're your friends. Don't you care about them?''

"Actually, Tran is more than my friend.'' Matt looked at her cryptically. "His name is Tran Van Hoa McCullough. He's my son.''

Elizabeth gaped at him, dumbfounded. Then her shoulders sagged helplessly. "Oh, Matt!'' she wailed. "Why didn't you *tell* me?'' She twisted her hands together in an agony of embarrassment. "I feel so...so insensitive!''

"Don't.'' He reached for her hands and held them firmly in his steady grasp. "It's my fault. Hey, listen to me!'' He ducked his head to look directly into her downcast, mortified eyes and smiled reassuringly. "It's my fault entirely. I didn't mention it because I didn't think it had any bearing on our working relationship, that's all.''

"Well, it doesn't, of course,'' Elizabeth moaned. "If I'd known, I wouldn't have said...I mean, I wouldn't have been so...''

"Honest?'' Matt finished wryly.

Elizabeth looked at him unhappily. "Something like that,'' she admitted. His son? The golden-haired child of her dreams vanished, leaving in its place the scowling visage of a surly, unpleasant adolescent with hard, angry eyes.

"Don't worry. I'm just sorry that you and Tran hit it off so badly. Not," he said, shrugging apologetically, "that that's so unusual. He hits it off badly with just about everyone."

"Problems from the divorce?"

"No. My ex-wife was never his mother."

"I don't understand. Who was his mother?"

"I don't know. Not even Tran knows."

"Then . . ." Elizabeth's forehead furrowed uncertainly. "Then he's not really your son."

"Not biologically, no. But he's really my son. I adopted him four years ago. You've seen him—those light brown eyes, that sandy hair. He's some American's son, that's for sure. No papers, no identification, nothing. But his face is his passport, as a refugee official told me. No one's even sure how old he is. I figure about fourteen or fifteen, but on his legal documents he's listed as sixteen. And he might be that old. He's small for sixteen, but malnutrition does that. The only thing that *is* certain is that he had an American father. He could be mine as well as anyone's." Matt's voice was grim. "Just part of the excess baggage left behind by a retreating army."

He could be mine. So he had fought in that bitter war. Elizabeth wanted to ask him about it, but there was a finality in his voice that sounded like the closing of a door.

"Where is Tran from?"

He shook his head and shrugged. "He came here from a refugee camp on the Cambodian border. He'd lived there most his life, except for a few years he says he hooked up with a group of soldiers and made his way to Saigon—Ho Chi Minh City, that is. But then he was caught in a government sweep of *con lai*—half-breeds, children of American fathers—and sent back to Dong Khoi Camp, until he finally came here.

"All I know is that he was found floating in the debris of a junk in the South China Sea. Everyone else was dead. Probably attacked by Thai pirates—raped the women, murdered the men, left them all to die. Tran was just a baby. They found him tied into a bamboo basket, nearly dead himself from dehydration and exposure. There was a little pouch of gold coins tied inside his clothes. That was all. No identification, nothing. Just that little pouch of coins." He paused. "Someone tried to buy a life for him, I guess."

Elizabeth's throat constricted, and her eyes filled with tears. "Poor Tran," she breathed. "I wish you had told me sooner. I could have been more...understanding."

"I told you I had a son," Matt reminded her.

"Yes, you did," she had to concede. Everything beyond that had been strictly conjecture on her part. Thinking about the story Matt had just related, the tragic image of an abandoned infant floating alone in the destruction of his world somehow took on a greater reality than the bitter, hostile boy he had become. She shook her head compassionately. "Poor Tran," she said again.

Matt smiled wryly. "Don't get too sympathetic," he warned. "If you do, he's bound to disappoint you. He's tough, and he can be mean. He'll do whatever it takes."

"Whatever it takes—?"

"To survive. He's a survivor, Tran is. The very fact that he made it this far proves that. But the same things that helped him survive in the refugee camps are the things that are dragging him down now. When he first came to live with me, he was totally amoral. Totally without conscience. And he hated me. He hated Deception Bay. He hated everything. There were more than a few times when I didn't think we were going to make it. It was months before he'd even try to talk, longer than that before he'd sleep in a bed or stop hiding food all over the house. Sometimes I used to go into his room at night and find him huddling in the corner, wide awake, staring out into the dark as if he were some kind of hunted animal."

"How awful," Elizabeth murmured. She heard the anguish in Matt's voice and wished desperately that there was something she could do to take the pain away. "For both of you."

"Well, it's better now. Tran is quite intelligent, you know. And he's come so far." Matt looked at her with the sheepish smile of a proud father who can't resist boasting about his child. "You can hear how well he speaks English—hardly any accent at all. And he goes to school. I have hopes that he may even graduate. But..."

Matt's face didn't change, it never did. It was his voice that provided the key to what he was feeling, and now his voice fell, becoming low and tortured. "But he'll *never* be everything he could have been, because of all those lost years when he had to use all his wits just trying to stay alive!"

Matt's fingers still clasped Elizabeth's, and now she turned their hands over so that she held his instead. Beneath his anger she heard something else, something she thought sounded like guilt. "You mustn't blame yourself, Matt. What happened all those years ago wasn't your fault, and now you've given him another chance at life. Whatever potential he *does* manage to fulfill will be because of you." She smiled reassuringly. "And he'll be fine. You'll see. Why, even in the short time I've known him, I'm sure I've already noticed him become a little less . . . antagonistic.''

And at least for the moment that it took her to say the words, it seemed to her that they were true.

CHAPTER SIX

PAINTING WAS a solitary pursuit, Elizabeth discovered. There were entire days when she didn't see or speak to another soul, and her only companions were the shrieking gulls and timid raccoons.

The kitchen became her studio. Although small, it had the best light and a northern exposure. She tacked her charcoal sketches to the cupboard doors and studied them carefully as she copied them in oils, hoping she possessed the skill to bring the old lighthouse to life.

Her first completed canvas showed a pewter sky over the rocky mass of Deception Head and its dark green mantle of stunted pines. What light there was in the painting seemed to radiate from the whiteness of the lighthouse tower alone. The crashing breakers hurled spume over the top of the cape, and the tower soared upward, as if freeing itself triumphantly from the primordial chains of the sea.

Elizabeth eyed it critically. The lighthouse had an abstract, three-dimensional perspective that pleased her, and the pine tree forest appeared to have the proper degree of mystery. The technique was a little rough, and the colors lacked subtlety, resembling the flat, gaudy tints of a color photograph. But to quote Matt, it "said something."

When the time passed in a succession of gray, overcast days, she spent them transferring her charcoal sketches to canvas, but the first thing she did every morning was walk out onto the porch and study the sky. Matt knew she wanted to sketch Deception Head Light under all conditions, so whenever there was a change in the weather, she knew she could expect a call from him.

Most of the time she and Matt had the *Chinook Wind* all to themselves, but once he telephoned her at dawn to invite her along on one of his fishing charters.

The day promised to be exceptional, he told her. Elizabeth could see that as soon as she looked outside.

Daybreak wasn't the normal sluggish graying of the sky, when the black grayed so gradually that it was hard to tell when night ended and day began. This particular dawn was breaking over the Cascade Mountains behind Deception Head Light with magnificent ribbons of orange and red streaming across the entire eastern sky. The fog bank that hung perpetually offshore was gone, leaving the air with a crystalline clarity rarely seen on the coast.

Already on board the *Chinook Wind* when Elizabeth arrived at the icehouse were eight fishermen on vacation from an accounting firm in Los Angeles. All but one were regulars, Matt told her. They came up for a week of salmon fishing every summer while their wives drove one hundred miles through the mountains to the annual Shakespeare Festival in the tiny, picturesque university town of Ashland.

Tran was also on board. Elizabeth was glad. It was the first time she had seen him in nearly a week. In view of everything Matt had told her, she was ashamed of her initial dislike of the boy and had determined to make a fresh start. But although she had stopped at his fish stand several times since then, she never found him there. She thought he had probably moved his base of operations to a busier intersection.

Tran was his usual churlish self when Elizabeth greeted him, although she noticed that he appeared to have a better rapport with Matt's regular clients. A third the age and half the size of most of them, he seemed nevertheless to have earned their respect. While Matt trolled the boat just inside the sandbar, Tran organized the fishing process.

"We're usin' flashers on the downriggers today," he announced authoritatively, the fact that English was his second language evident only in the slight hesitation of his speech. "They ain't been strikin' on feather plugs all summer." He reeled in the huge downriggers, one at a time, while the men watched, baited them and then reeled them over the side again.

"We got cut herring and anchovies," he then advised them. "You can try 'em both, but we been havin' better luck with the anchovies." He handed chunks of bait to the men lined up at the rail, and then, with patient, step-by-step instructions, helped the one novice bait his hook.

The day grew warmer. The fishermen switched from coffee to beer. They shed their cold weather garb, layer by layer, in favor of shirtsleeves. Along about midmorning, when everyone had caught the limit on salmon, the men went below for lunch and an instant replay of the day's events, which was as integral a part of the male bonding ritual as the fishing itself.

Only Tran stayed on deck, diligently cleaning the enormous chinook the eight fishermen had caught, for five dollars per fish. He was slicing open the rounded bellies of the fish to reveal the dark red meat, then scooping the entrails out onto the deck. When he came

to a female full of eggs, he would set the bright pink eggs
sacs aside to be made into bait later.

Elizabeth closed her sketchbook and walked aft to
where Tran sat on the refrigeration unit that extended the
full width of the stern. It was really a rather revolting
process, she thought with a shudder as she watched. She
sat down in the fish-fighting chair next to Tran and
folded her hands on top of the sketchbook in her lap.

"Nice day," she observed.

The boy didn't reply.

"You're very good at that."

"What's so good about it?" he muttered ungraciously. "You cut 'em open, you pull out their guts.
There ain't nothing to it." He shook his head as if he
couldn't believe her stupidity.

Elizabeth looked down at him unhappily. This wasn't
going the way she'd planned. Focusing resolutely on the
image of an abandoned, starved baby tied into a bamboo basket by someone who must have treasured him
above life itself, she smiled with determination.

"They keep you pretty busy, don't they?"

"That's what I git paid for," he retorted without
looking up.

"Yes. And you're very good at it, too." She'd already
said that. Conversation ground to an uncomfortable
standstill. Uncomfortable, that is, from Elizabeth's point
of view. Tran didn't seem to notice that she was still sitting there.

She tried again. "I remember that your father told me
you know all about the ghosts in the lighthouse," she said
pleasantly. "Someday, if you have time, I'd like to hear
about them."

Tran glanced at her with contemptuous eyes. "There
ain't no such thing as ghosts," he scoffed.

Elizabeth backpedaled furiously. Had she sounded patronizing? She hoped not—that certainly hadn't been her intention. "Well, of course not. I just meant, well, I'd like to know more about the lighthouse, that's all. Something about its history, maybe—"

He uttered a single syllable that was hardly more than a surly grunt, but sounded a bit like "Why?"

"Well, I think it would help me in my painting," Elizabeth replied. "A painting is more than just a picture— it's sort of a... *feeling*... don't you think? I'd like to capture that feeling if I can."

He gave her a look that said, *Why tell it to me?* Hefting a gargantuan silver salmon, he slung it across his knees and slit open its belly, letting the entrails spill out onto the deck.

"Nobody cares about your pictures," he said nastily. "Nobody wants you here, anyway. Whyn't you just go back where you came from?"

Elizabeth looked at his bent head. She fought to keep her temper under control. "Well, I'm sorry you feel that way, Tran. But maybe you should know that I won't be going back where I came from for a while. I came here to do a job, and I won't be leaving until it's finished. Tran," she added, "I'd like to be your friend."

He eyed her with hostility and grunted again. "Why?"

Why? That was a good question. Elizabeth grappled with several hackneyed reasons and discarded them almost as quickly. Tran observed her with a jaundiced eye.

"Don't bother," he snorted contemptuously. "I know why. You just want to get next to my father, that's why! Do you think I was born yesterday, or what?"

"Yes, Matt and I are friends, that's true," Elizabeth acknowledged. "And I'd like to be your friend, too."

"Don't need no friends," he stated in no uncertain terms.

"Everybody needs friends," she countered mildly.

Tran didn't deign to affirm or deny that one. He simply picked up the gutted fish by the jaws and tossed them into the cooler, then sat back down and hauled another one onto his knees. The deck around Elizabeth's feet was slick with the bloody viscera of fish.

"Anyways," Tran spoke up unexpectedly, keeping his eyes fixed on the flashing steel blade of his knife, "there ain't no ghosts at Deception Head. There's only rats."

"Rats?" She remembered with a loathsome shudder the afternoon in the lighthouse when her flashlight had fallen down the stairs.

"Rats," he repeated succinctly. "Place is full of 'em. Big. Big as cats, some of 'em." He looked up at Elizabeth, and his lips stretched into a semblance of a smile. It was an unpleasant smile, only a baring of his teeth, really, and cold almond eyes above. "I seen 'em myself, lots of times. Big as dogs, even, some of 'em." He studied her insolently, his smile becoming wider. "You can eat rats, too. You know that? I done it lots of times. Don't taste bad, either, long's you skin 'em good and get their guts out clean."

To illustrate his point, Tran scooped a fistful of greasy, gray entrails out of the salmon on his lap and thrust them toward Elizabeth. Some of the dripping effluvia spattered her face, and she recoiled in horror. Her hands flew upward to scrape the slime from her cheeks. Then, looking down, she saw that the putrid, bloody residue also covered her hands, and she rubbed them against her jeans with squeamish disgust.

Tran's smile became almost cheerful as he watched her face turn a sickly green. Standing, he threw the remaining fish into the cooler, then picked up a bucket from the deck and lowered it overboard. He filled it with seawater and hoisted it back up. Then, looking deceptively innocent, he bent over and sloshed the water across the deck.

Still shuddering from the first onslaught, Elizabeth was unaware of his intentions until suddenly the bucket of cold seawater washed across her feet. The water and the foul, slimy offal it carried with it soaked her jeans clear up to her knees.

She scrambled frantically out of the fish-fighting chair, and in the process dropped her entire morning's work into the slime. Dismayed, she watched it float across the deck in a grisly, pinkish-gray tide.

Tran looked on impassively. He picked up the sketchbook as it floated past, and handed it to Elizabeth. Slime oozed from between its pages. She held it suspended from thumb and forefinger and regarded it with revulsion.

"Sorry," Tran muttered.

It was his face that bothered her the most, she thought afterward—the false bravado had disappeared, and now he just looked . . . frightened.

"It's all right, Tran," she said, ashamed of her gnawing suspicion that the deed had been intentional.

"I was only swabbin' down the deck," he added defensively.

"I know that." She looked at the drowned, slimy sketchbook that she still held squeamishly between two fingers. An entire morning's work wasted, she wailed inwardly, and probably the most beautiful morning I'll see on this coast all summer! She tossed it onto the fish-fighting chair and wiped her fingers distastefully on her jeans. The lower part of her legs were cold and clammy in the brisk ocean wind, and she began to shiver.

"I think I'll go below," she said, "and try to get dried off."

"So now you're gonna tell my father?" Tran accused jeeringly. It was more a statement of fact than a question.

"What's to tell?" Elizabeth replied evenly. "It was an accident, Tran, that's all." She forced her chattering teeth to hold steady. "We don't need to mention it again."

Tran refused to meet her eyes. Suddenly her suspicions were confirmed. She knew that it had been no accident, and more than that, she knew that he knew she knew it.

Keeping in mind Tran's deliberate misrepresentation of the wild animal situation in Deception Bay, Elizabeth decided to ask Matt about the rat report.

"Rats in the lighthouse?" he queried in surprise. "Where did you get that idea? No, there aren't any rats in there. What would they eat? There are probably whole colonies of field mice, a few spiders maybe, but that's about all."

Elizabeth decided not to bring Tran's name into the discussion. She had as much as told Tran that she wouldn't. Besides, Matt knew his own son. He himself had said that Tran was a tough nut, and he certainly didn't need an outsider only here for the summer pointing out what he already knew.

Her heart ached for Matt, and it ached for Tran, the two of them caught up in some macabre drama that promised to end in tragedy for both of them. And in some only half-understood way it ached for the unknown woman who had been Tran's mother. She wished that the woman's sacrifice could have proved more worthwhile.

CHAPTER SEVEN

ONE MORNING Elizabeth woke to a drizzling mist, too fine to qualify as rain, but definitely with that potential. The trees that surrounded the cottage dripped moisture, and the sea grass was blanketed by rising gray vapor that looked like steam.

Wrapping her black silk kimono snugly around her body, Elizabeth weighed the possibilities as she ate her breakfast. The weather would have to be a judgment call, she finally concluded. If the drizzle remained mist, Matt probably wouldn't call. If, on the other hand, it turned into something more substantial, it might be her first opportunity to sketch Deception Head Light in the rain.

It doesn't need to be a cloudburst, she thought hopefully as she contemplated the wet world beyond the kitchen window. *A shower will do.*

Obligingly a peal of thunder rumbled across the sky.

Thank you! Quickly she finished her breakfast and put the dishes in the sink, then went into the bedroom to change.

She dressed in layers, which she had learned was the best way to cope with the fluctuating coastal climate— black tights followed by jeans, a heavy, cable-knit sweater over a long-sleeved camp shirt, and finally thick white socks with her running shoes, which were now suitably disreputable.

By the time Matt's anticipated call came through, she was ready to go.

"WE'RE IN LUCK," Matt said when Elizabeth boarded the *Chinook Wind* and joined him in the main cabin. "There's a storm coming in, and I knew you'd want to see it." He handed her a mug filled with the thick black brew that was his version of coffee.

He must live on this stuff, she thought with amusement, ladling sugar into the mug to neutralize the bitterness. Matt was wearing the jeans and black turtleneck that appeared to be his uniform when he was at sea, and Elizabeth noticed, as she always did, how the basic simplicity suited him.

"I suppose it's safe to be going out in a storm?"

"It's only a little bit of a squall," Matt said confidently. "And it's not even due until late morning. It might be a little choppy on the open sea, but I figure we'll be safely tucked away in Whale Cove when it hits." His eyes twinkled as he leaned against the counter and crossed his ankles, regarding her with the proud smile of a magician who had just pulled a rabbit out of a hat.

"Whale Cove," Elizabeth repeated. "Isn't that where Jory said you get the best view of the lighthouse?"

"Yep," he drawled in his slow-paced twang. "And when you see it, I think you'll agree. It's small and shallow, and the headland protects it from the wind and wave action, so we'll be able to see everything and hardly be affected, ourselves."

When he drained the last of his coffee, he reached for the slicker that hung on a hook beside the door. It draped him from shoulders to ankles in bulky yellow oilskin, and when he fastened the hood around his neck, his entire head disappeared inside its commodious folds.

Elizabeth laughed. "You look like a giant fire hydrant."

"You'll look the same if you want to come topside," he warned with mock severity as he turned and lumbered awkwardly out the door.

MATT SAILED OUT of the harbor, picking up speed once he passed the jetties and then circling the tip of South Jetty, hugging the coastline as he worked his way south. Through the windows of the main cabin Elizabeth saw rows upon rows of clouds scudding across the sky. They darkened very quickly from a soft gray to the drab color of lead.

Beyond the jetties the sea became choppy. The *Chinook Wind* lurched from the crest of one green-marbled wave into the trough of the next. An occasional gust of wind sent spume across the bow, and Elizabeth clutched the edge of the counter uneasily as she leaned over it to watch the seawater wash the deck.

She tried to quell a thrill of fear. A person could drown out here, she thought uneasily. A boat could just disappear and leave no trace except a little oil slick on the surface of the water.

Of course, she trusted Matt completely. He had to know what he was doing. This was the way he made his living, after all!

And, of course, she wanted to see Deception Head Light in stormy weather. But she wondered how she would be able to sketch with the deck pitching beneath her this way. She also wondered if she'd even be able to *see* the lighthouse through the rolling mist.

She smelled the rain before she saw it—a thick, earthy odor—and then big drops began to pelt the windows. The sky was gunmetal now. The *Chinook Wind* measured her progress in inches as Matt struggled to keep her quartered into the wind.

A person could drown... Unsteadily Elizabeth stumbled toward the wooden bench where Matt stashed the life jackets. She pulled one out and fastened it around her middle, then sat down on the bench and braced her feet against the bucking deck. Her white-knuckled hands gripped the bench with a determination born of panic. The minutes ticked by—they could have been hours.

Then, as quickly as it had started, the storm seemed to abate. The *Chinook Wind* ceased its savage lurching and subsided into irregular rolls that were, if not exactly calm, at least less violent. No longer driven by the force of the wind, the rain drummed a quiet tattoo on the deck.

The diesels shut down and Elizabeth heard the clank of the cable that indicated Matt had lowered the anchor. A minute later the cabin door opened and he walked in.

He threw back the hood of the oilskin and ripped open the snaps that fastened it down the front. Shrugging it off, he hung it on the hook by the door. Water streamed in rivulets from the rubber surface and made puddles on the floor. His hair and beard were plastered to his skin and his face was wet.

"We're here," he announced.

"Whale Cove?" She glanced past his shoulder and saw that the windows were filled with greenery—the dark green of cypress, the blue-green of the pines and the bright spring green of the willows.

"Yep. Want to come topside and—?" Suddenly Matt noticed the bright orange life jacket secured around Elizabeth's waist. "You were scared," he said in a voice full of contrition. He crossed the cabin hurriedly and put his arms around her. "I'm sorry, Elizabeth. I really am." He hugged her closely, rocking her as he might rock a child waking from a nightmare. "I wouldn't have frightened you for the world."

It was an embrace he meant to be comforting, but when his arms encircled her shoulders, Elizabeth felt something more. He made her feel small and vulnerable, and at the same time safe and secure. The final traces of fear left her, but she found that she still trembled. The wall of his chest was broad and solid. She rubbed her cheek against it, and the rough texture of his black sweater was a tantalizing counterpoint to the softness of her skin.

His lips moved softly in her hair, whispering kindly words intended to buoy her spirits. "It's all right now," he crooned soothingly. "It's all over. When we go back, it'll be as smooth as glass. I promise."

He leaned backward and looked down at her, wearing his usual down-turned smile. His green eyes were as calm as the water in a millpond. "Are you okay?" he asked affably.

The degree of her desire was frightening and a little shameful, especially since it obviously wasn't reciprocated. *He doesn't know,* she wailed inwardly. *He doesn't even suspect!*

She felt as though she were trying to corrupt him. He was so unworldly, so innocent. There was that word again. It seemed an inaccurate description of someone who possessed Matt's intense masculinity, but it kept recurring just the same. What he offered was friendship, simple and innocent, to which she seemed incapable of responding without perverting it into something very different.

Fool! she berated herself harshly. *You've spent so much time with singles bar types that you've forgotten*

*people can sometimes be just plain... decent. Without
any ulterior motives. Without trying to get you into bed.*

Carefully she withdrew and pushed herself upright,
stumbling momentarily until she found her footing. "I'm
fine," she replied firmly.

"You're a good sailor," he said, smiling his approval.
"A lot of people would have hit the head the minute we
passed the jetties and not surfaced again until we got
back."

"Oh, it wasn't all that bad," Elizabeth replied. She
chose to forget, for the moment, the terror that had taken
her breath away every time the boat listed into the wind.
"Did I hear you say something about going topside?"

To an outside observer Matt and Elizabeth both
might have looked like two giant fire hydrants standing
side by side on the deck in the pouring rain. Turning
clumsily in the bulky rain gear, Elizabeth looked up at
Matt. "Oh, it's lovely!" she exclaimed. Her eyes shone
through the rain that drenched her face and ran in a
stream off the tip of her nose.

The minuscule cove was almost a perfect circle. Steep
walls of smooth rock surrounded water that was tur-
quoise-blue even in the rain, and it was a precipitous drop
from the top of the cliff to the sea below. Here there were
no twisted, wind-sheared trees. The cove was ringed by
brooding cypresses and stately pines, while the limbs of
graceful willows arced downward to trail in the water.

"Deception Head protects this cover," Matt explained. "That's why it's so calm here, and the trees grow
so tall."

"It's very peaceful," Elizabeth said. "It's almost like
being inside a house looking out at the storm." She

glanced around curiously. "But where is the lighthouse?"

Instead of replying Matt turned her around so she faced the narrow inlet that formed the entrance to the cove. She gasped in surprise. Directly behind the *Chinook Wind* was Deception Head, half hidden in the gray rain. The lighthouse was unexpectedly close, so close that Elizabeth could distinguish the texture of its rough walls, so close that she couldn't even see its tiled roof unless she tilted her head and looked straight up.

Beyond the protected cove the storm still raged. Angry waves broke against the base of Deception Head, hurling surf halfway up the rocky headland, where it curled back on itself for a moment and then fell crashing into the sea.

The beauty and the raw, primitive power rendered Elizabeth speechless. Wordlessly she turned to Matt and found that he was gazing, not at the lighthouse, but at her.

"Do you like it?" he asked. Then he answered his own question without waiting for a reply. "Of course you do. I *knew* you would!" He sounded as pleased as if he were making her a gift of this magnificent view and of the storm itself.

"Thank you, Matt," she breathed. Standing on tiptoe, she planted an appreciative kiss on his wet cheek. It was a spontaneous gesture, clumsy in the bulky oilskins they both wore, and since much of his face was concealed by his rain hat, the kiss landed partly on his cheek and partly on the rubber hood.

Her eyes closed for a fraction of a second, and raindrops touched her eyelids. She fell back down on her heels. "I think I'll go inside and get to work," she said, and left him alone on the deck.

THE STORM RAGED ON for the rest of the morning. Once Elizabeth looked up from her sketchbook to see Matt come into the cabin. He shook the water out of his oilskin and hung it over hers on the hook by the door.

"Coffee?" he asked.

She shook her head. He filled his own cup and then stretched his long body out on one of the wooden benches to watch her work. In spite of herself Elizabeth found that she was listening for his controlled breathing behind her. In and out, inhale and exhale. It was deep and regular.

She wondered if he might be sleeping. She had never seen him asleep, of course, and wondered how he looked without his self-protective smile. Relaxed? Or gaunt and older, the way he had looked the day she had drawn his portrait?

Then she heard the click of his lighter and knew that he wasn't asleep. It made the skin on the back of her neck prickle to feel his eyes fixed on her from behind.

With superhuman effort she put him out of her mind. She concentrated instead on the storm breaking over the headland, the way storms must have broken over it for thousands of years—the power and the awesome, primitive magnificence of nature unrestrained. She portrayed it in the violent greens of the sea, the glittering silver of the spume, the writhing browns of the rock and the drab, terminal gray of the falling rain.

Gradually the storm began to abate. Elizabeth's last few sketches showed the grayness becoming tinged with yellow, and suddenly the sun broke out from behind the clouds. The wet headland shimmered.

She tossed her sketchbook onto the counter and flexed her fingers stiffly. Matt came up behind her, and she felt his hands on her shoulders as he began to massage her tense muscles with strong fingers. He was very good at it, kneading with exactly the right amount of pressure to drive away the tension.

He has talented hands, Elizabeth thought. She arched her back and stretched luxuriously, almost purring like a sleek, contented cat.

"Finished working?" he asked.

She turned around and smiled. "Yes. And I think I'd like some of that coffee now."

She filled the mug she had left in the sink and spooned in the requisite amount of sugar. The first sip made her shudder, as usual, but then her stomach accepted it, and her stressed-out body welcomed the caffeine.

"How would you feel about some lunch?"

"Is it that late already?" she said, looking in surprise at her watch. It was two o'clock. "Come to think of it, lunch sounds good." But she was disappointed. Lunch entailed going back to Deception Bay, and for reasons she didn't examine too closely, she hated to see this day end.

Matt took a brown paper bag out of the tiny refrigerator, and from it he unloaded an assortment of white cardboard take-out boxes. From the same brown bag he produced a stack of chilled paper napkins and two sets of cold chopsticks.

"Chinese!" Elizabeth exclaimed.

"You like Chinese? Good. I had Tran pick it up before we left. Let's see, what have we got here?" He poked a chopstick into each box. "Sweet and sour tofu. Garlic tofu. Tofu in oyster sauce."

He laughed at her dubious expression. "I'm only kidding. Shrimp, chicken and only one tofu. I didn't know what you liked, so I told Tran to get a little of everything." He poured the contents of the boxes into several separate saucepans and began to heat them up.

"I'll set the table," Elizabeth volunteered.

She opened the drop-leaf table and placed two green army surplus plastic plates, napkins and chopsticks on it. In the brown paper bag she found several packets of soya sauce, and she tossed them onto the table, too.

After filling the mugs from the seemingly bottomless coffeepot, she sat down on one of the wooden benches that flanked the table and watched Matt prepare lunch.

He appeared to enjoy his stint as cook. It was odd to see this golden bear of a man stirring and tasting, as much at home in the galley as he was on the bridge.

When Matt decided the food was sufficiently heated, he poured the contents of each pan into green plastic bowls and carried them to the table. Then he squeezed into the bench across from Elizabeth.

It was a very close fit. Maybe the fishermen wouldn't be bothered, Elizabeth thought, or maybe they never sat down to eat, but every time her knees bumped Matt's under the table, she became more and more flustered. Normally able to pick up a grain of rice with chopsticks, she found that she could hardly convey a bit of chicken or a wedge of tofu to her mouth without dropping it.

Matt didn't seem to notice. He used his chopsticks expertly, all the while filling her in on the history of this section of the coast in general and Whale Cove in particular. He punctuated his conversation with sharp jabs of his chopsticks in the air.

When lunch was finished, Matt stacked the dishes in the sink. "Let me help you with those," Elizabeth offered.

Matt shook his head. "I'll take care of them later. Right now I have something else in mind for you."

From the way he was beaming expectantly she knew she was supposed to guess, but she didn't have a clue.

"Have you ever gone fishing?" he prompted.

"Not really." She had a hunch he wasn't talking about the bluegill she used to catch with her father on the shores of Lake Michigan.

"Well, how'd you like to give it a try? Maybe bring in a trophy salmon you can hang on the wall in your office to remember me by?"

I don't think I'm going to have the slightest bit of trouble remembering you, she thought. *Forgetting you is going to be the problem!* Aloud she only said, "I'd love it! Jonathan has a gigantic marlin on his wall, and I happen to know he gets seasick whenever he walks past the water cooler."

"Well, let's go get 'em then." Matt started the diesels, then went out on deck to weigh the anchor. When he returned, he put the *Chinook Wind* in gear and increased the throttles. Soon they were sailing through the narrow inlet of Whale Cove and out into open sea.

As Matt had promised, the return trip was as smooth as glass. Elizabeth was surprised how quickly they got back to Deception Bay now that the weather was with them.

They came upon the first boat a mile south of the reef. In another few minutes they were surrounded by a dozen craft trolling for salmon. Matt turned off the diesels and let the boat drift. He chose one fishing rod out of the dozen or more racked in the cabin's storage locker, then took Elizabeth on deck and gave her a few rudimentary instructions.

"Jig—"

Oh-oh, I'm in trouble already, she moaned inwardly. "Jig?"

"Bounce the rod," he said, which he did after attaching a plug of herring to the line and flinging it over the side. "When you see the tip of the rod bend forward, that means you've got a strike. Pull back hard to set the hook."

He demonstrated, jerking the bait out of the water. "Hold the rod steady until he completes his initial run. Then reel him in until you feel him turn and run again. Reel and let him run, reel and let him run. You want to tire him out. Got that? But don't give him any slack. You don't want to let him thrash the hook loose. When he tires out, we'll reel him in and I'll net him."

Elizabeth took the rod in her own hands and dutifully hung it over the side. *Set the hook. Okay. Reel and let him run, reel and let him run. Okay, got it.*

She didn't know how long she stood there, running Matt's directions over and over in her mind, when suddenly the rod tip plunged downward. The line began to feed off the spool so fast that she could hear the clicking whir of its unwinding.

"I've got one! I've got one!"

"Strike it! Strike it!" Matt shouted. "Set the hook!" Excitedly he grabbed for the rod and jerked it sharply backward.

The fiberglass rod vibrated in Elizabeth's hands as the line streaked out.

"He's going down! He's going down!" Matt shouted. The rod began a series of sharp bounces. "He's smashing his jaw on the bottom! Don't give him any slack!"

Everything he had told her slipped through her mind like a sieve. She jerked back on the rod, remembering belatedly that she had to set the hook. *Now reel. No, let him run. No, reel. No, wait—*

In an instant Matt was behind her. He reached around her shoulders, his arms surrounding hers, and clamped her hands to the rod.

"Let him run," he said in a voice that struggled for restraint but failed completely. "Let him run! Steady, steady now. Okay, the line's going slack. Reel him in, reel him in. Okay, he's getting ready to run again. Let him go. That's right. Good. That's the way."

Holding the rod with one hand and guiding her reeling with the other, he thrust his arms forward and nearly dislocated Elizabeth's shoulders. He bent her forward in a tense embrace while he guided her movements. She found herself squeezed roughly against his chest, his lanky body glued to hers from behind.

Every movement he made forced her to move in unison with him. When he lifted the rod to reel line in, he pulled her arms with his; when he bent forward to let the fish run, his big shoulders hunched around her. His hips thrust against her with hard intimacy.

"Okay, okay," Matt announced finally. "He's getting tired."

"Getting tired?" Elizabeth repeated skeptically. "How can you tell?"

"See, he's not taking so much line out when he runs. Look over there. You can see him swimming."

Matt turned his head, and because his cheek was pressed against hers, Elizabeth had no choice but to immediately turn in the same direction. For the first time she caught sight of her fish—a shimmering silver shadow just below the surface of the water. "It's enormous!" she cried.

Matt grinned down at her for a fraction of a second, enjoying her excitement, then turned his attention back to the fish. "Watch him, watch him! He sees us. Now he's going to porpoise!"

The fish sailed out of the water. Its body made a silver arc in the air, then dived beneath the surface again. It porpoised once more, and then a third time, while Elizabeth stared, openmouthed with amazement.

The salmon fought for another ten minutes, but it was exhausted. It only thrashed lightly near the surface. Matt, his arms still around Elizabeth, played it carefully.

Now that she had time to catch her breath, Elizabeth began to notice a few things. The first thing she noticed was that she and Matt fitted together like spoons. His body curved over hers with an instinctive expertise that both thrilled and startled her—it held a promise that had nothing to do with the innocence she had heretofore associated with him.

Her hips were pressed tightly into his, and she noticed his involuntary reaction to the pressure—and that, too, had startling potential. She also noticed that the fish was no longer fighting and that Matt could have released her if he wanted to, but he didn't.

She twisted her head so that she could see his face, and her heart began to race. He was looking at her, too, and he wasn't smiling. Their eyes locked. His were unfamiliar, an unlikely fusion of black and jade. Their intensity proved that the provocative response of his body to hers wasn't entirely involuntary.

Elizabeth swallowed convulsively. She found herself in far greater danger of drowning in the depths of those green eyes than she had ever been in the storm.

Matt turned away. "I'd better get ready to net him," he said gruffly. He let Elizabeth take the rod. "Reel him in. Lift the rod. That's right." The fish was heavy, and she had to struggle to hold the rod aloft. "Lift, yes, slowly. Slowly, that's it."

He readied the net over the side of the boat. When the fish broke water, he scooped it into the net and threw it onto the deck. Quickly he seized a billy club from a hook in the gunwale and rapped the fish smartly on the head.

The brutality shocked Elizabeth. She hadn't associated such violence with Matt. Appalled, she looked from the fish to Matt and then back to the fish again. It lay inert on the deck. Its eye was already filming over.

All the excitement drained out of her. The salmon was so big. It had been so beautiful, arching its silvery body in the air. Somehow she hadn't realized that it was fighting for its life.

Matt put his hands through the fish's gills and grabbed its jaw. He held it suspended in the air, carefully avoiding its rows of tiny, sharp teeth as he regarded it proudly. "He goes thirty pounds, I'd say. Not bad for your first catch. Not bad at all!"

Elizabeth shrank back imperceptibly. She forced a weak smile. "What...what are you going to do with it now?"

Matt extended the fish toward her. "Don't you want me to take your picture?"

"No!" She beat a hasty retreat, backing into the gunwale with a bone-jarring thump.

Matt studied her silently for a moment, then with his free hand opened the fish locker astern and tossed the fish inside. "He was a magnificent fish, Elizabeth," he said quietly. "And a fighter."

Elizabeth sank down on the fish-fighting chair. "It was so beautiful before," she mourned. "Now it just looks...dead."

"I know. There are times when I feel the same way." He slouched backward against the gunwale and folded his arms across his chest. His face looked kind.

Elizabeth stared down at her hands, which were twisting unhappily in her lap. "Then why do you do it?"

"It's my job, Elizabeth."

"It's just that . . . it seems so personal, somehow, killing it with your bare hands like that. Something that big." She shuddered.

"It's not personal at all. It's just the way it is. That's the way it has to end." The corners of his smile deepened. "A Spanish philosopher once said, 'Man does not hunt in order to kill. He kills in order to have hunted.' I think it applies to fishing, as well."

"José Ortega y Gasset." Elizabeth looked at him curiously. "I read him in college."

"So did I." A look of amazement at his own words flickered across his face and instantly disappeared. It was obviously something he hadn't intended to say. He laughed instead. "Why are you looking at me like that? Don't you think a fisherman can have a college degree?"

"Well, yes, sure. Of course, but . . ." *Oh, to hell with it!* "No! But then I'm beginning to realize you're no ordinary fisherman."

"That's exactly what I am, Elizabeth." He smiled his crooked smile, but the words were serious, all the same. "And it's all I want to be. Come on, let's go up to the bridge. Have you ever driven a boat?"

WHY DID HE DOLE OUT information about himself the way he did—so sparingly, in bits and pieces, a little at a time?

Elizabeth recalled the look of surprise that had flitted across his face when he mentioned college. He seemed amazed that he'd told her. Why? He was so reluctant to volunteer anything at all about himself, and then there it was, sneaking past his lips against his will, things he'd obviously never meant to say.

A college graduate, was he? Well, at least it was another clue to the mystery. She'd add it to the tour of duty in Vietnam that he chose not to discuss, the hostile Amerasian boy who was his son, the boat whose name didn't fit and the enigmatic smile. The sum total was still zero.

CHAPTER EIGHT

DECEPTION BAY BOASTED an active art colony, and Matt invited Elizabeth to the July Fourth Street Fair held there every summer.

For the first time in nearly a month Elizabeth focused her attention on the mirror in the bathroom. She was surprised to note that she had acquired a genteel tan, and a scattering of freckles had appeared across the bridge of her nose. Her glossy black hair had taken on a reddish cast, and the sleek, geometric cut had become a bit ragged around the edges.

Devoid of makeup, the hoyden she saw in the mirror looked more like Lizzie than the Ms. Elizabeth La Salle who had moved into this cottage just a few short weeks ago.

She set about reconstructing her image. After a long, luxurious bubble bath in the chipped enamel tub, she polished her fingers and toes a vibrant red. Then she slipped into a red silk blouse even more vibrant and a pair of white sharkskin slacks that fell in sharp creases down the long curves of her legs. She draped a collection of gold chains around her neck and fastened heavy gold hoops in her ears.

When she looked into the mirror again, she was gratified by the metamorphosis reflected there. The excitement she felt at the thought of seeing Matt had given her face a natural glow that made blusher unnecessary, and her eyes shone with anticipation. Not a Lizzie, she said to herself as she slipped into a pair of strappy white sandals that added inches to her height, *definitely* not a Lizzie! Maybe even a Liz.

THE ARTISTS' QUARTER consisted of a cluster of shabby storefronts on Bay Street in the old section of town. The street was cobbled and narrow, flanked by broken curbs and authentic, old-time gaslight lanterns, and just now closed off to automobile traffic by striped yellow barricades.

Elizabeth was greeted by a riot of sight and sound and smells that had the flavor of another era: men in ponytails and tie-dyed jeans and women with long, straight hair and granny dresses, the scent of incense, and folk music sung by tuneless, earnest voices.

"It's like going back to the sixties," she exclaimed to Matt as they wandered down the long rows of tables displaying arts and crafts—pottery, leatherwork, jewelry and a variety of other handmade wares. Barefoot children romped on the grassy knolls surrounding Bay Street, and guitar players serenaded from the street corners.

"I told you this is where the flower children came when they grew up," Matt replied. His arm draped companionably around Elizabeth's shoulders, they zigzagged among the crafts and food booths.

Although it was already July, the beginning of the dog days of summer, the sky was overcast and a keen wind blew in off the water. The warmth of the big body next to hers and the protection it afforded from the sharp breeze were undeniably pleasant. And the friction of sharkskin on denim as Matt adjusted his long strides to her shorter ones was considerably more than that. His lean flank moving against her hip with unintentional inmacy made her exquisitely aware of his body along the full length of hers. The secret place in the pit of her stomach coiled.

Don't be ridiculous, she admonished herself. *He's as alien as if he were from the moon, and those drop-dead good looks have nothing to do with it. We have nothing in common, and besides—*

She stopped short. She was ashamed of herself and this mental, one-sided discussion of a situation that had never even come up. This cynicism, steeped as it was in the hard-eyed lust of singles bars, had no place here. This wasn't Rush Street, after all. And this wasn't a man on the make.

She glanced up at him. His eyes were fixed on an assortment of necklaces on one of the tables, and she saw in the rugged profile a purity and an innocence that touched her. But there was also silver at the temples of his yellow hair, and a little in the beard, as well. The unlikely combination of innocence and experience was intriguing.

"Which one do you like?" Matt asked, gesturing at the colorful collection of handmade necklaces displayed on the table.

Elizabeth inspected them carefully. Some were worked silver, others were enamel and beads and chains, and each was more exquisite than the one before. Unable to decide between them, she picked up several, one after the other, and turned them over in her hands, marveling at the intricate patterns and painstaking workmanship. "It's a hard decision," she declared finally. "They're all so lovely!"

Matt picked up one of the silver pieces she had admired, an old-fashioned filigree heart suspended on a silver chain so fine that it appeared made of gossamer. "I like this one. It's the same color as your eyes."

Elizabeth looked at him, then down at the ornate silver heart suspended from his big hand. The choice said a lot about him, she thought. Old-fashioned. Romantic.

"I like it, too," she immediately decided, and watched as Matt took a bill out of his pocket and gave it to the jewelry maker behind the table. Smiling, he put his hands behind Elizabeth's neck to fasten the delicate chain. It hung inside her collar, the silver heart reaching just as far as the tender, blue-veined hollow of her throat.

"There," he said with satisfaction. He looked down at the necklace where it rested against her skin. Her eyes followed the angle of his, and she saw that his glance had flickered lower, down to where the curve of her breast rose inside the neckline of her red blouse. "Beautiful," he murmured.

"It *is* beautiful," Elizabeth replied. She reached up with both hands to touch the filigree heart. "And I love it. Thank you."

"I didn't mean the necklace," Matt said, and his voice was very low. Then he smiled, and draping his arm across her shoulders, ushered her on to the next table.

Elizabeth saw that his attention was fixed on a display of colorful baskets. They were woven of pine needles, some dyed and some left natural. Elizabeth recognized them as fine work, and very expensive. She had seen them often in the better gift shops around Chicago, and she was surprised to note that they weren't any less expensive here.

The man who sat behind the table was obviously an aging hippie. He was balding now, with what was left of his hair hanging in a braid down his back, and a beard that looked like a lion's mane. His eyes peered, owl-like, from behind round, wire-rimmed glasses.

As Matt and Elizabeth approached, he placed the sandwich he was devouring on the table and carefully wiped his hands on his ragged dungarees. "Peace," he said, extending one hand cordially.

"Fret," Matt replied, giving the none-too-clean hand a friendly shake. "I'd like you to meet Elizabeth La Salle."

Fret's teeth flashed in his shaggy beard. "I've heard a lot about you. Peace."

Elizabeth smiled uncertainly. From the reception she had encountered elsewhere in this town, his noncommittal remark could mean anything. Or nothing at all.

"You're painting the lighthouse, right? Groovy. That's going to bring a lot of business into this little burg, let me tell you."

"Most of the people around here seem to think that's not such a good thing," Elizabeth said.

"Not me. I love tourists! Takes a tourist to pay the outrageous prices I charge for these baskets!" He grinned broadly. "Besides, like, I was lucky enough to find this place, and anyone wants to come here, it's okay by me. The land belongs to the people, man. Right?"

The buzz words of the sixties rolled off Fret's tongue with a practiced naiveté. The quaint, outdated jargon may have been the language of his youth, Elizabeth thought, but she got the distinct impression that it was now his stock-in-trade. His eyes behind the round lenses were shrewd, probably figuring to the exact penny what "picturesque" was worth, and she wouldn't have been surprised if his basket-weaving was a thriving cottage industry, complete with employees and an accountant and tax shelters.

"Where's Hannah?" Matt asked.

"Oh, she's around here somewhere. Hannah!" he bellowed.

From behind a velvet-covered table on which were arranged crystal pyramids of various sizes and colors, a woman rose and walked toward them. "No need to shout, Fret," the woman admonished him calmly. "I'm right here."

"Hannah," Fret said, "my...er...lady."

The woman was large but moved with regal dignity, and when she stood beside Fret, she towered over him by several inches. She wore a bright dirndl skirt, flattering in spite of her girth, and a white peasant blouse that revealed strong, sunburned arms. Several large pieces of jewelry, obviously garnered from other vendors at the street fair, adorned her fleshy neck and wrists and dangled heavily from her multipierced ears.

Hannah leaned forward from the waist, letting her long, gray-threaded brown hair fall to one side, then caught it up in one hand and flipped it expertly behind her back. Her mellow smile embraced Fret and Matt, and then widened to include the tall, elegant brunette who stood between them. "You must be Elizabeth. Our daughter has told us so much about you."

"Hannah and Fret are Celebration's parents," Matt explained.

"An accident of genetics, that's all," Fret interjected. "Actually, Celebration is a child of the universe, a free spirit." He said it as though issuing a policy statement, and then he smiled benignly. "We 'are the bows from which our children as living arrows shoot.' We 'house her body but not her soul, for her soul dwells in the House of Tomorrow, which we cannot enter, not even in our dreams.' Kahlil Gibran, *The Prophet,*" he elaborated at Elizabeth's blank look.

"Oh. Yes. Well, it's very nice to meet you." What could Celebration *possibly* have said to these people, Elizabeth wondered, considering the girl hadn't exchanged a civil word with her since Matt had introduced them? "I've spoken with Celebration many times! She is...she's...I mean—" She stopped in consternation.

Hannah laughed. "I know what you mean! She's been giving you a hard time, right? She's in love with Matt, you see, and I'm afraid she sees you as competition."

Elizabeth smiled in return. "I'm sorry she feels that way but, of course, she's mistaken."

"Is she?" Hannah mused, eyeing Elizabeth thoughtfully. Her voice sounded a little smug, as though she knew something no one else did, and Elizabeth suddenly remembered that Matt had said that Hannah was a psychic. Not that there need be anything clairvoyant about Hannah's assessment of this situation. It wouldn't take a psychic to know that Matt was probably the most eligible bachelor in town. No doubt there were plenty of women besides Celebration who viewed Elizabeth as competition.

"Of course, Matt *is* the most eligible bachelor in Deception Bay," Hannah continued blandly, while Elizabeth shot her a startled look. "There are quite a few women who probably see you as competition."

"Cool it, Hannah," Fret interrupted with a laugh. "Can't you see you're embarrassing her?"

"No, not at all," Elizabeth assured him. "It's just that, well, I'm only here for the summer, that's all, and of course I'll be going back home soon. In September. I'm not the least bit interested...I mean, I'm no competition at all...I mean..." *Stop!*

She knew she was talking too quickly and too much, a disquieting tendency that seemed to beset her more and more often since she'd left the well-defined parameters of the corporate world she knew so well. Hannah wouldn't need to be a psychic, she told herself ruefully, if all her clients volunteered as much trivial information as Elizabeth did!

"Oh, well, it really doesn't matter," Hannah pronounced complacently. "Love is never wasted." Her soft, unfocused eyes had the beautific look of total and indiscriminate affection.

After promising to drop by their house another time for some home brew, Matt and Elizabeth took their leave of Fret and Hannah and continued down the street.

They bought Corny-dogs-on-a-stick and colas in cardboard containers at one of the food booths, then strolled to the bottom of Bay Street, which ended at the shoreline. Concrete blocks formed a sea wall against waves that would have washed the pavement away at high tide. The tide was out now, but the surf still sent occasional spindrifts over the top of the barricade.

"What do you think of Fret and Hannah?" Matt asked as they sat down on the sea wall to eat their lunch.

"I like them."

"I thought you would. I wanted to show you that not *everyone* in Deception Bay is paranoid about outsiders."

"They aren't like anyone I ever knew before. Do you suppose Fret meant all that stuff he said about parents and children?"

Matt laughed. "Well, you've got to understand Fret. It's hard to be a middle-aged hippie and have all your chickens coming home to roost! Fret makes it a point to sound radical—he may even believe he is, but underneath I think he's every bit as conservative as any other father of daughters!''

Elizabeth couldn't help comparing Fret's laid-back attitude to the one displayed by her own very Victorian father. Interviewing hapless suitors had been Emil Pulaski's particular specialty. He would pace around a quaking boy like a drill sergeant, firing point-blank questions at him with the rapidity of a machine gun. While Elizabeth wrung her hands in an agony of embarrassment, Daddy would quiz the unfortunate young man about his grades, his ambitions, his driving record—everything but his mother's maiden name, Elizabeth used to think despairingly!

She could only guess how he must have felt when, despite his best efforts, his only child had married a man who ended up breaking her heart. Glancing at Matt, who was devouring his hot dog with simple enjoyment, she suddenly found herself wondering what her father would think of him. Daddy would approve, she thought.

And what do I think of him? she asked herself. But for that one she had no answer.

IT WAS NEARLY DARK when Matt pulled his old blue truck into the yard in front of the caretaker's cottage. Caught in the headlight beams, a family of raccoons gazed solemnly at the truck from the porch. Their masked bandit faces considered the newcomers gravely, but not fearfully, then they crept down the steps and disappeared into the woods.

"They're probably wondering where their supper is," Elizabeth remarked. She unlatched her seat belt and reached for the door handle. "It's been a wonderful day. I enjoyed meeting your friends...."

Matt twisted so that he was leaning backward against the door on his side, one arm draped casually on the steering wheel and the other extended along the back of the seat. "Are you in a hurry?"

In a hurry? She had never felt less hurried in her life. "Not at all." She released the door handle and settled back in the seat.

"The firemen will be putting on a fireworks display." He jerked his head at the back window, where the signal beacon on North Jetty flashed. "They'll start as soon as it's dark."

As though emphasizing his words, a series of firecrackers exploded in quick succession from somewhere down on the beach.

"I'd love it," Elizabeth said. It wouldn't be the lavish demonstration the city of Chicago set off in Grant Park on the Fourth of July, shooting the rockets out over the dark waters of Lake Michigan, but Elizabeth suspected she would enjoy it even more.

Matt reached into the crew cab for a blanket, then got out and walked around the truck to open the tailgate. Elizabeth followed.

"The bed's none too clean," Matt said, shaking out the blanket. "The last thing I hauled in it was hay."

Elizabeth took one end and helped him spread it on the tailgate. "You keep horses?"

"Yep. And cows. A few chickens for eggs."

"Sounds like a regular farm!"

"Not really," Matt replied. "It's just an old A-frame and some acreage. Small, but it's perfect for Tran and me—lots of old-growth forest land, and a meadow that backs right up to the Cascades. On a clear day from the crest of the butte right behind my cabin you can see for miles in every direction."

"Sounds beautiful."

"It is. There was a time when I thought about building a house out there."

"Why haven't you?"

"Well—" he smoothed the wrinkles out of the blanket "—I thought it would be a great place to raise a family, for one thing. But now, with just the two of us, Tran and me, the A-frame is plenty big enough."

He sat down on the tailgate, one foot propped on the inside edge of the truck and the other planted on the ground. "Come on up," he said, extending his arms to assist her.

The oversize tires made the tailgate a bit of a jump. When Matt's big hands grabbed her waist, Elizabeth pushed herself up and scooted backward, and unexpectedly found herself firmly positioned against his upraised knee. He slid his arms around her waist and pulled her snugly into the wide V between his legs.

"Comfortable?" he asked. His voice was so close behind her that his beard tickled her ear.

Being captured between Matt's legs wasn't what she would call comfortable. Thrilling, yes. Arousing, definitely. Incredibly erotic, of course. But comfortable? No. "Yes," Elizabeth managed to croak in a tone that suggested exactly the opposite.

An owl hooted and swooped. The silhouettes of bats darted jerkily in front of the rising moon, skimming insects just above the tops of the trees. The stillness was filled with a thousand night noises—the chirruping of crickets, the distant howl of what might have been a coyote, the constant rustling interaction of predator and prey.

Elizabeth nestled deeper between Matt's legs. She was drawn to his masculinity intuitively, the way the moths were drawn to the heat of the yellow globe that lit the porch. "I'm going to miss this place when I go back to Chicago," she sighed wistfully.

"Why talk about leaving? You still have all summer."

"I tell myself that, too, and it sounds like forever. But then I remember that it's already July."

"You still have... what? Two months?" His hand dropped to her lap, and he squeezed her folded hands companionably. "A lot can happen in two months."

That's true, she said to herself. *Look what's happened already!*

With just a slight shift of position his big hand could reach up and cover her breast. He would feel the heaviness of it filling his hand through the red silk. Its peak would harden in his palm.

His hands, so skillful at everything he did, wouldn't fumble on the buttons of her silky blouse if he decided that it was in his way. He would find her wisp of a bra and push it up, not bothering to unsnap it as his expert fingers claimed the throbbing nipple and pinched it gently between thumb and forefinger.

Or, her hyperactive imagination continued shamelessly, his hand could move down to caress the hot, waiting juncture of her thighs. He would understand what she wanted from him, and all the ways she wanted it. But would he give it to her? After all, she had only one tentative kiss to go on. That, and a single, electrifying glance exchanged over the body of a dead fish.

She shifted uneasily on the hard metal tailgate.

If this were her own turf, she would... what? She didn't know—she had never let down her guard enough to find out. The reputation of La Salle and La Salle was inextricably intertwined with her own—Elizabeth knew that, and she accepted the limitations it placed on her behavior. Even in her exalted position at the top of the corporate ladder, she wasn't exempt from the rules of sexual exploitation.

Once she capitulated, she would become just another conquest, another topic of sniggering boardroom conversation on Monday morning, and all references to La Salle and La Salle would be colored with thinly veiled innuendoes about her appetites and availability.

With men, of course—with Jonathan, for example—it didn't work that way. A little salacious gossip only heightened their standing. But a woman in love was vulnerable, so went the conventional wisdom. She was compromised.

But here it seemed like a different game, with a different sort of man and a different set of rules. Could she play the game here the way she had never dared play it in Chicago? How would it feel just to let go, to give in, to ride the waves of passion with no reservations, no limits and no thought to the morning after?

A fiery burst of color split the sky, then another, a fountain of sparks that cascaded into the air and fell earthward like a galaxy of shooting stars. Rockets streaked across the bay with shrill, high-pitched whistles. Starbursts like giant sparklers. Sunbursts. Pinwheels. Gold and red and blue and green and blinding, glaring white.

The finale, when it came, was a blazing intermingling of red, white and blue that painted a phenomenal American flag on the dark horizon, the colors twisting, writhing and undulating as they separated into red and white stripes and a blue background studded with brilliant, white-hot stars.

But they were nothing, nothing at all, compared to the fireworks exploding in Elizabeth's head.

The sea breeze carried a residual scent of gunpowder across the headland. A few clouds drifted across the face of the moon. Ground shadows, like tiny night animals, scurried among the trees. In a damp patch of earth that was sometimes a seasonal creek a bullfrog croaked monotonously.

"That was a fantastic show," Elizabeth said, twisting around to smile at Matt.

"I'm glad you enjoyed it."

"Would you like to come in for a drink? Or a cup of coffee." Even to her own ears her voice suggested something more.

"I'd better not." Matt cleared his throat. "I have an early charter tomorrow."

Regretfully Elizabeth slid down from the tailgate, supporting herself briefly on Matt's thigh as she did so. Away from the warmth of his body the night air was cold on her back.

Side by side, barely touching, the two of them walked to the porch. "Well, I had a wonderful time today," she said. "I enjoyed meeting your friends. Uh...maybe I could reciprocate sometime." She stopped, took a deep breath, then plunged ahead. "Maybe I could make dinner for you one night?"

In the yellow glare of the porch light Matt hesitated. "I don't think I should..." he began slowly. Then his expression cleared. A "throw caution to the winds" grin lighted up his face, and he suddenly looked boyishly eager. "Sure! Why not? When?"

"Oh, one day this week would be good for me, I think," Elizabeth replied, as if mentally consulting her social calendar. She tried to make it sound like a thing of no real importance, but she couldn't keep her voice from rushing on with an eagerness of its own. "How about tomorrow?"

Matt nodded. "Tomorrow's good."

"And," Elizabeth felt obligated to add, albeit reluctantly, "bring Tran, too, if he'd like to come."

Matt looked pleased but doubtful. "I'll invite him, but I don't think he will. He's probably got other plans. You know kids that age."

As a matter of fact, she knew nothing about kids that age, but she did know Tran! She'd invited him to please Matt, but for several reasons, a few having nothing at all to do with the boy himself, she sincerely hoped Matt was right and Tran would have other plans.

CHAPTER NINE

"Looks like rain," the grocer observed as he transferred Elizabeth's purchases from basket to cash register and then to a brown paper sack.

"Do you really think so?" Elizabeth asked. The sky beyond the plate glass window was sunny and blue.

"No doubt about it," the grocer grunted. "When the night's clear like it was last night but there's a circle around the moon, it always means rain. Besides, I got this ankle was broke once, and whenever there's a storm coming it commences to throbbing something fierce! Broke it back in '22 when I fell out of McDermott's old apple tree. I . . ."

Rather like Gran's rheumatism, Elizabeth thought, and just about as reliable. She gave the garrulous old man her undivided attention. The grocer was one of her success stories. She had made a concerted effort to overcome his innate distrust of outsiders, shopping at his store almost daily with an air of determined friendliness despite his lack of response.

It had taken several weeks, but her persistence had paid off. Now the grocer treated her like one of the locals, filling her in on rumors and bits of juicy gossip about people she didn't even know.

She loaded her groceries into the back of the station wagon, then drove on to the vegetable stand at the edge of town where the owner, unfortunately, was one of her failures. He watched her pick through his artichokes and salad vegetables with an aggrieved expression on his face.

Surprisingly, because she usually ate fast food at her desk or drawing board, Elizabeth loved to cook. Her virtually unused kitchen was stocked full of blenders, food processors, mixers and fine, French enameled cookware that she hoped to have the time to experiment with someday. For now, though, the black cast-iron skillets and worn, wooden-handled utensils in the caretaker's quarters would do just fine.

A real ethnic feast was what she had decided to prepare for Matt, straight from the émigré neighborhoods of Chicago, the sort of thing he probably hadn't experienced this far away from the population centers of the East.

First, Italian stuffed artichokes of the kind found in restaurants along Twenty-fourth Street and Wentworth, then a Greek salad with feta cheese and marinated olives. For the entrée she had decided on braised Polish sausage with gravy, served on thick chunks of French bread. For dessert there were apple wedges and slices of cheddar cheese, very British. And everything would be accompanied by a light Oregon zinfandel.

She had just pulled away from the vegetable stand when the first fat droplets of water hit her windshield. She saw the owner of the stand, moving a good deal faster than she had ever seen him move before, let down plywood flaps to cover the sides of the stand and pull a tarp across the top, then fold his arms over his chest and gaze with resignation at the darkening sky, while the wind ballooned his canvas tarp like a parachute.

The air was thick with the damp, earthy smell of rain. Easing her foot off the gas, Elizabeth rolled up her window and reached across to roll up the one on the passenger side. A bolt of lightning split the sky, followed in a few seconds by an ominous burst of thunder. Suddenly buckets of water were spilling from the lowering clouds that completely cloaked the tops of the trees.

The downpour made the roads slick and treacherous, and very quickly the shoulders became muddy. With headlights, defrosters and windshield wipers all going at the same time, the alternator of Elizabeth's old car was pushed to its limit. The lights were dim, while the wipers swept only sporadically.

She crept along at a snail's pace, reaching up frequently to clear the foggy windshield with her sleeve. "When there's a ring around the moon..." the clerk in the grocery store had said. Come to think of it, Gran's rheumatism hadn't always been wrong, either!

With the highway hidden in sheets of rain, Elizabeth found it difficult to see the curves in the road until she was almost on top of them. She kept her eyes glued to the solid yellow line directly in front of her left front fender. The rain sluicing down met the water splashing up from the tires, and they combined to make an impenetrable gray cocoon all around the car.

After what seemed like an eternity, she came to the Stop sign that marked the turnoff to the lighthouse. She breathed a sigh of relief. Flipping on her turn signal, she began to maneuver the station wagon to the right when she glanced up into the rearview mirror and saw headlights approaching from behind.

They were bearing down on her very fast despite the rain-slicked road. Who would be driving like that in this weather? she wondered uneasily. The headlights were coming closer at an alarming speed and showed no sign of slowing down.

Through the driving rain the yellow lights filled her rearview mirror, and in a sudden, panicky instant it became blindingly clear to Elizabeth that the driver wasn't going to stop.

She jerked her wheel wildly to the right. The station wagon spun around in the middle of the highway, then looped onto the muddy gravel road, spinning again and flinging mud and stones high into the air. It came to rest facing the wrong way on the gravel road.

Through the flying mud and the sheeting rain Elizabeth saw the vehicle that had been following her shoot past the intersection. Her eyes widened. It was Matt's old blue truck. But it didn't look like Matt behind the wheel. As the truck had careened by, she had glimpsed a dark smudge that barely reached the top of the dashboard, a thin silhouette that was almost invisible through the sheets of rain.

The confusion in her mind focused on the image in the truck, and suddenly she recognized it with crystal clarity. *Tran! My God, that was Tran driving Matt's truck!*

In a paroxysm of fear and relief Elizabeth rested her forehead against the steering wheel and took deep, regular breaths, trying to quell the frantic beating of her heart. After a minute, she realized she was still out in the middle of the road, so she backed the station wagon up and turned it around, heading for the safety of the caretaker's quarters.

Her fear at her narrow escape turned to anger. He could have killed her! He could have killed himself! And who knew what unsuspecting motorist was going to be at the *next* intersection!

Once inside the cottage, she picked up the telephone with shaking hands to dial the police or Matt or anyone who could stop that crazy kid before he hurt someone.

Predictably the phone was dead. The storm must have washed out lines from here clear to Portland, she thought sourly.

She eyed the soggy paper bags on the counter with a baleful glare. Puddles were accumulating on the linoleum around her feet. The day was turning out somewhat differently from what she had expected.

Matt. Dinner. Of course. No sense allowing that surly little criminal to ruin the romantic evening she'd planned.

Resolutely she turned and hurried into the bedroom, unbuttoning her damp shirt as she walked. She flung it over the doorknob, then sat on the edge of the bed to peel off the jeans that clung to her legs like a soaked second skin.

Glancing quickly into the mirror, she ran her fingers through the dripping tendrils of her hair and saw that it was definitely going to need the attention of a hair dryer. With a decisive flick of her wrist she plugged in the dryer and turned it on.

The lights immediately went out.

FOR THE REST of the afternoon raindrops beat down on the shingled roof with a monotonous rhythm. Elizabeth could hear it rushing through the gutters and spewing out of the waterspout just below the kitchen window.

When she pulled back the curtain and looked out, the rain made another curtain just past the eaves of the cottage, a translucent but impenetrable gray wall that hid the world beyond every bit as effectively as the fog did.

Elizabeth prepared her dinner by candlelight. The burners on the range were very small and the oven was very, very soiled, but at least it worked. She was grateful to the farsighted occupant who had, at some time in the past, converted the vintage wood-burning stove to gas.

She was also grateful that she remembered having seen a box full of candles on the shelf in the bedroom closet. She groped around the shelf in the dark, her fingers encountering decades of dust, and a few relics of things undoubtedly distasteful that she refused to let herself think about. Apparently, she observed wryly, once her cautious fingers had located the box of candles, losing the electricity wasn't an uncommon occurrence.

ELIZABETH LOOKED at her watch. Matt was late. She arranged and rearranged the dinner and salad plates, aligned the silverware into even more exact parallel lines and refolded the paper napkins into sharper creases. Then she looked at her watch again. What could be keeping him?

In the dim firelight the snowy tablecloth disguised the tarnished chrome of the dinette set and rendered almost unnoticeable the torn vinyl of the chairs. A pair of heavy silver candlesticks also found on the closet shelf held candles with tiny flames that flickered due to an unseen draft.

Elizabeth paced restlessly from the living room to the kitchen and then back to the living room again, pausing every so often to listen for Matt's truck in the front yard. The moan of the foghorn on North Jetty and the croak of the bullfrogs were the only sounds that penetrated the dreary tattoo of the rain.

The dark cap of her hair was still damp. She tried to fluff it with her fingers, then gave up and smoothed it flat against her head. With the hair scraped away from her face the fine bones stood out whitely in the subdued light. Her gray eyes, reflecting the silver candlesticks, had the same luminous sheen of sterling. A furrow appeared between them as she paced, trying to determine what could be keeping Matt.

Her elation gradually subsided into concern, which quickly progressed to worry. Matt had said he could drive these roads blindfolded, but could he *really*—especially with screwballs like Tran out there?

Tran. Another of her failures.

The boy skulked around the edges of her mind in much the same way that his slight, undernourished body skulked around the streets of Deception Bay—eyes darting furtively from side to side, hands shoved into his pockets, neck pulled like a turtle's into the collar of the scruffy army surplus jacket she had never seen him without, not even in the warmest weather.

He was always hurrying, as if late for some urgent appointment, and he was always alone. His lack of companionship somehow saddened Elizabeth, even though she had to admit that she understood it. She wondered if his familiarity with the ghosts wasn't simply a substitute for the human relationships that seemed to be beyond his capabilities.

A sudden knock at the door caught her unaware. She reached for the dead bolt, then frowned uneasily. It could only be Matt, but why hadn't she heard his truck? Or seen his headlights in the window?

She peeked through the curtain. An indistinct shape stood in front of the door. As she stood rooted uncertainly to the floor, the dark shape shone a flashlight up to illuminate its face.

"Matt!" she cried. Elizabeth threw open the door and pulled him inside. Rain and wind entered with him. A gust caught the door and battered it wildly against the doorjamb before Elizabeth was able to catch it and force it closed.

Matt stamped his feet to shake off the mud that coated his boots and shook his head like a wet puppy. Then he stood on the throw rug in front of the door and dripped. Water ran down his forehead and streamed in rivulets off the tip of his nose. He gave Elizabeth an apologetic look and smiled his shy, down-turned smile. "Am I late?" he asked.

Elizabeth stared at him, dumbfounded. "Matt! What on earth happened to you? Where's your truck? How—?"

Matt held up one hand to stop her. "Maybe I could dry off first?" he asked tentatively.

"Oh, yes, of course!" She hurried to the bathroom and returned with several towels. He took one and began to dry his face, then threw the towel over his head and rubbed his drenched hair and beard.

"Matt, what—?"

"You won't believe it," he replied, eyes peering out from beneath the towel that covered the rest of his face. He leaned against the wall to pull off his mud-encrusted boots, then set them side by side next to the door. "I, uh...well, as a matter of fact..." He shrugged, his smile turning farther downward and becoming slightly abashed. "I ran out of gas."

"Oh, Matt!" He looked so woebegone that she dared not laugh. "Where?"

"In the middle of nowhere naturally. Isn't that always the way? Just north of the turnoff."

"But that's nearly three miles from here!"

"Yep."

"You're so...so...wet! Why didn't you call me? I could have picked you up!"

"Well, even if there had been a phone nearby, the lines are probably down. They usually are in a storm like this.

I figured it was just about as far to walk here as it was to walk back to town, so I came on ahead. I hope you don't mind."

Elizabeth knew for a fact that the turnoff was a good deal closer to town than to the lighthouse. She smiled happily. "Not at all. I'm glad you came. I was getting worried."

"What I can't figure out," Matt said in a puzzled voice, "is how I managed to run out of gas. I could swear I had a full tank yesterday."

"I'm afraid I can tell you," Elizabeth informed him reluctantly. "I saw Tran driving your truck today." Briefly she described the incident at the intersection. "I wouldn't have thought he was even old enough to drive," she finished. "But even if he is, he could certainly use some driver's education."

Matt's face darkened. "Oh, he's old enough, all right. He learned how to drive in an old army troop truck in Saigon when he was about five, he says. But I didn't know he was driving like that, and I sure didn't know he had my truck—"

"Matt, I'm sorry. I know it isn't any of my business, but I thought you'd want to know."

"I appreciate your telling me. I'm sure it can't have been easy for you. And I'll see to it that nothing like that ever happens again."

It was probably the closest Matt ever came to anger, Elizabeth thought, noticing the few, almost imperceptible changes in his face. The down-turned smile narrowed just a little, while his jaw tightened and his eyes became a more opaque shade of green. That was all. *It really* is *a mask,* she realized suddenly, wondering what cataclysmic sort of event it would take to remove it, to reveal what was *really* going on in his mind.

His green parka was waterproof, but apparently nothing could withstand this cloudburst. When he took it off, Elizabeth saw that rain had seeped inside the collar and soaked his clothes.

The water made dark streaks down the front of his gray plaid Pendleton, and it had the peculiar but not unpleasant odor of wet wool. Instead of his usual jeans he was wearing gray pleated slacks that must have been pressed when he put them on but now hung in damp wrinkles from his waist down to his stockinged feet.

He removed the dripping parka and hung it on the coatrack by the door. Belatedly Elizabeth realized that he was still standing by the drafty front door, dripping onto the throw rug.

"I'm sorry," she exclaimed contritely. "You must be freezing! Right now we'd better get you out of those clothes." Immediately she bit her tongue. The "we" had been a Freudian slip on her part, and she hoped Matt hadn't caught it, but the quick, involuntary grin that flickered across his face indicated that he had, and it flustered her.

"I mean, if you'll take them off. I'll..." That didn't sound any better. She gestured in the general direction of the fireplace. "I mean, I'll dry them for you. There. By the fire."

"Maybe you've got something I could put on," he suggested gently as the astute grin was replaced by his usual diffident smile.

"Oh, yes. But..." She glanced around the living room in confusion. "What do you think...?"

"An old robe or something maybe?" he suggested again.

"Of course." Grateful to have something to do, Elizabeth headed into the bedroom for the only thing she had

that could conceivably fit him—her floor-length black
silk kimono.

When she returned, Matt was standing in front of the
fireplace, his back to the room. He had untucked his shirt
and was tugging it out of his trousers. She watched him
peel it off and drape it on the back of one of the rocking
chairs that flanked the hearth.

Still facing the fire, he crossed his arms in front and
removed his T-shirt, pulling it up and over his head with
one lithe twist of his torso. The strongly muscled back
that was thus revealed to Elizabeth was framed and ac-
centuated by the firelight. It was broad and triangular,
tapering from wide shoulders to narrow waist where it
disappeared into the waistband of the gray slacks. The
long shadows thrown across the room by the fire highlighted his flesh tones to the patina of a new penny.

The firelight rippled across skin that was still damp
from the rain, outlining and defining each individual
muscle as he moved with the sinuous grace of a prize-
fighter. He draped the T-shirt over the chair. Elizabeth
drew a breath that was almost a gasp. She wanted nothing at that moment except to watch him. But in the very
next moment she knew she wanted more than that.
Much, much more.

Strength was implicit in the athletic physique, and it
somehow seemed all the more virile for having been developed, not by sports or games, but by hard physical la-
bor. Unconsciously her fingers tensed, imagining how the
tight bunches of sinew would feel beneath them, going
with the flow of the spinal column, one vertebrae at a
time.

He took a wallet out of one pocket and a handful of
change from another and placed them on the mantle,
then reached down to undo his belt. Abruptly he stopped,

becoming motionless for a moment as his attention was riveted by something on the mantel.

Elizabeth groaned inwardly as she realized what he was looking at: over the fireplace she had tacked one of the charcoal sketches she had done of him aboard the *Chinook Wind*.

In her own mind she likened him to the heroic men in the old photographs—the abstracted look of listening intently to sounds no one else could hear, eyes peering great distances at things no one else could see. He belonged with them, she thought privately, and she had intended to use the sketch in a painting someday. Too late she realized that she probably ought to have taken it down.

For a rash instant she hoped against hope that he hadn't noticed it. Then, when he slowly pulled the belt through the belt loops and absentmindedly let it hang from his hand to the floor while his face remained fixed on the mantel, her heart sank. No such luck.

Matt sensed her presence and glanced over his shoulder. Then he turned—it seemed to Elizabeth that he moved in slow motion—and in the firelight his blond hair and beard took on a warm, reddish cast. His chest was as copper-colored as his back and was covered by a mat of fine, light hair. It gleamed with the same moist sheen that could be rain or perhaps perspiration from the heat of the fire.

Still moving in slow motion, he walked toward Elizabeth, dropping the belt on the sofa as he passed, where it slipped unnoticed to the floor. Backlighted by the fire, his face was a dark oval framed by a pale gold ring of light, and the emerald of his eyes disappeared beneath the craggy shadow of his brow.

She stood very still, the kimono clutched, forgotten, between her hands. Her eyes widened as he came closer. Then he was directly in front of her, only inches from her, almost touching her. She wondered if he could hear the frantic beating of her heart in the stillness of the room, broken only by the crackling of the fire and the drumming of the rain on the roof. The shadows that fell across his face concealed his expression as effectively as his habitual mask.

When he reached toward her, her whole body sprang to attention, and when his hands touched hers, she jumped again. Her eyes became saucers. Gently he lifted the robe out of her hands. "Thank you," he said, smiling courteously as he took it in his own and slipped past her into the bedroom.

"THAT WAS A WONDERFUL MEAL." Matt split the last of the wine between Elizabeth's glass and his own. "What was that spice you put in the sausage? I don't think I ever tasted it before."

"Fennel. It's Polish."

"And those artichokes—kind of hard to get at, but well worth it when they're stuffed with whatever it was you stuffed them with!"

Elizabeth smiled. "Italian bread with oregano and chopped olives," she informed him. "Thanks, Matt. I like to cook. I don't get to do nearly enough of it."

"Well, if you're out of practice, it doesn't show. Where did you learn how to make all these things, anyway?"

"In Chicago. It's like the United Nations there—every race and nationality you can think of, and some you've probably *never* heard of. There's so much cultural diversity—it's one of the things I like most about living there."

"There's some of that here, too." He twirled his wine-glass between his fingers, watching the play of candle-light on the white tablecloth. "The Mexican influence. The Chinese who came out with the railroad. But every-thing gets kind of moderated by the time it reaches the West. Food. People. Ideas. You can still find real, au-thentic ethnic food, of course, but you also find a lot of things like ravioli made with wonton skins and tofu ta-cos. As a matter of fact, you can probably find *every-thing* made with tofu around here. It's one of our staples. Also brown rice. We eat a *lot* of brown rice!"

With the kimono knotted around his waist, its length reaching only midcalf and its flowing, deep-cut sleeves broadened and squared as they draped over his shoul-ders, he looked like a Chinese mandarin. The candle-light cast flickering designs of light that looked like jewels on the rich black silk.

And it was evident that he was enjoying himself. He laughed loudly and often. He made Elizabeth laugh, too. She felt a little light-headed and didn't know whether it was the wine or the company. She marveled that she could be this close to an exciting, attractive man, clad only in the simplest of robes, and be talking about brown rice, much less laughing about it with an ease that was completely spontaneous.

When she got up to clear the table, he helped. She tried to protest that she'd clean the kitchen tomorrow, but he demurred, insisting that he didn't want her to spend time washing dishes when she should be working, so they heated water in the teakettle and did the dishes together by candlelight.

A dishwasher would be a distinct disadvantage, she decided, hands buried in suds while Matt stood next to her, drying the plates and sliding them back into the cupboards. She tried not to let her emotions get the upper hand, but she found she couldn't be this close to him without experiencing some very pleasant and disturbing sensations.

When the kitchen was finished, Elizabeth put on a pot of coffee. Matt picked up one of the heavy silver candlesticks and walked around the living room, studying her completed canvases by the light of the tiny flame. She tried to act nonchalant, but watched his every move out of the corner of her eye. Suddenly it mattered very much to her that he approve of what she had done with his lighthouse.

She made several trips from the kitchen to the living room, carrying the coffee and dessert she planned to serve by firelight. When everything was arranged on the low table in front of the sofa, she sat on the edge of the cushions, her anxious eyes following Matt as he moved the candles slowly from one painting to the next.

He hunkered down on his heels and held the candlestick close to the floor to examine the last few that were propped against the far wall.

"Well?" she demanded impatiently.

Silent, he tightened the knot of the robe at his waist. Still silent, he walked around the sofa and sat on the opposite end, sinking deeply into the plump cushions.

"Well?" Elizabeth said again.

Automatically he reached up to pat his chest where his shirt pocket would normally be, and Elizabeth knew he was looking for a cigarette.

His security blanket, she remembered. Her shoulders stiffened. What was he nervous about? "As bad as that?"

"Bad? God, no! How could you think that? They're wonderful! I just can't come up with the right words to tell you how great they are!"

She expelled the breath she hadn't even known she was holding. She felt weak with relief. With hands that trembled only a little she poured a cup of coffee and handed it to him—black, the way she'd learned he liked it. She poured herself a cup, too, then sat back and crossed her legs.

"Thanks," she said demurely.

"I'm not sure what I expected. Pictures, I guess. But these are more than that. They don't just look like Deception Head—they *feel* like it, too. The lighthouse looks like it's a natural extension of the cape, as though it's been there as long as the rock itself. The perspective is a little off sometimes, but—"

"I know I have a lot to learn," Elizabeth interrupted hastily.

"Maybe. But you have an empathy—an affinity—that's more than just a matter of technique. That sunset where the sky is almost purple—that's not a color most people would be aware of in a sunset, but it's one that's definitely there. And that sun!"

The coffee sloshed dangerously in Matt's cup as he gestured to one of the canvases against the wall where a red fireball occupied most of the painted sky. "It isn't just another pretty sunset—it's so bright and fierce, it looks like the end of the world!"

"Well, I only hope that's what the Lighthouse Society is looking for."

He looked at her earnestly. "You have too much talent to let someone else dictate how you should paint." He crossed his legs, propping the ankle of one on the knee of the other, and the sash that was wrapped around his waist slipped precariously.

Elizabeth's attention was riveted. It wasn't much fabric, she thought fleetingly, to cover so much man. It did hide the most essential parts—but not by much. Or, she amended more frankly, by *too* much.

"Yes, but I have to support myself," she pointed out faintly as her voice became huskier and her breathing a little too rapid. She forced her eyes upward, hoping that the sudden violent wanting that coursed through her body from its secret female core didn't show in her face.

Elizabeth wondered for the rest of the night what Matt said next, but she was never to know, for his reply was drowned out by a savage pounding on the door. She glanced questioningly at him. He raised his shoulders and spread his hands in a gesture that said he had no idea who it could be. He stood and pulled the robe around himself like a surplice, then stood behind the door and turned back a corner of the curtain.

The rain was still falling steadily, gusting into a frenzy when the norther whipped it erratically. Even if there had been a moon, its light wouldn't have pierced the sodden sky. Elizabeth put down her cup and seized the candle Matt had placed on the coffee table. She walked to the door and opened it a few inches. In the meager light a dark shape loomed on the doorstep.

"Jonathan!" she cried in the exact second that a gust of wind blew the candle out.

CHAPTER TEN

THE COLLAR of his raincoat was turned up, almost completely concealing his face. Water poured in a steady stream from the brim of his hat. "May I come in?" he asked, one eyebrow cocked quizzically. He lounged casually in the doorway, his arch smile indicating he knew exactly the effect that his unannounced appearance would have on Elizabeth.

And his calculations were correct. She stared at him speechlessly as she braced the buffeting door with both hands. "Yes, yes, of course, come in," she finally said, but she made no move to open the door any farther.

Jonathan La Salle enjoyed her astonishment for another brief moment, then took the doorknob in one hand and gave her another quizzical smile. "May I?" he repeated.

Still speechless, Elizabeth stood aside to let him pass.

His astute glance flickered over her shoulder as he stepped inside, and his eyes narrowed. Then, with a barely perceptible pause, he turned them back to Elizabeth. "I hope I'm not interrupting anything," he said smoothly.

Elizabeth found her tongue. "What are you doing here?" She forced the door closed behind him, noticing with relief that Matt had disappeared from the corner of her vision.

"Shouldn't you tell me first how happy you are to see me?" Jonathan lifted the hat from his head and shook the water out onto the floor. Unhurriedly he took off the dripping tan raincoat and neatly folded it shoulder to shoulder, then hung it on the coatrack next to the door. He dropped his hat on the hook next to it. His quick, observant glance fell to the mud-encrusted boots by the door, but he said nothing.

There wasn't a hair out of place on Jonathan's perfectly molded head. His hairline was receding, but so artfully did his barber style his sandy hair that it was impossible to tell unless you saw him first thing in the morning. His three-piece tussah Palm Beach suit was impeccable. Only his tie was a little askew, and he straightened it meticulously, smoothing it beneath his understated diamond tiepin with loving care.

"But what on earth are you *doing* here?" she asked again.

"Actually, I had a meeting in San Francisco, and since I was in the neighborhood, I thought you might appreciate a little company." He flashed a charming smile. "I hope I was right."

Elizabeth eyed him suspiciously. "San Francisco is over two hundred miles away from here."

"Tell me about it! You'd never believe what a time I had getting here! Do you know there's not an airport within fifty miles of this town? What's it called—Disappointment Bay?"

"Deception Bay."

"Yeah, right. I flew into some place called Coos Bay—Coos Bay, right?"

"Coos Bay, yes."

"Named for Captain Coos, no doubt! Anyway, I got that far, then found that I couldn't get here from there."

"So how did you get here?"

"I'm coming to that." He strolled, uninvited, into the living room, where his keen glance noted the rustic surroundings with exaggerated distaste. "I tried to get one of those puddle-jumpers—you know, one of those little commuter lines?—to bring me down, but it seems no one was willing to fly in this weather. What's going on, anyway? Doesn't it do anything else but rain around here?"

"Why?"

"It looks like it's been raining forty days and forty nights! At least! The entire front of your house is a lake! You didn't know that? Why? Haven't you been outside in the month or so you've been here?" His voice had the caustic edge she remembered so well. "That wouldn't surprise me a bit. I can't imagine why you'd *want* to go outside, except that this inside is so much more—" he paused, scanning the cottage with contemptuous eyes "—depressing."

"Jonathan..." Elizabeth warned.

"Okay, okay. So, anyway, I hired a cab."

"A cab? All the way from Coos Bay? That must have cost a fortune!"

"You got that right. Two hundred and sixty bucks. And I had to give the guy another fifty to keep going when the rain got so bad that he wanted to turn back. Hel-lo—" he interrupted himself, looking over Elizabeth's shoulder with feigned surprise.

Elizabeth turned just in time to see the bedroom door swing open and Matt walk out. He had taken his not-quite-dry clothes from the fireplace and dressed in the bedroom and was just fastening the last cuff of his shirt as he came through the door.

"Uh, Jonathan, this is Matt McCullough. Matt, Jonathan La Salle, my ex-husband."

Jonathan smiled like a co-conspirator as their hands met in a brief acknowledgment. Matt didn't.

"Elizabeth, I'll be going now," he said shortly. "I'll call you in the morning."

"Wait. Let me drive you home. Jonathan will be all right here by himself."

"I'd just as soon walk, thanks."

"Take my car then. You can bring it back later."

Matt hesitated.

"Wait a minute, pal!" Jonathan said with artificial jocularity. "I've got a cab outside. I told him to wait," he said, turning to Elizabeth, "because I wasn't sure that you'd be here, what with no lights or anything. Go ahead, take it. I'll even pay the fare." He made a subtle movement toward his back pocket—Elizabeth recognized the gesture for exactly what it was: a simple but effective display of dominance. She was relieved to see that Matt didn't rise to the bait.

"No need." Matt's voice was as calm as his eyes. "But I will take the cab. Thanks."

Elizabeth saw him to the door while Jonathan watched with an amused expression on his handsome, florid face.

Matt retrieved his parka from the coatrack and pulled on his boots. "Is everything all right?" he asked in an undertone as Elizabeth opened the door.

"Everything's fine, Matt. Don't worry." But she had an uneasy feeling that everything wasn't all right, or else why would her ex-husband have come two thousand miles, unannounced, to visit her practically in the middle of the night, practically in the middle of the worst storm she had ever witnessed?

"I'll call you tomorrow," Matt said again. "If you need anything..." He didn't have to finish. He pulled the parka over his head and ran with long, awkward strides over the puddles in the flooded yard to the waiting taxi.

Elizabeth slammed the door behind him. Then she turned and leaned against it. "All right, Jonathan. What's going on?"

Jonathan didn't answer immediately. He sauntered around the living room, hands in his pockets, idly studying Elizabeth's paintings, which were only dimly visible in the dusky half-light from the fireplace.

"Who's the lumberjack?" he asked, his voice deceptively casual.

"They call them *loggers* up here," Elizabeth corrected him coolly. "And he's not a logger. He's a fisherman."

"Slumming, Liz?" He turned to look at her with mocking eyes.

Elizabeth's own eyes narrowed angrily.

Jonathan didn't appear to notice. "Got anything to drink?"

"Coffee."

"I'll take it."

She poured a cup and handed it to him black, feeling a bit childish because she knew from years of experience that he liked it with cream and a lot of sugar. To her surprise he didn't object. He leaned against the kitchen counter and crossed his tussah-clad legs at the ankles.

He seemed nervous, which was uncharacteristic. Jonathan had a reputation in advertising circles as a shark— he enjoyed the fight and he enjoyed the kill, and sometimes he did both just for the fun of it.

"Haven't they heard of electricity up here, either?" he asked with a thin, sarcastic twist of his lips.

"The lines are down."

"Of course. Telephone, too, I'm sure. That explains why I haven't been able to reach you all day."

"Well, you're here now, Jonathan. And I don't believe you came all the way up here from San Francisco just to make small talk."

He set the cup down on the counter with a decisive clatter. "I want you to come home, Liz. Right away. The whole ball of wax is falling apart without you." He fixed her with steely eyes—eyes she had seen annihilate an opponent at twenty paces without even blinking. She recoiled slightly. Jonathan could be a formidable enemy.

"I can't come back now. You know that. I have a job to do."

"You have a job back in Chicago, too, and it's a good deal more important than whatever it is you think you're doing up here."

"I'll be back in September."

"I need you now."

"Jonathan, we made a deal."

"I was wrong. I didn't realize how much—"

"Come on! I held down the fort for the whole three months you and your new bride honeymooned in Europe!"

"Yes, but you forget that was also a business trip. This is different."

"The hell it is!" Elizabeth exploded. Angrily she whirled around and strode into the living room, twisting her hands together in a nervous habit she'd had since childhood whenever she felt her back was to the wall. Her back was to Jonathan—it felt like the same thing.

Jonathan stalked around the sofa to stand in front of her and gripped her by the shoulders. "You're going to seed, Liz. Look at you. What happened to your hair? Don't they have *scissors* in Disappointment Bay? Look at your clothes! Here you are, entertaining your cur-rent...*lover*—'' he made the word sound like an epithet ''—in jeans and a sweatshirt! And that from a woman who used to serve dinners by candlelight with only a silk negligee on, and nothing at all underneath.''

''That's not fair, Jonathan!'' It was a low blow. The words hurt more than she could have believed possible. ''That was a very long time ago. And my personal life is none of your business!''

''It's not?'' His voice was dangerously low. ''I don't agree. I know you, Liz. I know everything about you. Hell, I *made* you! Every time I see you out there cut-ting the competition or giving some poor joker a knee to the groin—figuratively speaking, of course!—I think, 'That's my girl!' ''

''That was never me, Jonathan. You only thought it was. Even I thought it was.'' She hesitated, not entirely sure what she wanted to say, even less sure that Jona-than would understand. ''But these past few years I've felt as though I was on some kind of mad carnival ride, whirling around faster and faster with no idea in the world where I was going.''

She could tell from Jonathan's expression that her words were totally incomprehensible to him. She won-dered why she even bothered to explain. He was born to the hype of the carnival, and he savored every scintillat-ing minute of it. The merry-go-round's gold ring was well within his grasp now. She wondered when she first be-gan to realize that it wasn't gold at all, only pot metal.

''I am coming back, Jonathan. Don't worry about that. La Salle and La Salle is my life. It's the only life I have, and I've got too much time and energy invested to turn back now. But we made a deal, and I won't let you back out of it. I'm going to stay here and finish what I've started with the lighthouse."

"The lighthouse?" He looked at her scornfully. "Okay, let's talk about the lighthouse!" He gestured to the canvases lined up against the wall. "You call this *talent?* You've got nothing here, Liz. *Nothing!* Look at that ugly, violent orange. No sun was ever that color! And that sky—it has *purple* in it, for Christ's sake! Who ever saw a *purple* sky?"

He pointed to the canvases, one after the other. "The lighthouse? All right, look at that lighthouse! It looks like a pile of rocks. You can hardly separate it from the boulder it's built on! That's not *art*, Liz. It doesn't soothe the way art should—it disturbs! You're wasting your time, babe. I *know* what will sell. It's my job! And I'm telling you, you'll never sell these."

She walked over to the wall where the canvases were propped and stood looking down at them—her children, in a way, insulted by a stranger who didn't even know them. "I don't know if they'll sell. I don't even know if they're good," she said reluctantly. "All I know is that it's what I have to do."

Jonathan unlatched his briefcase, which lay on the kitchen table. He lowered his voice to a calm, persuasive tone. "Come back. If it's cash you need, we can renegotiate the contracts. I'm a reasonable man, Liz. Talk to me. Look, I bought you a ticket. Nonrefundable. That's how sure I was that you'd come back with me."

He thumbed the ticket envelope enticingly. "Come on, babe. Just throw your stuff in a suitcase and we'll be out of this sleepy hollow on the nine o'clock to San Fran. What d'you say?"

"You're not listening to me, Jonathan. *This* is what I say." She marched across the room and snatched the ticket envelope out of his hand. She tore it smartly in half, then marched back across the room and threw it into the fire. It flared briefly, then crumbled to a wisp of ash.

"I don't know why you came all this way to give me a hard time, anyway," she said in the brittle tone of voice that she saved for especially distasteful situations. "As far as I'm concerned, we had this all settled before I left."

With mournful eyes Jonathan watched the ticket burn. "I'm only thinking of you, Liz. I like you. I loved you once, remember? And we get along so well—not many couples can say that after a divorce."

She gave a bitter laugh. "We get along so well only at the office, and only because we *both* want what's best for La Salle and La Salle. But if our ideas ever diverge, you'll walk. I learned that in our marriage, Jonathan. That's what *I* remember."

He bowed his head. *He's checking out the toes of his Pierre Cardins,* Elizabeth thought for a moment with extreme annoyance. *Probably making sure his expensive shoes hadn't got any mud spattered on them.*

"Leslie wants to come to work at La Salle and La Salle." His voice was almost inaudible.

"What did you say?"

He cleared his throat. "Leslie says she wants to go to work. She's bored. Says she's tired of being at home with the girls all day and having people think she's an airhead."

"But I thought that's what she wanted!"

Jonathan looked at her, chagrined. "So did I."

"Go ahead and hire her. I don't care. She can be your secretary."

"Well, that's the problem." He shoved his hands into his pockets and fell heavily into the depths of the sofa.

"She wants me to buy you out." He grimaced apologetically. "She wants your job."

Elizabeth looked at him in disbelief. "*My* job? What does she think—that she can just step in and do my job?"

"I don't know what she thinks."

"It took me *years* to make the design department what it is today! Doesn't she know that?"

"I was as surprised as you are," Jonathan assured her. "She's been coming in every day since you left—just to help out, she said. But now I don't know. She's on some kind of power trip or something."

He shook his head helplessly, looking comically like every other husband who ever married a girl and found a headstrong woman underneath. "I thought maybe if you came back, you know, and she *had* to go home, maybe she'd forget all this foolishness."

Elizabeth eyed him suspiciously. "Are you sure this isn't all your own idea, Jonathan? You aren't just trying to keep the profits in the family?"

"Me? Hell, no! I know she could never do your job! Besides," he said, smiling sheepishly, "I *like* having her at home. I *like* having her meet me at the door every night with my slippers and a martini. That may make me a male chauvinist, but I *like* being treated like a king in my own home."

Elizabeth glanced away uncomfortably, unwilling to be made privy to the secrets of Jonathan's marital life. "You can spare me the details. I know what you like."

"Well, anyway, I like things just the way they are, that's all. But—"

"But?"

His voice fell. "I don't want to have another failed marriage, either."

Elizabeth was surprised by the rare display of sincerity. "I hope it won't come to that," she said more kindly. "But you can tell Leslie—"

"Tell her what?" Jonathan looked at her hopefully.

"That I won't sell. I've got ten years of my life tied up with that place, and I'm not about to give it all up just because Leslie is bored!"

"You'll come back then?"

"I'll come back, Jonathan. In September, just as I had planned."

"But...but what'll I tell Leslie?"

"*That,* my dear Jonathan, is *your* problem!"

LATER THAT NIGHT, with Jonathan bunked uncomfortably on the sofa, Elizabeth had her first, faint doubts.

It was unthinkable, of course. Leslie couldn't possibly handle the design department at La Salle and La Salle! Still...

She played the "what if" game. What if she didn't go back in September? What if she decided to stay—oh, not forever maybe, but for a little while longer?

She could paint Deception Head Lighthouse in the fall when the scrub oak behind it would be a brilliant and extravagant red, when the hills back of town would be covered with snow, when the sun would be shining all day long, not peeking coyly from behind a fog bank every now and then.

When Matt's guide service slowed down a bit and he would have more time...time for...for what? Unbidden, her mind went back to the broad expanse of his damp skin gleaming golden in the firelight, to the length of thigh and the lap barely covered by the black silk kimono.

The same pleasure that was almost pain plunged through her, and she tossed restlessly from one side of the double bed to the other. She was very hot in spite of the chill in the room, and she threw off the blankets until only one thin coverlet remained over her body. Perspiration formed in the creases beneath her breasts and slid down the smooth, heated flesh to the thin sheet below.

If Jonathan hadn't arrived when he did, she was very much aware that she might not be lying alone in this bed tonight. Her mind skirted that disturbing line of thought and returned to painting.

If the Lighthouse Society liked her preliminary work, she might have a contract that would keep her busy for many summers to come. But could she absent herself from La Salle and La Salle for three months every summer? Jonathan wouldn't allow it—and his refusal would be perfectly justified.

Another option crept into her mind. Okay, then, what if she didn't go back at all? What if she were to sell her interest to Jonathan? She would realize enough profit to keep her going for a long time, with proper investments possibly for a *very* long time. Jonathan could hire Leslie, or anyone else he chose....

But how could she turn the reins of La Salle and La Salle over to Leslie's inexperienced hands? It was inconceivable. Still...

Her mind played the "what if" game most of the night, scurrying around in the maze of possibilities until the small hours of the morning.

Sometime after midnight the rain stopped.

CHAPTER ELEVEN

THE RINGING of the telephone awakened Elizabeth long before she was ready to get up. When it stopped, she breathed a semiconscious sigh of relief and burrowed deeper into her pillow.

"Liz?" A voice she hadn't heard first thing in the morning for years called her name from the doorway. "Liz, telephone."

She opened one eye. "Who...? Who...*Johnny?*" Her voice was groggy. Only half awake she sat up in bed and rubbed her eyes. The oversize nightshirt she slept in was pulled to the side, exposing one shoulder and the curve of one full breast.

"Telephone," Jonathan said again, his voice suddenly rough. He was wearing only a T-shirt and the trousers of his Palm Beach as he lounged in the doorway. He walked over to the bed and sat on the edge.

While Elizabeth watched him confusedly, as if she couldn't quite remember who he was, he reached out with careful fingers and adjusted the neckline of her nightshirt. Involuntarily his eyes fell to the deep V of the unbuttoned neckline. Then, with more self-discipline than anyone who knew him would have given him credit for, he smoothed her rumpled collar, looked directly into her sleepy face and gently shook her shoulder. "Yes, it's Johnny, Liz. Are you awake?"

Elizabeth stretched her arms over her head and yawned thoroughly, then dropped her hands to her head and ran her fingers through her disheveled hair. She noticed sunlight streaming in through the tattered shade over the bedroom window and heard the quarrelsome chirping of birds.

The rain must have stopped, she thought vaguely. Then she saw Jonathan and her eyes snapped open. "Jonathan!" she exclaimed. Her hands shot down to pull the coverlet up to her chin.

"Telephone," he said, concealing his momentary lapse into gallantry with a suggestive leer. He pushed himself up from the edge of the bed and walked out of the room.

Elizabeth stumbled from the bed. She grabbed the black kimono from the hook behind the bedroom door, then jammed her arms into the sleeves and wrapped it snugly around her body, quickly securing the sash as she walked into the kitchen.

She smelled coffee. It dawned on her that Jonathan must have brewed it—Jonathan, who had lived with her for seven years and never even learned how to operate the coffeemaker! Leslie was obviously having better luck training him than she had! Jonathan handed her the telephone receiver with a most aggravating smirk on his face.

"Hello?" Her voice brightened when she heard Matt on the other end.

"I see he stayed the night," Matt began without preamble.

"Well, yes, I mean, why not? Where else was he going to go?" Matt surprised her. She had never heard him speak in that curt tone before. She suspected he wasn't smiling his mellow, laid-back smile, either.

"I'm sorry. I had no right to say that."

"It's all right." She heard a hint of something in his voice that she might have interpreted as jealousy in anyone else, but which she knew to be completely out of character for Matt.

"When is he leaving?" Again the slight hint of uncharacteristic sharpness in his voice.

"Ah...I don't know. We just got up." There was silence at the other end of the line. "I mean..." Damn! For a woman renowned in the business world as unflappable, she seemed to have a great deal of difficulty finding the right words to use with Matt! "He hasn't said yet...."

"Is it up to him or up to you?"

"I don't know. Why?"

"I didn't get around to mentioning it last night, but that cruise we talked about up the coast to Florence? To Heceta Head Light? Well, I spoke with Will and he thought we might come on up today."

"Today?"

"Well, this might be our only chance this summer— Will keeps himself pretty busy. But if you can't make it..."

"No, no, today will be fine. I'm sure today will be fine. Yes. What time?"

"How soon can you be ready?"

Elizabeth's eyes flickered momentarily to Jonathan. "I just need to get a few things together. It won't take me long."

"How does noon sound?"

"Sounds perfect."

"Okay, why don't I meet you at the diner? We'll have lunch and take off afterward."

When she hung up the phone, Jonathan gave her a dour look. "I take it you want me out of here?" he growled.

"No. You can stay if you want to," she said gaily. "But I won't be here." She couldn't keep a happy grin from lighting up her face.

"They're not going to believe this back in Chicago," Jonathan said, shaking his head disapprovingly. "Liz La Salle, Elizabeth the Hun, the Bitch Goddess of Michigan Avenue—did you know they call you that?"

Elizabeth smiled thinly. "I'd heard the first. I surmised the second."

"Elizabeth La Salle . . . and a lumberjack!"

"Fisherman, Jonathan. And I really don't care what they believe." She poured herself a cup of Jonathan's coffee and sat down at the dinette table, mentally sorting what she needed to pack.

"Can you at least give me a ride to the airport?"

"I don't have time to take you to Coos Bay," she replied in a preoccupied tone. "But I can take you to the airpark just south of here, and maybe you can get one of the crop dusters to give you a lift!"

Jonathan failed to see the humor in that. "Take me into town and I'll get another cab," he said in a long-suffering voice. He took his silk shirt with the monogrammed cuffs from the back of the chair where he'd hung it and slipped it on.

"Liz," he began gingerly, fastening the buttons from the bottom up, which he had timed and found to be faster and more efficient, "won't you reconsider? Leslie...who knows what will be on her mind with you gone another two months? Why not just come back now before things get out of hand? You'll get tired of this fisherman. You know you will."

With unselfconscious nonchalance he unbuttoned his trousers and lowered the zipper, then tucked his shirt in all around and fastened the trousers up again. Elizabeth watched with a curious detachment. Something in her marveled that so intimate an action could have finally become nothing more than an unthinking habit.

"I don't suppose your bearded . . . *fisherman* . . . keeps a razor here?"

"No."

Jonathan sighed as he slipped into his jacket. "No matter. Maybe I'll run into a flight attendant who likes the Don Johnson look!"

THE ONE HUNDRED MILES of coastline between Deception Head and Florence were uniformly breathtaking. Matt hugged the shore as much as possible, steering the *Chinook Wind* out beyond the continental shelf only when it was necessary.

"Give me a holler if you see anything you'd like to sketch," he had said, but Elizabeth soon realized that if they stopped at every magnificent vista that opened up before her, they would never get to Heceta Head.

The contrast of the sea and the shore captivated her artist's instincts—the endless battle between the solid basalt walls that looked seaward and the eternal, restless waves trying to break them down. Of course the sea eventually won, she concluded, judging by the irregular crags of basalt where the relentless breakers had worn the cliffs away. But maybe not, the cliffs were still there, after all, broken and battered but still standing.

The *Chinook Wind* sailed past nameless inlets and busy seacoast towns. On the chalky cliffs of Cape Blanco, the most westerly point of the Oregon coast, sheep and horses grazed, wandering down from inland ranches to feed on the salty sea grass.

As the boat traveled farther north, the cliffs were sandstone, scarred by wave tunnels and eroded by the encroaching sea. Narrow peninsulas jutted out into the water, some not much more than outcroppings of rock with the sea still clawing away at their base.

"How do you like it?" Matt asked, joining Elizabeth at the rail. His Basque fisherman's cap was tipped at a rakish angle, and a cigarette dangled in the corner of his mouth. He propped both hands on the brass rail, arranging the long, lean lines of his body into an angular slouch against the gunwale.

"Well, I can certainly understand why they needed lighthouses along this coast," she said. "To someone from the flatlands of the Midwest this is really an experience!"

Matt put his arm around Elizabeth's shoulder and turned her in the direction his other hand was pointing. "Look over there." Her eyes followed the line of his finger, and she saw a tiny point of land in the distance.

Upon closer inspection she realized that it was an island, separated from the mainland by a narrow inlet. The sun glanced off a white structure at the extreme western end of the weather-beaten islet.

"Cape Arago Light," Matt said. "You can only reach her by footbridge." His arm stayed around her shoulders, as if he'd forgotten all about it altogether, and his eyes remained fixed on the tiny islet.

"It's in much better condition than Deception Head," Elizabeth noted. The Light itself wasn't at all like majestic Deception Head Light. It was short and squat, its octagonal tower only about twenty-five feet of stoutly built, reinforced concrete.

"Actually, it's the third lighthouse built there, so it's not nearly as old."

"What happened to the first two?"

"Well, the first one was built on the eastern lee, along with a lifesaving station. Its tower was much taller than this one. Then erosion undercut the cliff and the lighthouse fell into the sea, so the Coast Guard build a second one farther from the edge. Unfortunately the erosion continued, and that one finally fell, too. They built the third one in what was the middle of the island then, but as you can see, it's right on the point now."

The sandstone cliffs were jagged and steep and precariously close to the foundation of the lighthouse. They looked as though they might crumble at any moment and let the lighthouse drop into the sea, just as the first two had done.

"What's to keep the cliff from collapsing under this one, too?"

"Theoretically the Army Corps of Engineers. They built the jetties north and south to protect the harbor. Of course, the Indians say the problem is that there's a curse on the island."

"More ghost stories," Elizabeth guessed.

"Right. Seems the footbridge was built on an old Indian burial ground. You can still see some of the mounds. They bring their dead here sometimes, even now, but instead of digging up the ground they bring the ashes and throw them into the sea from the cliff."

"And what do you think? Which one is correct?"

He appeared to study the question seriously. "Who knows? Science would explain it by talking about geography and prevailing ocean currents. But, of course, it may be that the geography and the prevailing currents *are* the curse! All I know for sure is that no part of the coast was more littered with shipwrecks than this stretch right here. Sometimes ships had to anchor outside the harbor and wait a month or more for weather conditions to allow them to cross the bar."

The squat white structure of Cape Arago Light was directly across from them as the *Chinook Wind* drifted past the tiny islet. The intermittent sun glistened off pockets of mist rising from the ice-blue water.

"You know how I'd paint this?" Elizabeth burst out suddenly. "I'd paint the Light just the way it is now, and over it I'd paint the first one, transparent, sort of, just a suggestion of how it must have looked." Her eyes blazed with inspiration. Her hands cut through the air, sketching her ideas on the wind with broad, decisive gestures. "The old tower, and then this one, like this—" her hand flew upward "—soaring above it like a phoenix rising out of its own ashes!" Her voice rushed on eagerly. "Yes, that's how it should be! And I'm sure I can get pictures of the old lighthouse from the library!" She turned excitedly to Matt. "What do you think?"

Matt regarded her with his usual down-turned smile. Behind his wraparound sunglasses his eyes squinted engagingly. "That's what I admire about you—your enthusiasm. You know what you want and you go after it. I bet when you were getting your ad agency going you slept a lot of nights on a couch in your office. Am I right?"

"And showered at the Y around the corner, yes." She looked at him curiously. "How did you know?"

"That's the way you are. I can tell. You don't do anything halfway." There was frank approval in the voice, and in the eyes that were barely visible behind the dark glasses. "I bet it's the same in the rest of your life, too. A hundred and ten percent. I bet you're a risk taker in everything you do."

"No," Elizabeth said thoughtfully. "I don't think so."

She knew how to walk the fine line between progress and the status quo, how to sense a trend in the making and run with it. Innovation was the name of the game in advertising—the minute you stopped taking risks you were no longer on the cutting edge and the competition would go for your jugular.

But in her private life she was very different. It had been a long time since she had curled up at night with anything riskier than the contents of her briefcase.

"No," she repeated, sorry she had to diminish Matt's opinion of her. "I don't take many risks in my personal life. I can't afford the time."

"Maybe you just haven't found...the person you'd be willing to take risks for," Matt suggested gently.

She looked at him sharply. "I was married to Jonathan for seven years," she pointed out.

"That has nothing to do with it."

"You're right, of course." She tried to remember how she had felt about Jonathan in the early days. Had she ever been willing to risk everything for him? Her love, her career, her life? Had she ever loved him to the point of total distraction?

The answer saddened her. "Maybe I was unfair to Jonathan," she said. "Maybe I didn't give him the kind of love that would have made him stay at home. I *thought* I did. He was certainly everything I wanted—intelligent, ambitious, hard-charging. He knew what he wanted out of life and he went for it, and I liked that. Besides..."

"Besides?"

Her silvery eyes flashed impishly. "He was a very passionate and...imaginative...lover. I liked that, too."

If she had been hoping to elicit some reaction from Matt, she was disappointed. He took a last, deep drag on his cigarette and then flicked the butt overboard.

"I'm not surprised," he said. His voice was gruff. "I figured you'd be the same way when you're in love. No holding back. I don't think you'd be capable of anything less."

No holding back. That was the fairy tale she'd been raised on. The fact that it had never been that way for her made her doubt, not love, but herself.

She glanced up at him. His eyes were fixed on the shoreline where Cape Arago Light was disappearing into the hazy sunshine. His patrician profile was chiseled like a bust in a museum, she thought, and just as inexpressive, whether talking about love or lighthouses.

Did he know anything about passion, Elizabeth wondered unexpectedly, with his austere, smiling face as pure and impassive as sculpted clay? She remembered his kiss, tentative and almost boyish, his total unselfconsciousness outfitted in her silky black kimono. Was it possible that he could be unaware of his own overwhelming virility?

From behind the barrier of sunglasses his eyes turned to hers, and she immediately lowered her own eyes in confusion. Without the calm green of his eyes to underscore the sweetness of his smile, his features looked different. Provocative. Sensual. She drew a deep, ragged breath. Unaware? Suddenly she doubted it.

"You took quite a risk coming here," Matt said into the stillness that was broken only by the steady splash of the bow as it cut through the water. "And that was personal, not only professional. Most people wouldn't take that sort of risk."

"You don't think so?" To her the decision to leave Chicago had felt like desperation. She was pleased that Matt saw something more positive in it.

"Most people would play it safe, stick it out to get their gold watch and their pension."

"It wasn't really such a risk," Elizabeth felt honor-bound to admit. "My career will still be there when I get back." She sighed wistfully. "Still, sometimes I think I'd like to just stay aboard the *Chinook Wind* and paint for the rest of my life."

Matt was silent for a moment. "What would your ex-husband think about that?" he asked finally.

"Jonathan?" She looked at him in surprise. "Well...I guess he wouldn't like it very much. Why do you ask?"

"He came all this way to see you. That must mean something."

"Yes. It means he wants me to return to Chicago."

"That's what I thought." Matt reached his free hand into his shirt pocket for another cigarette and inserted it between his lips.

"No, it's not what you think," Elizabeth hastened to add. "He says the office is falling apart without me."

"Seems like he could have told you that by telephone," Matt offered mildly. He dug a lighter out of his pocket and lit the cigarette. The smoke was carried upwind by the brisk breeze.

"Well, it was more than that, actually, but it doesn't matter. I'm entitled to a life away from La Salle and La Salle, too." She set her chin firmly, and her voice took on a stubborn edge. "Jonathan promised me this summer, and I'm going to hold him to it."

"Good for you." Matt's arm fell from across her shoulders, and he lazily uncoiled his long legs. "I'd better get back to the bridge. Maybe you'd like to go below and relax for a little while? We'll be heading out toward open sea now, and there won't be much to see until we get to Florence."

"I don't want to miss a minute of this," Elizabeth told him with a smile. "Why don't I make us some coffee? I'll run you up a cup."

"That would be great." With his arm around her waist Matt escorted her to the hatch that led to the main cabin. In another minute she heard his feet running up the ladder to the flying bridge.

SUNBEAMS GLINTED OFF the long windows surrounding the main cabin and made tiny prisms on the varnished wooden bulkheads. Beyond, the world was washed in the pale yellow of the afternoon sun. Elizabeth reached into one of the upper lockers and found a can of coffee. Her reflection was an indistinct smear of color in the dull luster of the bulkheads as she filled the coffeemaker and plugged it in.

The gusty sea air had made her eyes feel very heavy-lidded, and the warmth of the cabin and the rhythmic motion of the *Chinook Wind* took over where the sea air had left off. She stretched out along one of the hard wooden benches, intending only to relax for a few minutes, and promptly fell asleep.

When she woke, the light had changed. It was dusk and the cabin was gray. The tiny red light on the coffeemaker glowed in the dimness, and directly above it the window looked out on a darkening expanse of sea and sky.

For a split second she wondered what had awakened her, and then she realized that the rotations of the *Chinook Wind*'s diesels had slowed. Instead of plowing through choppy seas the boat now rose and fell on tranquil swells. The churning wake had become a gentle splash.

She reached above her head and switched on the light. The windows instantly became glazed black walls that faithfully duplicated the cabin around her. Peering past the reflection, she saw lights in the distance—lights that grew larger and gradually multiplied into a picturesque seacoast village. A short wooden wharf extended over the water, and the running lights of a dozen boats moved slowly in the dark.

The *Chinook Wind*'s engines groaned as Matt rocked the boat in a series of back and forth motions, walking her closer to the wharf, and then she heard his voice shout down, "Hey, Chino! Tie me down, will you?" One end of a thick rope hurtled past the window and was caught by someone still out of sight on the wharf.

A minute later Matt's cheerful face appeared in the hatchway. "We're here."

THEY STOPPED for dinner at the Pier, a small, seedy tavern on the waterfront. After the hours spent at sea, Elizabeth found that she couldn't take a step without automatically compensating for the roll of the boat. Even when she sat down at a table covered with a scrubbed, red-and-white checked oilcloth, she kept expecting the earth to pitch beneath her. The diesels still droned in her head, competing with the din of the noisy tavern.

On the table where Matt and Elizabeth had seated themselves, a candle in a red glass container guttered fitfully. A bored waiter slouched on one hip between them.

"What do you recommend?" Elizabeth shouted to Matt over the drone of the diesels and the noise of the crowd.

Matt pointed to a blackboard above the bar. It said Steamed Clams. "The owner doesn't concern himself much with variety." He grinned. "He cooks whatever his boys happen to bring in that day."

"Well, then I guess I'll have the clams." Elizabeth smiled at the bored waiter, who looked as though he'd just as soon stab them as serve them. "And a glass of white—"

"Beer," Matt interrupted. "It's all they serve."

"Er, a Bud Light," Elizabeth amended.

"We only got draft, lady," the waiter replied, shifting impatiently from one hip to the other.

Elizabeth shot Matt a humorous glance. "That's fine."

"Make that two," Matt instructed as the waiter slouched away. Then he crossed his elbows on the table and leaned closer. "No atmosphere, but they make the best seafood on the coast."

"Oh, I'd say it has *plenty* of atmosphere," Elizabeth countered dryly. The tavern smelled of spilt beer and un-washed bodies, and a blue haze of cigarette smoke hung in layers on the air. There was sawdust on the floor and moth-eaten, fly-specked animal heads mounted on the walls. A jukebox wailed a dirge about unrequited love from the far corner of the room, its tinny music barely audible over the cacophony of loud voices and raucous laughter.

The men who lined the bar looked as rough as their laughter and their voices. Above their heads flew a trio of mounted glass-eyed ducks, doomed to hang sus-pended forever in this smoke-filled room where no bird was ever meant to fly.

Matt leaned closer and covered her fingers with his. "You must think I'm totally without class," he shouted into her ear. "Someday I'm going to take you to one of the really fine restaurants here on the coast. We'll have a nice, leisurely nine-course meal from soup to nuts, just like you're used to in Chicago. Would you like that?''

Elizabeth tried to picture him in Chez Paul or Cricket's. With his sun-bleached hair, curling blond beard and open, honest manner, he would look decidedly out of place, she concluded. "Actually, I like this," she shouted back. "I've never been in a place quite like it before."

Their waiter slammed two foaming glasses of beer on the table. A minute later he brought plates, silverware and paper napkins, and a three-foot loaf of French bread that he carried under his arm. Finally he returned with an enormous black kettle, and when he lifted the lid, the potent smell of garlic wafted upward in the steam.

Eyeing the contents of the black kettle with relish, Elizabeth realized that it had been a very long time since lunch. Matt broke the length of bread in half and handed one end to her. "Dig in," he commanded.

CHAPTER TWELVE

THE MAN MATT introduced as Chino gave them a lift to Heceta Head Lighthouse. His truck was an antique Ford four-on-the-floor, and whenever he shifted gears he bumped Elizabeth's knees, which caused him to sweat profusely and apologize in a strangled voice every time it happened.

Chino drove down a rough asphalt road that coiled through the woods. It was an old logging trail, and it wound along the side of the cliff in a series of hairpin turns.

Here were more wind-sheared pines and twisted scrub oak, flanked on the south by mountainous white sand dunes. The sand shifted like fluid in the misty moonlight. At a fallen log the asphalt came to a dead end, and Chino brought the truck to a halt.

"Thanks, Chino," Matt said as he opened the passenger door and slid out, giving Elizabeth a hand as she followed. He slammed the door shut, and Chino took off, still sweating in an agony of embarrassment. His spinning tires precipitated a whirlpool of leaves and pine needles at their feet.

Ahead on the rugged cape was the white turret of Heceta Head Light, which had tantalized Elizabeth with brief glimpses of its soaring tower during the past fifteen minutes of the trip, revealing itself when the road curved toward the sea and then disappearing again when it wound inland. Closer than the lighthouse was the keeper's dwelling. The house faced the Pacific. It stood in startling white contrast to the brush and rock that surrounded it.

Although larger than the caretaker's quarters at Deception Bay, Elizabeth saw that the weathered clapboard construction was familiar. Even the rocking chairs on the porch were familiar, gently creaking to and fro in the still night air as if propelled by some ghostly occupants.

Moths beat their wings frantically against the porch light, and the sound of canned laughter drifted faintly from inside. Matt rapped on the window. Through the shade Elizabeth saw a stooped shadow rise and walk to the door.

"I'm coming, I'm coming," a voice barely discernible above the blare of the television said.

The old man who opened the door had faded blue eyes and wrinkled parchment skin. He wore a dingy thermal undershirt, its neckline stretched out of shape, and baggy blue dungarees held up by striped suspenders. A bushy gray mustache hid his upper lip and drooped down into the jowls of his chin.

"Matthew!" he exclaimed, clapping Matt on the back with one gnarled hand and pulling him inside. "As I live and breathe! Whyn't you tell me you was comin'?"

"It was kind of a spur-of-the-moment thing," Matt told the man blandly. Elizabeth shot him a surprised look.

"Never mind, never mind, you know you're always welcome here! Come on in! It's good to see ye, good to see ye! And this must be...?"

"Elizabeth La Salle. She's come to paint Deception Head Light. Elizabeth, I'd like you to meet Guillaume Aubergine."

"Come on in, gel, come on in!" Guillaume Aubergine aimed his rheumy old eyes at Elizabeth. "Make it snappy. Make it snappy now. Don't want to let the bugs in!" He hustled them inside and slammed the door behind them.

With a jowly grin that stretched his mustache from ear to ear, he hung their jackets on the bentwood coatrack beside the door. Then he stood back and clasped Matt's shoulders with both hands, regarding him with an appraising look. His voice was loud and bombastic. "Lookin' good, Matthew, lookin' good! Ain't gettin' any younger, though. I can see that!"

He turned his attention to Elizabeth. "This is the one you told me about, eh? Not bad, not bad." His glance roved over her with frank speculation. "Well, she's a looker, all right, Matthew, just like you said. Ain't as young as she might be, but she's got some good years left in her yet. Could give a man some fine lookin' young'uns before she's through, I warrant!"

Matt laughed. "Will, you're incorrigible!" He turned to Elizabeth. "He's been trying to get me married off for as long as I can remember. Don't pay any attention to him."

"I'm happy to meet you, Mr. Aubergine," Elizabeth said, and offered her hand.

The old man grasped her hand with both of his and shook it energetically. "Well, bless your heart, gel, bless your heart! No one's called me 'Mr. Aubergine' since I retired from the merchant marines! You call me Will, hear? Like everyone else does, eh? None of this 'mister' business. Makes me feel old!"

He chortled at the absurdity of that thought as he paused to turn down the volume of the sitcom rerun that was blaring from his television set, then ushered them toward the threadbare couch in front of the hearth.

A potbellied wood stove, black with polished nickel trim, was built into the fireplace—probably a real improvement in its day. The stovepipe ran into the wall above the mantel, and a vriac fire—driftwood and seaweed, a "poor man's fire"—glowed dully behind the sooty glass door, filling the room with the brackish aroma of burning salt.

"What can I get ye?" Will demanded. "Are ye hungry? Thirsty?"

"We just had dinner down at the Pier," Matt said.

"Well, then ye must be thirsty. A little blackberry brandy? Good for what ails ye, blackberry brandy! Yes, sir!"

Will disappeared into the kitchen, returning with two glasses of a thick purple liquid. He handed one to each of them and then eased himself stiffly into a sagging leather recliner that was molded to the shape of his body.

"Drink up, drink up!" he ordered heartily as he beamed at them across the blackened stove. "Take the chill off'n your bones!"

While Matt and Will caught up on old times, Elizabeth studied the room curiously. It was the same eclectic combination of old-fashioned and contemporary that characterized the keeper's quarters at Deception Head.

In one corner a painted whatnot shelf was full of the souvenirs of life on the coast—a large green Japanese fishing ball, a pearly conch shell that enclosed the sound of the sea, several smaller shells, a ship under full sail in a whiskey bottle.

There were also a few relics of Will's days in the merchant marines—brassware from India, a walrus tooth, an old admiral's spyglass. And the walls were lined with photographs.

"I see you're looking at my rogue's gallery," Will interrupted his conversation with Matt to remark.

"Yes. They're fascinating."

"Well, go on, go on! Take a closer look-see. That's what they're there for!"

"Elizabeth is interested in the history of this place," she heard Matt explain as she stood and walked to the wall where the photographs were displayed. "I told her you know more about it than anybody."

"And so I do, so I do!" Will heaved his bulk out of the armchair and came to stand behind Elizabeth. "That there," he said, pointing at one photograph, "see, that's me when I was fifteen. First time I ever went to sea. Look at those brass buttons! I was so full of myself I could have split right open with pride!"

Elizabeth peered closely at the out-of-focus image in the ancient photograph. She could see no resemblance in the bright-faced boy to the old man Will Aubergine had become.

"And that one," Will continued, "that's me right after the war. And that's old Hazen. Me and him was in Honolulu picking up a load o' copra bound for China."

He led her down the wall, one photograph at a time.

Some were pictures of ships—tramp steamers, cargo ships, tankers—anchored in nameless foreign ports or tied up at tired-looking docks. Others were of men in shabby uniforms—men standing on dazzling white sand with palm trees in the background, men leaning against a ship's rail or against a lifeboat on the beach. They were young, most of them, their arms linked together or thrown around one another's shoulders, laughing faces squinting into the sun.

There were women in a few of the photographs, too, most of them surrounded by children. Only one was alone.

"Who is this?" Elizabeth asked, pointing to the stained, faded tintype of a solitary woman posing stiffly in front of a lighthouse. She was a stout creature, grim and unsmiling, and outfitted more somberly than the others in dark boiled wool trimmed with braid.

"That? Why that's Mrs. Juliet Nichols." Will gazed fondly at the old photograph. "Spent some thirty years in the Lighthouse Service. Longer'n most men."

"I didn't know women could be lighthouse keepers."

"Weren't many," Will had to admit. "Mostly they didn't think ladies was up to it. Except Mrs. Nichols here, o'course. She was a fine figger of a woman. There warn't no doubt she could handle the job better'n most men! She was stationed down at Angel Island in San Francisco Bay, was Mrs. Nichols. Lot o' ships reached their port of no return on that bar, let me tell you. The old-timers used to tell about the summer of 1906, fog so thick it weighed on you like a bad conscience, and the foghorn broke down.

"That little lady took a sledgehammer and pounded the giant fogbell by hand for over twenty hours to warn ships away from the island. Two days later the foghorn broke again, and she did it all through another night." He lumbered back to his armchair and lowered himself into it. "Yep, musta been quite a woman," he ruminated. "Don't make 'em like that anymore."

Matt was settled comfortably in one corner of the couch. His long legs were crossed at the ankle, stretched out toward the wood stove. A cigarette burned forgotten between his fingers, and the ash was long at the tip. When Elizabeth sat down beside him, he looked up and smiled.

Will reached for the cold pipe that was sitting in an ashtray next to his chair. He filled the bowl from a pouch of tobacco also beside the chair, then carefully lit it with a long fireplace match. "So you want to know about Heceta Head?" he finally demanded, peering sharply at Elizabeth through the rising smoke.

"All the lighthouses up around here," Matt clarified. "She's going to be painting all of them in the next few years."

"I *hope* I'll be painting all of them in the next few years," Elizabeth corrected modestly.

"Are you any good?" Will asked.

"She's good," Matt said before she could reply.

"You ain't gonna prettify 'em, are you?" Will grumbled. "Make 'em into something they're not?"

"Not at all," Elizabeth assured him.

"You'd approve of what she's done, Will," Matt added.

"Well, just so's she ain't gonna prettify 'em," Will grumbled again. "Clean 'em up for the public that don't know nothin' about 'em, anyway. Give 'em a facelift, take away all their character…" His voice trailed off. He hooked his thumbs in his suspenders and looked into the fire with a disgruntled expression in his rheumy blue eyes.

"Matt tells me you were the last keeper at Deception Head Light," Elizabeth said.

"That I was, that I was." Will brightened. "In fact, I was there in '61, the only time in nigh onto one hundert years the light ever went out."

"What happened?" Elizabeth asked, as if he needed any encouragement at all to talk. Will's eyes had the same distant expression she had seen sometimes in Matt's—a look of being tuned into something far away or long ago.

"It was a bitter storm, bitter storm." He wagged his head, relishing the memory. "Yep, we had seawater in the lantern room that night, let me tell you! We had an emergency generator, but that failed, too. The assistant keeper got hold of an old oil lamp from somewheres, and me an' him took turns walking around the gallery with that old lamp from midnight to morning."

Guillaume Aubergine was indeed an adventurer. He had savored the feast of life at tables never even dreamed of by most men. Like Scheherazade, he had a thousand and one stories, and also like Scheherazade, he was a born storyteller. He seemed to forget that he was old, and his stories took on the immediacy of the here and now.

The piebald tabby napping against the warmth of the stove rose and stretched. The fire in the grate burned low.

"Fire's almost out," Matt announced unnecessarily. "Do you want me to get some wood?"

"Ain't got none," Will replied. "That's why I'm burning vriac. Arm's been bothering me—got cut in a fight with a Malay up along Pitcairn years ago," he explained, turning to Elizabeth, "and it ain't never been the same since."

"Well, let me go split some for you, then," Matt said. "You'll be needing it." He downed the last of his blackberry brandy and walked to the door. When he opened it, whorls of fog drifted in and the tabby stalked aristocratically out.

"Well, well, well," Will said when Matt was gone. "You're the first of Matthew's lady friends he ever brought out here. What do you suppose that means?" He hooked his thumbs into his suspenders and eyed Elizabeth shrewdly.

"I have no idea," she replied.

"Must mean he thinks you're something special. That's the onliest reason I can figger. Fine boy, Matthew, fine boy. You could go a lot farther and do worse."

"Why don't you call him 'Matt' the way everyone else does?"

"Me? I knowed Matthew all his life. Used to take him out fishing when him and his ma came down to the coast in the summer. Fine boy, fine boy." The old man's voice trailed off as a small golden-haired child from the past skipped across his memory.

"What about his father? Didn't he come, too?"

"Old Doc McCullough? Didn't know him well. No one did, least of all Matthew. Drove down from Portland, old Doc did, ever' so often. Thought his patients couldn't get along without him. Died from a heart attack few years back." He paused and sucked his pipe meditatively. "Getting along without him now, I guess."

"Matt's father was a doctor?" Elizabeth said thoughtfully. "I imagine he was pretty disappointed when his son became a fisherman."

"Toward the last he was, I think. But he never gave up hope that Matthew'd go back to medicine."

"Matt wanted to go into medicine, too?"

"Never wanted t'do nothin' else."

"What happened, then?" Elizabeth remembered her own youthful ambitions and the way she had let herself be sidetracked. She was sorry to hear that the same thing had happened to Matt. "Why didn't he become a doctor like his father?"

Will looked at her as though she were a not-very-bright child. "He did. The two of them was 'Old Doc' and 'Young Doc' when his daddy was alive. Ever'one thought he'd hang out his shingle with his daddy one day. Never did, though." Will chuckled at the blank look on Elizabeth's face. "Never told you that, did he? Ain't that just like him! Well, it was a long time ago. Most everyone's prob'ly forgot. Prob'ly he's forgot it himself by now."

"Matt is a *physician?* Then why on earth is he fishing for a living?"

"Why not? It's good, honest work."

"Of course it is. But you don't spend ten years in medical school preparing for it!"

Will leaned forward in his armchair and emptied his pipe into the fireplace, tapping it methodically on the stone hearth until all the ashes had fallen out. While Elizabeth watched, full of questions, he refilled the bowl with ritualistic concentration and ceremoniously lit the tobacco. He sucked on the stem of the pipe deeply and with great satisfaction.

"You may be right," he granted finally, puffs of smoke accompanying the words. "Fishin' takes a lot o' skills, but you don't learn 'em from a book."

"Why doesn't he practice medicine anymore?"

"Dunno. Reckon no one does, 'cepting Matthew."

"But didn't you ever *ask* him?"

Will fixed her with a reproving eye. "We leave each other be up here, young lady. World'd be a lot better place if more people did the same. He don't *want* to be a doctor, he don't *have* to be a doctor. He wants to fish, he can fish. Ain't no one gonna be telling him what he can do and what he can't. It ain't our way."

Elizabeth felt politely but firmly rebuked. She looked down at her hands, twisting unhappily around the jelly glass of purple brandy she still held in her lap. "I didn't mean to pry," she said. "It's just that..."

Will leaned forward and patted her hand. "I know, gel, I know. You think you've found your man, and now you find out that there's a whole other side of him you don't know nothing about.''

Elizabeth took a long, slow sip of the brandy. It made her mouth feel sticky and sweet. ''No, it isn't that....'' But when she looked up into Will's wise old eyes, she saw that he understood her possibly better than she understood herself. ''Maybe...'' she admitted in a voice suddenly shy.

''Well, I ain't never asked him about it, no more'n anyone else has.'' His voice fell to a confidential whisper. ''But he went off to Vietnam. It was volunteer or be drafted for young docs in those days. And when he came back, he warn't the same. Oh, it warn't nothin' you could put your finger on, mind you. He seemed like that same fella he's always been—always ready with a smile or a joke, do anythin' for you, give you the shirt off his back if'n you needed it. You know how he is.''

Elizabeth nodded. She knew how he was. Or at least she'd thought so until a few minutes ago. She kept her eyes fixed on Will. His own faded blue ones stared into the dying fire.

''But he was different, too,'' the old man continued after a moment. ''Hell, I practically *raised* that boy, summers, and I *knowed* he was different. And I warn't the only one, neither. His wife got tired of it and she divorced him. No great loss. That's what I told Matthew, and I told him right to his face, too. I ain't one to talk behind a man's back. She married a doctor and a doctor was what she wanted him to be. Never mind what *he* wanted! But it was somethin' more than that, even...''

''What?'' Elizabeth whispered. She concentrated on the old man's words, wondering if he was giving her the key to the riddle that was Matthew McCullough.

"Well, you couldn't get close to him, like. He didn't talk so much anymore. Oh, sure, about the weather and such. He'd even talk about Vietnam if'n you asked him, or anything else if'n you asked him. But... it's like he went away in his own mind, and he ain't never come back. Ever'body thinks Matthew's a good old boy, the salt of the earth—and he is, too. But there's somethin' missin'. Somethin' that used to be there and now it ain't anymore. And all those refugees he's brought over here, even that poor misbegotten youngster Tran ain't helped him none, neither."

"I know about Tran, but... refugees?"

He looked at her pityingly. "He ain't told you nothin', has he? Ain't that just like Matthew? Well, I guess if he'd a wanted you to know, he'd a told you."

That disclaimer out of the way, Will proceeded to tell her the story himself. "Before Tran there was a whole string of Vietnamese refugees Matthew sponsored. Owed 'em, he said. Always had two or three or a family living with him. Don't know where he found room for them all. None of 'em stayed long. Mostly they moved on down to San Francisco soon's they got a little money ahead— whole passel of Vietnamese refugees living down around the Bay area. Then Tran came, no more'n a kid, and Matthew figured he could do somethin' more for him, so he adopted him. Been cluckin' over him like a hen with one chick ever since."

Will cleared his throat several times, then made a great production of locating his handkerchief in one of his pockets and blowing his nose noisily. "Maybe I'm just a used-up old codger with too much time on my hands," he grunted after a moment. "And maybe I ain't got no business tryin' to figger out another man. Hell, I ain't even got *myself* figgered out yet! But I love that boy, practically raised him summers, and I *know!* He left something back there in Vietnam, and he ain't never found it again.''

Elizabeth leaned back into the couch. Her forehead furrowed as she tried to reconcile the Matt she thought she knew with this new information.

A physician? That big body that looked as natural on board the *Chinook Wind* as if he'd been born there? The man who favored old jeans and plaid Pendletons and turtleneck sweaters? Whose hands were rough and callused and brown, whose arms and strong back bulged with the muscles of a workingman, a laborer who earned his living by the sweat of his brow?

Why? Her mind kept circling back to the same question. Why would he keep such a thing a secret? He seemed so forthright and honest—what you saw was what you got. And then there was *this!*

Was it something to do with the war, as Will suspected? Certainly Matt wasn't bitter; quite the contrary. He was always good-natured, always smiling that slightly off-center, down-turned smile. Always that relentless good nature, she thought with a vague, half-formed suspicion suddenly lurking in the back of her mind, just beyond her ability to grasp it. Always that impenetrable smile...

The door burst open and Matt came in. Cold air blew in around him. Jonathan should see him now, Elizabeth thought. He looked more like a logger than ever with his arms full of wood and his shirt covered with wood chips. He shoved the door shut with one elbow and lowered the armload of split logs to the hod beside the stove.

''Going to need another cord by winter,'' he said to Will. He piled several logs on the ashes of vriac, and the fire flickered to life. The heavy woolen gloves that covered his hands were filled with splinters, and he tossed them onto the mantel as he held his hands toward the flames in the grate.

"Ought to wear a coat out there," Will grumbled. "Don't want to take a chill."

Matt gave Elizabeth a conspiratorial wink as he slouched into the couch beside her. After rolling his sleeves up past his elbows, he stretched his arm along the back of the couch, and his fingers trailed idly in the shaggy wisps of hair at her neck. She leaned her head against the back of the couch and found herself nestled in the crook of his elbow. He still exuded an aura of cold, fresh air.

"I don't need a coat. It's the middle of July," Matt reminded the old man.

"Don't make no never mind if'n it's July or it's January. Person can still get a chill." Will sucked furiously on the stem of his pipe, little puffs of smoke rising indignantly around his face. "And you living alone down there with no wife like a man ought to have to tend you proper...."

Matt looked at Elizabeth and winked again. Apparently this was territory he and Will had been over before.

Will laid his pipe in the ashtray and stretched his arms above his head in an exaggerated yawn. "Well, you young folks can burn the midnight oil if'n you want to, but it's past my bedtime, 'way past my bedtime. Matthew, why don't you show Elizabeth where the guest room is? There's bedclothes in the chest by the window—you can make a bed up on the couch if'n you want."

Will got to his feet and walked stiffly to the door, which he opened to allow the tabby to streak inside with an indignant jerk of its tail.

"My room's *all* the way on the other side of the house," he continued pointedly to Elizabeth. "And I sleep real sound. Ask Matthew." He looked at Matt guilelessly. "Ain't that right, Matthew? I don't never hear *nothing* once I get to snoring. And I sleep *real* late, too. Prob'ly won't even wake up till, oh, at least noon or so, I reckon."

Will's words were innocuous enough, but his old eyes twinkled and his underlying meaning was clear: he was telling Matt and Elizabeth that they would have the privacy to make whatever sleeping arrangements they chose without need for explanation nor worry about interruptions.

Preceded by his little cat, which wove itself agilely between his feet as he walked, Will gave Matt a savvy wink, then ambled through a door on the other side of the room, closing it with exaggerated finality behind him.

His departure left tension in its wake. It was made up in equal parts of the dimness of the light provided through the glass door of the wood stove, the intimacy of the cozy living room and the clear implications of the guest room that waited up the stairs.

Will's obvious assumption that she and Matt would want to share that room flustered Elizabeth, but even more than that it excited her. She tried not to let it show, but suddenly she didn't know quite where to put her eyes.

Matt sensed her discomfiture. "Don't let Will's lack of subtlety bother you," he said with a naturalness that immediately put her at ease. "He likes to talk. He says it's one of the rewards for getting old—you can say what you like and no one dares argue with you."

"He's quite a talker, all right," she agreed, knowing full well that it wasn't Will's lack of subtlety that bothered her. "As a matter of fact, he talked quite a bit about you while you were outside."

"Oh?" Matt's voice was noncommittal.

"Yes. He said..." She hesitated. *We let people be up here, young lady.* "Well, he worries about you."

"I wish he wouldn't," Matt said. "But I know he can't help it. I'm probably the closest thing to family he's got."

"Didn't he ever get married? Or have any children?"

"Married, yes, lots of times. Not always with the benefit of clergy, either, from the way he tells it. He never had children, though—at least none that he knows of, he says. Probably didn't stay around long enough to find out! I get the distinct impression he must have been quite a ladies' man in his younger days."

No doubt, thought Elizabeth, who hadn't missed the man-to-man wink the old man had aimed at Matt. She took a deep breath. "He said...well, as a matter of fact, he also told me you're a physician."

The fingers on the back of her neck stopped abruptly. "Sometimes Will talks too much. You should take what he says with a grain of salt."

"Are you?"

"No."

Elizabeth frowned. "Then why would he say that?"

The fingers began to massage her neck again. "I was. Once. But that was a long time ago. I'm surprised Will still thinks about it."

"Why did you give it up?"

"I wasn't suited to medicine, that's all."

"You prefer to fish for a living?"

"Something like that."

"But...to waste all those years, all that training!"

"I'm content. Isn't that enough?" He smiled. It was his usual gentle smile, but there was a coolness in his eyes that warned Elizabeth the subject was one he didn't choose to discuss. There was something he wasn't telling—even Will felt it. What else was he concealing behind that inscrutable smile?

"It's enough," she said, "if it's true."

"It's true enough." He continued to run his fingers lightly along the back of her neck. She moved her head back and forth, intensifying the prickly sensations his fingers were creating. When she idly turned her face toward him, she saw that he was watching her. In that instant his eyes informed her that Will's expectations weren't lost on him, either.

He reached over and took her hand, letting it curl upward in his rough brown one. "I shouldn't have brought you here," he said in a low voice as his thumb made tiny, self-conscious circles on her palm.

"I'm glad you did." She turned her hand over and fitted it to his, palm to palm, extending her fingers along the full length of his. How small her hand was against his, even the long oval nails not reaching the tips of his fingers! "You said Will is a fascinating person, and he's definitely that."

Tentatively Matt's fingers closed on hers. "That's not why I brought you. Not really. I know how crazy it sounds, but it bothered me a lot, your spending the night alone with Jonathan. Someone you once loved. Someone you used to sleep with."

"You needn't have worried. There's nothing between Jonathan and me."

"I'm glad. It's none of my business—but I am." He stood, not letting go of Elizabeth's hand. "Maybe I'd better show you the guest room."

The staircase was lighted only by the flames that flickered inside the wood stove. At the top of the stairs was a low door that opened into a tiny loft. Matt stooped and stepped inside, holding the door so that Elizabeth could enter in front of him.

The low ceiling slanted to the floor. The room, really no more than a corner of the attic, was simple and unadorned with only the most basic furniture—a bed, a bureau, a hard-backed chair. There was a single lamp on the bureau, a brass antique with stained glass shade and painted flowers on its ceramic base.

Two dormer windows reached only as high as Elizabeth's waist. They were bare and admitted the moon in a broad shaft of light that fell across the goose down comforter on the bed.

Elizabeth crossed the room and switched on the lamp while Matt stood in the doorway, his hand still on the doorknob. His big body was only a looming shadow, disappearing with the other shadows into the darkened corners of the room.

As she watched, he turned and walked over the creaking floorboards to the sea trunk beneath the window. He opened the lid and took out a pile of afghans, topped by a pillow encased in blue mattress ticking.

"Matt. Don't go." The lid of the trunk fell with a heavy thud. Matt straightened. He didn't turn around, and for an improbable moment Elizabeth thought he hadn't heard her. "Please. I want you to stay."

"Elizabeth . . . I can't."

The words hung in the air. They sounded so final. *I can't.* Elizabeth's heart quivered like a captive bird in the cage of her ribs.

Matt dropped his armload of bedclothes on top of the trunk and turned, crossing the tiny room in several swift strides. He wrapped his arms around her, holding her carefully, as if she would break if he held her too tightly. Or as if he would.

The pounding of her heart was replaced by a sinking feeling that would later, she knew, become humiliation. He wasn't going to stay, that much at least she understood. He wasn't going to make love to her. The why didn't matter.

"I want to, Elizabeth," he said, his chin resting on top of her head. "You must know that. I want you more than I've wanted any other woman in my life, and I have since the moment you walked into Milt's office. But it's not as simple as that."

He spoke slowly. It was apparent that he was choosing his words with great precision. "It was, at first. You were so beautiful—any healthy male would have responded the same way. And I could tell that you found me...not unattractive. I hoped that, if you were willing, we could have gotten something going between us. It would have been very nice for a little while. Just for the summer."

Elizabeth remembered the intensity that had smoldered in his green eyes that morning in Rodney Milton's office. Even in the bright daylight of the Coast Guard station, it had suggested darkness and excitement and compelling sensuality.

"But then it got complicated. I guess I waited too long to make my move." He gave a small, ironic chuckle. It sounded as though he were laughing at himself. "And all of a sudden I realized that, if I was ever lucky enough to have you, I wouldn't be able to bear giving you up when the summer was over." He tilted her head up with one finger under her chin. "And I will have to give you up, won't I?"

Elizabeth had no answer for that. Of course he would. This wasn't her reality—this was temporary, a three-month respite from life in the fast lane. She had never intended anything more than that. Had she?

Besides, she'd already learned one thing about lighthouses—they weren't usually located in population centers. Although the Lighthouse Society had hired her with the promise of future assignments if they liked her work, was she really willing to give up the excitement and stimulation of city life for the rustic simplicity of a place like, say, Deception Bay? Or another town very much like it? She sighed heavily. There seemed to be no solution to the dilemma.

"You see?" he said when she didn't reply. He tilted her head higher so that she couldn't avoid looking directly into his eyes. "You're everything I ever wanted in a woman and I have no right to you. I'm a coward, Elizabeth." He smiled down at her with a wry, humorous expression that made the word sound even more preposterous.

"Coward?" Elizabeth repeated.

"I'm not like you. I don't rise to challenges the way you do. I avoid them. That's why I came to Deception Bay in the first place—to avoid real life."

"But...why?"

"I had my reasons. They seemed like good ones at the time."

Elizabeth's eyes searched his face, puzzled. "Are you saying you're *not* happy here, after all?"

"I'm content." He smiled gently. "It's not the same thing."

He continued to smile, belying the bleak censure of his words. "I knew it would be a trade-off. I knew there were things I'd have to give up in exchange, but I thought it was worth it. Maybe I was wrong. I don't know. But I do know that I've long since reached my port of no return."

"But you can *always* change your mind," Elizabeth said, feeling as though she were fighting in a fog, unsure even what she was arguing about. "As long as you're alive, as long as you *want* to!"

"No, it's not always a matter of wanting or not wanting." His voice was very patient. "When you make certain decisions and they result in certain other decisions, it's not always possible to go back. Besides, I have commitments that make other commitments...unlikely."

She knew he must be talking about Tran. She sighed again.

"I have what I wanted," he continued. "Peace, of a sort. It's not what I had hoped for, but it's more than I expected."

It was very peculiar, some corner of Elizabeth's mind thought vaguely, to be on the coast in all this fog and not hear a foghorn. She listened for it with some sensitive inner ear that had become attuned to its monotonous regularity at Deception Head.

There had never been a foghorn at Heceta Head, Will had said. The unusual rock formations off the coast made for inaudible dead spots at sea, deadly when ships were listening for a signal to warn them away from the dangerous shoals.

That was the way she felt now. She was listening for a sign of some sort to help her understand what Matt was saying. But he was transmitting mixed signals. His words were bitter, but his voice was light and teasing, and he still smiled that interminable smile. The beating of his heart, which she could hear as she pressed her face against his chest, was slow and regular, unlike the shallow rapidity of hers.

He let his arms fall to his side. Elizabeth stepped away from him and walked to the window, where she stood looking down into the yard. A gnarled old apple tree threw grotesque blue moon shadows on the side of the house.

The moon had risen higher in the night sky, and the shaft of light that had fallen on the bed now fell at a shorter angle. It highlighted every peg in the square foot of flooring beneath Elizabeth's feet.

"Matt," she burst out all at once, turning away from the window to confront him with baffled eyes, "you sound like a spectator to your own life! You're . . . you're talking about your life as if it belonged to someone else!"

He shrugged, still smiling, a slight raising and lowering of his shoulders that indicated it was something he chose not to discuss. Then he walked back to the trunk, where he gathered up the assortment of bedclothes and disappeared out the door.

CHAPTER THIRTEEN

IT WAS A RARE DAY on the coast. The nighttime clouds had gone and not even the perennial fog bank darkened the horizon. The empty sky stretched out overhead like a sun-washed blue canopy.

The outcropping of rock where Elizabeth sat was warm, and its heat radiated throughout her body. Her sketchbook lay open and untouched on her lap.

Directly in front of her jutted Pyramid Rock and the Dead Indian, two enormous basalt crags that helped make this part of the coastline nearly unnavigable. They were white with a millenium of bird droppings. And a little farther north on the rugged, rock-bound headland was what she had come here to see.

Heceta Head Lighthouse. "Old Faithful," Will had called it. It stood two hundred feet above sea level, its beacon flashing over the Pacific for nearly one hundred years, first with an oil lamp, then with gas and finally with electricity the equivalent of one million candle-power.

The last keeper left in 1963, Will said, when the light was automated, but that didn't mean the lighthouse was uninhabited. Old Rue was still there. Old Rue would always be there, as long as the lighthouse remained standing.

The footless, floating apparition had been sighted by dozens of believers over the years, in the lighthouse itself as well as hovering on the road behind it, although it was in the old caretaker's quarters that she made her home. No one knew exactly who she was, but legend had it she had been the wife of an early keeper, who had lost a child to the sea and was waiting for it to be returned to her.

Elizabeth had shuddered last night when Will narrated the bizarre story of Old Rue in a sepulchral voice. She had shuddered again this morning, remembering, as she watched the stealthy fingers of the sea creep around the offshore crags to clutch at the base of the headland with some sinister purpose of their own. Thinking about poor Rue and her lost child, Elizabeth hoped, would keep her mind off her own situation, which seemed just as unlikely to have a happy ending.

It was strange how the sea mirrored your own moods, she thought as she gazed out across the open water. It could be as voluptuous and seductive as a tropical beach, and as harsh and forbidding as an iceberg. It could be the jeweled blue of a sapphire or the dun color of stone.

Just now it was a pale and indistinct shade of blue, reflecting the washed-out color of the sky. The waves broke beyond the reef and sent the surf shoreward on the incoming tide. You didn't notice the tide, Elizabeth thought, invisible but inevitable, whether going out or coming in.

Like Matt. He had erected a barrier between himself and the rest of the world, invisible but inviolate. She had discovered how inviolate last night when she reached out to him and ran smack into it.

Elizabeth wasn't accustomed to rejection. It wasn't something she had experienced often in her life. But she was sure there was more at work here than wounded pride. He *had* wanted her. He had said so himself, and the proof of his body was indisputable. This fisherman—no, this-doctor-turned-fisherman, she quickly amended—was turning out to be a great deal more complicated than she had first suspected.

Before the sun had cleared the top of the apple tree in Will's backyard she had been up and dressed. Creeping down the stairs, she'd seen that the wood stove was out and the living room was chilly. Matt was lying on the couch, half hidden beneath a mound of rumpled blankets.

Although the room was filled with filtered morning sunshine, he was asleep. The television was still on, its sound turned low as Will had left it, and its images cast a flickering black-and-white pattern on the blue-striped ticking of Matt's pillow and on his face.

Quietly Elizabeth descended the stairs, sketchbook tucked under her arm. She tiptoed cautiously, keeping her eyes fixed on Matt's motionless form. A stair creaked under her foot, and she stopped short, holding her breath as he muttered something unintelligible and rolled over.

She breathed a sigh of relief. Her luck was holding. The last thing in the world that she wanted this morning was to have to face Matt in broad daylight.

Once down the stairs, she backed noiselessly around the couch. Matt had removed his woolen shirt and was wearing only a T-shirt. At the other end of the couch his feet burrowed into the cushions, and Elizabeth could see Will's piebald cat curled up behind his flexed knees. One arm lay bent under his cheek, and the other was thrown forward, as though reaching for the warmth of the wood stove.

His face looked so peaceful, so vulnerable. And, in spite of the crinkled lines at the corners of his eyes and the scattering of gray in his beard, so young. Elizabeth resisted the urge to go to him and tuck his arm back under the covers. What would he say if he woke and found her there?

Worse, after last night, what would *she* say?

She eased open the door, being careful not to make a sound. Restlessly Matt turned again. The cat leaped down from the couch and dashed outside with a peevish purr. After a final, troubled look at what was now the back of Matt's head, Elizabeth followed the cat and pulled the door quietly shut behind her.

She'd found the ground damp with dew. Turning her collar up against the chilly morning air, she had headed down the narrow footpath toward the ocean.

Now the sketchbook still lay open on her knees. Its blank pages mocked her. Sighing, she spread her chalks on the ground beside her and tried to go to work.

Heceta Head Light refused to cooperate. It stood alone and aloof at land's end, deriding her attempts to bring it to life on paper. She turned under sheet after sheet, and every sketch was only some variation of brown and white—the white tower, its brown roof; the white surf, the brown rocks. Even the sea seemed to be turning an uninspiring shade of beige.

Farther down the beach a boy was running along the tide line. He moved like a young child, his body held erect while his little legs churned like pistons beneath him. Looking ahead, Elizabeth saw a black dog, almost as large as the boy, trotting toward him, carrying a stick of driftwood in its mouth.

When it reached the boy, the dog dropped the stick at his feet and barked ecstatically. The little boy picked up the stick and threw it down the beach, and the dog bounded after it.

Absentmindedly Elizabeth sketched the boy into the corner of her drawing. She roughed in his spiky blond hair, his bright blue jacket, the cutoffs that were rolled up to his knees. She wished she could get a closer look at him so that she might include the lively colors of laughing eyes and rosy cheeks.

The boy and his dog disappeared, and Elizabeth quickly forgot them. A short time later, however, a blond head popped up from behind a large rock, and a moment later she saw a pair of curious eyes regarding her from beneath unkempt yellow hair.

She and the boy studied each other for a moment, then he walked over to stand beside her. He had an urchin's face and an impish glint in his blue eyes. His bare feet were caked with sand.

"Hey, that's me in that picture!" he exclaimed suddenly, pointing to the blue jacket in the corner. "Hey," he yelled, beckoning excitedly toward someone still out of sight under the cliff. "C'mon up here! Come see what this lady's doing!"

In a moment another blond head appeared over the big rock. It was quickly followed by a chubby, round figure that proved, upon closer inspection, to be a little girl. She was dressed identically to the boy, except that her jacket was red and looked to be several sizes too large for her. It hung down past her knees, and the sleeves were rolled up into bulky cuffs. She was also barefoot.

"Hey, look over here, Chrissy," the boy cried. "See, the lady drew me in her picture!" The little girl hung back, apparently not as sure of her welcome as the boy. "I'm Danny. That's my little sister," he added offhandedly.

Shyly Chrissy edged over to stand beside her brother and took a timid peek over his shoulder. Her eyes widened when she saw the picture on Elizabeth's lap.

"You *did* draw him," she accused Elizabeth. "And there's Jigs." With one fat finger she pointed at the romping black dog, then her eyes clouded up. "But where's me? Why didn't you draw me, too?"

"Well, because I didn't see you, Chrissy." Elizabeth explained gently. She smiled at the twosome, completely charmed.

"But I was there," the child argued. "Right behind that rock." She couldn't seem to understand the fact that Elizabeth couldn't have seen her beneath the cliff. "I was *right there*," she repeated tremulously.

"Don't be a baby, Chrissy," Danny instructed with a haughty air. "If she doesn't want to draw you, she doesn't have to draw you. Maybe she just wanted to draw me."

The little girl's eyes filled with tears. She poked a thumb in her mouth and looked mournfully at Elizabeth. She sniffled.

"Of course I want to draw you, Chrissy. Come over here."

Chrissy pulled the thumb out of her mouth and inched closer to Elizabeth.

"Now you just stand still for a minute," Elizabeth told her, and smiled as Chrissy straightened up, puffing out her little red chest like a robin. She pasted the self-conscious smile on her face that even adults did when having their pictures taken and watched Elizabeth out of the corner of her eye.

Never having done portraits before, Elizabeth wasn't sure how to begin. But she had seen other people do

them, after all, and she had certainly done enough man-
nequins for fashion layouts. How hard could it be?

The child was a sturdy little thing. First Elizabeth
sketched in the round, cherubic face, surrounded by the
nimbus of white-blond hair. Then she looked for distin-
guishing characteristics, such as the dimples on either side
of the sweet, self-conscious smile and the smattering of
freckles across the bridge of the nose.

The mouth was puckered into a shy grin, revealing two
rows of small, even baby teeth, and the eyes were big and
blue, fringed by lashes still damp with recent tears. Even
in the dusty chalks the little girl's delicate skin seemed to
glow.

As a final touch, Elizabeth invented minuscule gold
rings in the earlobes, so tiny as to be almost invisible.
Then she wrote "Chrissy" across the bottom of the page
and handed it to the little girl.

"Oh, it's so beautiful," Chrissy breathed, accepting
the sheet of paper almost reverently. "Look, Danny, I
even have earrings!"

"Do me! Do me!" Danny demanded eagerly. He
jumped up in front of Elizabeth and snapped to attention in a pose that was decidedly Napoleonic, even at his
young age.

The hair was the same color as his sister's, only shorter.
Being older, his features were more pronounced, the
bones already hinting at the man he would someday be.
His small jaw was squared and his lips sealed into a
straight line, in what was probably his best superhero
imitation.

With a flourish and a smile Elizabeth scrawled
"Danny" on the bottom of the finished portrait and
handed it to him.

"Gee, thanks, lady," he mumbled, unsealing his lips to show a wide, toothy grin.

"Children!" a slightly harried-sounding voice called from the beach. "Come away now. Let the lady work."

"She's not working, Mom!" the boy shouted back. "She's just drawing pictures!" But he took his little sister's hand and began to retreat.

"What about that man?" Chrissy announced suddenly as Danny pulled her away. She pointed a stubby finger over Elizabeth's shoulder. "Are you going to draw him, too?"

Elizabeth whirled around. "Matt!"

He was sprawled on an outcropping of rock. He looked very comfortable, leaning back on his elbows with his legs extended in front of him and crossed at the ankles. He also looked as though he'd been lying there for quite some time.

"What on earth are you doing here?"

"Watching you work, of course." He grinned at her from his supine position. His hair, only a little darker than the children's, ruffled in the ocean breeze. Beside him on the rock was his Basque fishing cap and a backpack. "I missed you this morning."

The knees of his jeans were faded and almost worn through, Elizabeth noticed as she also perceived the snug way they rode his flanks. Her throat worked convulsively. "Yes . . . well, I wanted to catch the good light."

"Oh, you mean one light's good and another's bad?" He nodded solemnly, only the corners of his down-turned smile twitching wickedly. "I never knew that."

His voice was light and teasing, just as it had always been, and in no way suggested that he even remembered her humiliation of the night before. She was grateful. Since it was inevitable that they were going to be spending more time together before this assignment was completed, it would be better if they could *both* forget last night.

Easier said than done, a taunting voice inside her head said, but she flashed him a smile that she hoped was properly superficial and turned back to her sketching.

"I made breakfast for us," he said after a minute. "Bacon, eggs, toast, the works. When it kept getting later and you didn't come down, I went upstairs to wake you and found you gone. You really must have gotten an early start."

"Yes, I did. I wanted..."

"To catch the good light. I know."

Elizabeth attended to her work with more concentration than she had shown so far that day. Rustling noises behind her told her that Matt had stretched his long body out on the warm rock again. Overhead, gulls swooped and shrieked.

"I was in Vietnam for a year and a half," Matt said quietly and unexpectedly out of the stillness. "I was in-country for a year—nine months at the Ninety-fifth Evac Hospital in Da Nang, and three months at the navy dispensary at Solid Anchor. Then I extended my tour of duty for six months on the hospital ship *Sanctuary*. When I came home, I gave up the practice of medicine. For good."

The voice behind her was flat, and the words sounded rusty, like the hinge of an old door that had been closed for a long time. Elizabeth found that her fingers were moving automatically across the paper, with no idea in the world what they were doing. She held her breath.

"Everyone's got a story. Mine's no different from a thousand others. One day I was an intern in a big-city hospital with a senior resident overseeing every stitch I made, every tongue I depressed, and the next day I was right in the middle of hell, broken bodies being thrown at me from every direction, and I was supposed to fix them.''

He gave a harsh bark, a pale imitation of a laugh that had nothing to do with mirth. ''That was my job. Fix them and send them home. Fix them and send them back into combat. Or close their eyes and move on to the next one. Sometimes there wasn't even time to close their eyes. I hope the nurses did. I hope someone did.

''I still hear the choppers bringing in the wounded. Do you know what triage means? It's a term left over from the French Revolution. It's when they separate the wounded into three piles—those who'll probably die no matter what you do for them, those who'll probably live even if you don't do anything for them, and those who, with care, have a chance of making it. And you separate them as they're loaded off the choppers—live, die, maybe. And you work on the last bunch.

''It's all you have time for. The rest you shoot full of morphine—if you have enough—and wait. Sometimes they scream. And sometimes they just look at you through the blood that's running in their eyes and the blood that's on you and they don't say anything, because they know it's no use, and there's not a damn thing anyone can do about it, anyway. The worst part...was deciding who was wounded badly enough to go home and who could be patched up and sent back into combat. I felt like an executioner whenever I had to send one of them back, and more than once I had some kid come across my table again later, dead.

''I got so tired of writing letters. 'He went quickly' or 'It was peaceful' is what you usually say. Christ, how many hypocritical letters I wrote to mothers and fathers and wives of men I never even knew, saying that, knowing it was a lie and wondering if they knew it, too.

"I used to lie awake at night and count incoming. We all did. And lots of times I'd forget whether it was the mortars that I was counting or the letters that I had written."

The voice behind her left shoulder fell silent, but Elizabeth didn't turn around. She sensed he was saying things that perhaps he had never said to another living soul, and she knew she mustn't interrupt him, mustn't make him stop before he had gotten everything out. After a moment, the disembodied voice began to speak again.

"It was the nights that were the worst. The men used to say, 'We own the day. The night belongs to Charlie.' It was true. They knew their way around the jungle better than we ever could. Hell, it was their country! A few of our people got as good as the VC at surviving in the jungle, but when they did that they changed somehow. Became more *them* than *us,* and everyone else got a little afraid to be around them. They were men apart. Marked. Like Cain."

His voice droned on inexorably, as if reciting a strict catechism of pain that he wasn't allowed to stop until he reached the end. "But the worst thing was the fear. From the first night I got in-country until I left a year later, I never stopped being afraid. I never stopped listening for incoming—rockets, mortars, artillery. Even when I was on the *Sanctuary,* I was listening for it. Sometimes I still do. It's like a nightmare you've woken up from but never forget how it made you feel. And you never forget what it made you see about yourself. I saw that I was a coward."

He stated it as a fact already well established and not subject to interpretation. "I was terrified. I never had to go out on patrols. I never even got shot at. I had a nice, safe billet in a nice, safe hospital in Da Nang, and all I had to do was try to put back together the men who were right in the middle of it all. But I never stopped being afraid. And living with that knowledge is the worst hell of all."

The self-recrimination in his voice was almost unendurable. "But, Matt," Elizabeth interrupted, forgetting that he needed to talk, forgetting everything except the anguish she heard in his voice, and her own need to make it stop, "*everyone* must have been afraid!"

"Maybe," the disembodied voice continued ruthlessly, "but I was safe, you see. I was never in any real danger. I never even had to shoot my .45, and I was *still* scared out of my mind every minute of every day that I was there."

"Did you ever talk to anyone about it? I'm sure they would have told you—"

"I couldn't talk to anyone. How could I?" His voice was dull. "I had to be infallible. I was the Doc. I couldn't let them suspect. I couldn't let anyone suspect. It would just have made it that much worse for them."

He paused so long that Elizabeth thought he had finished. The only sounds she was aware of were the shrieks of the gulls and the beating of their powerful wings overhead as they came sweeping down out of the sky.

"I developed quite a skill over there," the monotone went on after a while. "I got so I could convince them they were going to make it. Right up until they died I could make them believe they would live. I thought it made them less...frightened. Sometimes that meant keeping the chaplain away from them until it was over, but I did that, too. Now I sometimes wonder if it wasn't just myself I was protecting.

"By the time I came home I'd had enough. Enough of horror and pain and suffering and blood and death. Enough of being so close to other people that I couldn't tell where I stopped and they began. I couldn't take it anymore, and so I gave it up. Medicine, I mean. I don't ever want to be that close to other people again. Now I just want to be left alone."

He pushed himself to his feet and walked to the edge of the cliff where he withdrew a cigarette from his shirt pocket and lit it with a hand that shook. A thin puff of smoke spiraled upward. "It's a coward's way out, of course, but . . . at least I don't have to listen for incoming anymore. There are even some nights when I don't hear the choppers." He exhaled heavily, sending another puff of smoke skyward. "It's a trade-off, as I said last night. I don't ask too much of life, and it doesn't ask too much of me."

Elizabeth looked at him unhappily. They were harsh words, and they hung awkwardly on the air, accompanied as they were by the gentle sounds of a warm summer afternoon.

She couldn't deny the truth of what he had said—she didn't know anything about it. The whole thing had passed into history without really affecting her. She didn't even know anyone else who had been there. And yet here it was, all these years later, as fresh and as ugly as if it were still going on. And it was. For him.

Her mind sifted through his words and scraped them away one at a time until, instinctively, she reached the crux of what he had said. "Why did you stay the extra six months on the hospital ship?"

The shoulders lifted and fell. "I don't know. They needed me."

"That doesn't sound like a coward to me."

"It doesn't matter now. It was a long time ago." He turned around to look at her, and Elizabeth saw his halfhearted attempt to fix a smile on his face.

"Don't, Matt," she said quietly. "Don't hide anymore. Not from me."

Without the smile his face looked very tired. For the first time she understood what a strain it must have been, keeping up that smiling facade for so long. Years.

"Why did you tell me this?" she asked quietly.

He shrugged again. "I just wanted you to know."

"I'm glad."

He threw the cigarette to the ground and crushed it purposefully with his foot. "Well," he said briskly, returning to the spot where he had left his backpack, "since you didn't have any breakfast, I brought you some lunch. Actually it was Will's idea. He was sorry he missed you this morning."

Matt laid out the contents of the backpack on the rock: the ubiquitous smoked salmon, a package of cream cheese, a box of stone-ground wheat crackers, a bottle of Oregon white Chablis and two plastic cups.

"A person would really be out of luck around here if she didn't like salmon, wouldn't she?"

"Wouldn't even be allowed in the state," Matt assured her solemnly. With his pocketknife he spread a dollop of cream cheese on a cracker, sliced a bit of dark pink salmon from the larger chunk and put it on top of the cheese, then handed the cracker to Elizabeth.

"Delicious!" she exclaimed, lips dusted with cracker crumbs. "But messy."

Matt spread a cracker for himself and popped it in his mouth, then he poured the two plastic glasses full of wine. "When we finish, Will asked if we'd pick some blackberries for him."

"Pick blackberries? I always thought they came in little cardboard boxes in the supermarket."

"Nope. They start out their lives on bushes—in vacant lots and alongside railroad tracks. And they're full of thorns, and naturally the ripest ones are always in the middle of the brambles. When I was a kid, my brothers and I used to go blackberrying with umbrellas. We'd open them up and use them like shields to push the thorns out of the way, and then we'd carry the blackberries home in them."

"How many brothers do you have?"

"Two, and two sisters."

"Big family," Elizabeth remarked, accepting another salmon-and-cream-cheese cracker. "I'm an only child. I always thought it would be fun to have brothers and sisters."

"It was. And still is. Big families seem to run in my family! Everyone is married and everyone has a raft of kids."

"Except you."

"Right."

"Maybe you will someday, too."

Matt smiled. "It's getting a little late for that, I'm afraid."

She tipped up her plastic cup and let the last few drops of wine slip down her throat, then silently extended the cup toward Matt. "Late, maybe," she teased, not certain why she didn't just let the subject drop. "But surely not *too* late."

He leaned forward to pour the wine. "I watched you with those kids. You really have a way with them."

"Oh, it's nothing," she said with an embarrassed shrug. "I really don't know the first thing about kids. It's just that everyone likes to have their picture drawn."

He smiled as if he didn't quite believe her, then proceeded to spread several more crackers for himself and for her. A swarm of gulls hovered over their heads, as persistent as ants at a picnic.

"You go ahead and draw," Matt said when they finished Will's picnic lunch and tossed the scraps to the gulls. "I like to watch you work." True to his word, he stretched out on the warm rock and propped himself on his elbows.

"Maybe I'll do another portrait of you. You look like a lizard lying there taking in the sun."

"Be my guest," he replied. "But no scales. And no earrings! When you're ready to call it a day, we'll take a walk down the railroad tracks and get Will's blackberries."

CHAPTER FOURTEEN

"BY THE TIME I got there the war was winding down. Everyone knew it was only a matter of time before the end. We just didn't know when. We were cutting back our troop strength, but the North was pushing us harder than ever to make sure we didn't change our minds. The fighting was fierce."

Matt and Elizabeth measured their steps to the irregular spacing of the wooden cross ties as they walked along the railroad tracks. They were searching for blackberry bushes not already denuded by local children.

The thin parallel lines of the rails were rusted out in spots, mute testimony to the fact that the Union Pacific had stopped running trains on this branch line many years ago. Weeds sprouted between the tracks. Sometimes they obliterated the rails entirely, and with them any lingering signs of civilization.

"I had been back less than six months when Saigon fell. I had another year to go in the navy after that, and then I went back to Portland and tried to pick up my life where I'd left off. I couldn't do it. So I quit. Finally I ended up in Deception Bay, and I've been there ever since."

"Why did you choose Deception Bay?"

"Just because I'd always loved the coast. Some of the happiest days of my life were the summers I spent fishing with Will as a kid. But it was a trap. I don't know if I meant to stay or not, but after a while it got easier to stay than to go. I let my medical license lapse. I let my marriage fail. And what you said last night was true—I felt like a spectator in my own life. I felt as if I were watching it happen to someone else."

Elizabeth paced the cross ties for a little while in silence. "Do you ever miss it?" she finally asked. "Medicine, I mean?"

"No," Matt replied shortly.

Much too shortly, Elizabeth thought. "I think maybe you do."

Matt paused at a blackberry thicket that grew straight up the side of the railroad embankment. The fringes were picked clean but, as he had predicted, there were scores of plump purple berries in the center.

"You hold and I'll pick," he instructed, handing Elizabeth a Baggie. Even with his long reach it was a considerable stretch, and he teetered precariously on the edge of the embankment as he leaned into the brambles. The thorns caught at his sleeves. Soon his hands were covered with scratches.

"Yes, I *do* miss medicine," he stated after a few silent moments of concentrated blackberry picking. "Is that what you wanted me to say? I've missed it every hour of every day of every year since I quit, all right? I'd planned to be a doctor all my life, and you can't devote that much time and energy to something without it becoming a big part of what you are. When I quit, I felt as though a chunk of myself was torn away, and I haven't had a waking moment since that I've felt like a whole person."

"Why don't you go back, then?"

"I've thought about it," he replied. "But it's the other times that stop me—the nights. I keep seeing those faces, those bloody, bloody faces. Sometimes it feels as if I can remember every single face—the ones I sent home, the ones I sent back, the dead. And there's not a damn thing I can do for any of them. I can't help anyone else. Hell, I can't even help myself!''

"I don't think that's true. What about the refugees you sponsored?''

"Will told you about that, too?''

"And then, of course, there's Tran. You've done a great deal for a lot of people.''

Matt smiled skeptically. "There are twenty thousand Amerasian kids still over there, and hundreds of thousands of refugees. What I've done makes no difference at all.''

"I don't think Tran would see it that way.''

He stepped away from the blackberry thicket and wiped his purple hands on his jeans. "Besides, I'm a different person than I was ten, fifteen years ago, and I can't go back to what I was then, even if I wanted to.''

Taking the Baggie from Elizabeth's hands, he hefted it judiciously. "I think that's plenty,'' he decided. "These should keep Will in blackberry brandy for a while.''

"The subject is closed,'' Elizabeth guessed.

Matt smiled as he put his arm around her shoulders and turned, heading back toward Heceta Head. "I don't want you to make more out of it than there is,'' he countered. "I am what I am. I'm like that old lighthouse—don't go trying to prettify me, as Will would say. Don't try to make me into something I'm not. You're sure to be disappointed.''

He may have tried to resign from the real world, Elizabeth reflected as they retraced their steps down the railroad tracks, but it was obvious that he hadn't been able to get his heart to cooperate.

Now she understood the secret behind the smile he wore with such fierce determination. It wasn't a smile at all; it was a grimace, with the rough edges honed away so that it resembled something very different.

Arriving back at Heceta House, they found Will sitting in one of the rocking chairs on the porch, moving himself back and forth slowly with the toe of one foot. The brim of his straw hat shaded his face, and he watched them through squinted eyes that only pretended to be asleep. When he heard their footsteps on the creaky wooden steps, he looked up with feigned surprise.

"Well, well, well," he grumbled, interjecting a note of irritation into his voice. "Took your sweet time about getting here, didn't you? I had to put supper back in the oven twice!"

He pushed himself to his feet and accepted the plastic bags full of blackberries that Matt extended toward him. "Where'd you go to get these, anyway?" He held the Baggies up to the light and inspected them critically. "Not much to 'em, is there?"

"Down by the old Union Pacific yard," Matt said, winking at Elizabeth. "And you know they're the best berries you've seen in years!"

Will harrumphed skeptically. "You two just sit down here and make yourselves to home," he ordered. "I'll go see if supper's still fit to eat."

After feasting on the venison Will had killed last winter and which was very definitely still fit to eat, Matt and Elizabeth shooed him out of the kitchen while they did the dishes. Will didn't object. He was, in fact, glad. The kitchen was very small, hardly big enough for two people to turn around in, really; and proximity, Will knew, although he would have phrased it in earthier terms, was a powerful aphrodisiac.

He settled himself in his favorite leather chair with his pipe and a glass of blackberry brandy, one eye on *Wheel of Fortune* and the other on the romance he fondly hoped was unfolding in his kitchen.

LATER ELIZABETH AND MATT sat side by side on the couch. His arm rested lightly on her shoulders. She had sipped her way through several jelly glasses of blackberry brandy, and the sweet, sticky stuff had made her pleasantly drowsy. Matt, on the other hand, had seemed uncharacteristically tense. He lighted one cigarette after another, then let them burn forgotten between his fingers while he gazed, preoccupied, at the fire in the wood stove.

As long as Will had been seated in his sagging leather chair, everything had been all right. His stories filled the room with the ghosts of people long departed from this world, but at least they were friendly ghosts, not the variety that haunted Matt. After Will rounded up his cat and went to bed, the silence in the living room became uncomfortable.

The fire glowed warmly in the grate. Elizabeth knew she could stay here all night, with Matt's arm around her and his face so close that she could smell his cigarette and his cologne, but her instincts warned her not to make a fool of herself twice. What she wanted he couldn't give, maybe would never be able to give. There was no point sitting here in the dusky intimacy of Will's living room and wishing things could be different.

After Will was gone, Elizabeth forced herself to stand, too. "I think I'll go to bed," she announced.

Matt caught her hand and looked up at her, smiling quizzically. "So soon?"

She hesitated, uncertainty in her eyes. "It must be the sea air," she hedged. Then she spoke more honestly. "After everything you told me today, I'm not sure I know what to say to you anymore."

"Just say the things you've always said." His smile broadened persuasively. "I'm the same person I was before."

Elizabeth felt gauche and inept. Everything she wanted to say seemed woefully inadequate under the circumstances. "That may be," she replied carefully, "but I can see that I didn't really know the person you were before."

His mouth tightened. "I had to tell you," he said in a voice that was lifeless and dull. "I didn't want to, but I figured you had a right to know." His fingers went slack and his hand fell away from hers. "But let me also tell you this—if you despise me, it can't be more than I despise myself."

"Despise you?" Elizabeth repeated. She was dismayed at her own ineptitude. "I don't despise you. I—" *Love you,* she almost said, and the realization stunned her. "I'm just so sorry..." Her words faltered as she found herself unable to speak around the lump that suddenly rose in her throat.

"That's almost as bad."

"Sorry for what you've been through," she finished. "Making small talk just seems so... trivial somehow."

He looked up with something like caution in his eyes and something else, more like hope. "You don't think any less of me?"

"Not at all. And I'll tell you something." She gazed at him seriously. "You think you've taken the easy way out, but that's not true. The way you've chosen is much, much harder. I hope someday you'll realize that. If you ever do, you'll go back to medicine and back to letting yourself...*feel*...again." Leaning over the couch, she kissed him gently on the mouth. "Good night, Matt. I'll put your bedclothes outside the door."

Elizabeth was nearly asleep when she heard a tap at the door. When it opened, a dark silhouette stood framed in the doorway. Matt. Highlighted from behind by the flames of the wood stove, his features were shadowed and indecipherable.

"Matt? I put your blankets—"

"I want to stay." His voice was brusque and pleading at the same time. He closed the door, and the room darkened, bathed only in the hazy, pale light of the moon. "Can I stay?"

Without a word Elizabeth threw back the comforter and held out her arms. Matt crossed the squeaky wooden floor, and she pulled him down to join her on the bed. He sat on the edge, facing her. Tender hands reached up to frame her face, lifting her tousled hair and letting it fall through his fingers.

"I want this to be very good," he whispered.

Elizabeth trembled when he touched her. She was ready—she was more than ready, but suddenly she didn't know what to say or what to do. She waited in unaccustomed docility for him to make the next move.

There was no urgency in him. He brushed gentle lips across her forehead and eyes and nose and cheek while his hands still cupped her face. Finally he reached her mouth and let his tongue slip inside, not forceful, not demanding, just tasting. She met him in a deep kiss, and the contact made her spine tingle.

He stood. The bulge in his jeans was at her eye level. He unbuttoned his woolen shirt, letting it fall to the floor, then twisted out of his T-shirt and let that fall, too. He kicked off his shoes and slipped his jeans and briefs down his long legs, where they dropped in a heap with the rest of his clothing.

There was unconscious pride in the way he held himself—straight and tall, arms at his sides, only the tension in his rigid fingers and his rising masculinity betraying what was in his mind. The columns of his legs were planted like tree trunks on the attic floor. His bronzed skin looked very dark, except for the bank of flesh across his hips gleaming white in the pale light.

He stood over her for a moment, and her eyes fixed on the long, hard length of him. Then he lifted the comforter and lay naked beside her.

One elbow was bent on the pillow, the hand propping up his head as he positioned himself on his side. He was smiling just a little. There was nothing tentative about him now as he prepared to explore her body, although his hands were gentle, as she had known they would be. He unbuttoned her nightshirt and pushed it out of the way, then curved his hand around her breast. It was a simple, sweet gesture, almost reverent in its tenderness.

"So many nights I've thought of you, of this, of how it would be to touch you like this...." He held each breast in turn in his hand and watched the brown buds tighten under the stroking of his thumb.

The light, caressing motion, the brush of his thumb over her awakening nipple, made Elizabeth quiver with anticipation.

Lying on their sides, their bodies faced each other, barely touching in the middle of the plump feather mattress. The hair on his chest, stomach and legs prickled against Elizabeth's skin like tiny jolts of electricity. She reached down, and a thrill of sheer animal pleasure coursed through her as her fingers found him and her hand cupped the hard, thick enormity of him.

She wanted him inside her. That was all. It was the only thing. She thrust one knee over his legs and pulled herself upright so that she straddled his hips. He rolled easily onto his back and folded his hands behind his head. He was grinning up at her, as if waiting to see what she would do next. She felt him, hot and throbbing, the sensitive, blue-veined skin caught momentarily between her pelvis and his.

She moved sensually over him, savoring the sense of power she had over his body, enjoying being the pacesetter. Then, bending forward at the waist to touch his lips with a tenderness that matched his own, she let her breasts brush his chest in sensual invitation. She leaned farther forward, offering them to his mouth. He caught the nipples between gentle teeth, one at a time, and flicked his tongue over them. She moaned with pleasure that was almost pain.

He unfolded his arms from behind his head and drew his hands over the lush curves of her body, from her shoulders down to her buttocks. His hands curved around them, lifting her so that she was open to him.

The tautness of his stomach rippled against hers when he pulled her upper body close against him and held her there. Her breasts flattened against his chest. She felt the straining muscles of his lean flanks between her thighs as she straddled him. He gripped her buttocks, holding her prisoner while he rotated her hips against his with his big hands in slow, incredibly erotic circles.

She picked up his rhythm and began to move with it. Her whole body writhed in the instinctive, pulsating tempo of love. She yearned toward him. The tension was becoming unbearable. She wanted it, wanted it inside her with a desperation that astonished her. She moaned again.

A rough sound tore from low in his throat. In the next instant he rolled them both over so that he was on top of her. Elizabeth caught her breath. The rules of the game had suddenly changed. He grinned briefly at the surprise in her eyes. Then his smile became as hard as his body. He spread her legs apart with strong, sure hands and entered her.

The penetration was slow and purposeful. His thrusts were unhurried, but each was deeper than the last, and his eyes never left her face.

To Elizabeth that was almost more intimate than the way his body moved inside hers. His fiery, probing gaze besieged her heart and her mind, searching out her innermost desires.

He grinned down at her wolfishly. "Tell me," he whispered. "Tell me what you feel." But when she opened her mouth to tell him, no words came—just a long, shuddering moan that drove him farther and faster into her with a tortured moan of his own.

He measured his thrusting to the response he read in her eyes, gradually increasing the tempo and riding high so that the friction carried her along with him. For an interminable length of time they hesitated on the edge of ecstasy.

For a panicky moment Elizabeth thought she couldn't do it. But he stretched her and filled her, coming at her faster and harder, and she couldn't turn away from his pounding loins or fiery eyes.

Her hips thrust against his with equal fervor, rising and falling to the rhythm he dictated. Then he felt her yield to what they both wanted, and his face and hers con-

vulsed at the same time as he released his passion into her
waiting woman's body.

HOURS LATER Elizabeth reached down sleepily and
pulled the comforter up from the floor where it had
fallen. Beyond the warm island of the bed the air was
chilly.

Dawn was breaking, bathing herself, Matt and the entire room with pale gray light. Elizabeth looked around,
trying to imprint every detail of the tiny attic room on her
memory.

It was comforting to be held. Her buttocks fitted
tightly into the juncture of Matt's thighs, and his knees
pressed the back of hers. She could feel the steady beat
of his heart. One of his big hands rested possessively on
her hip. Even in sleep he held her close.

How strange and yet how wonderful that the two of
them, so opposite in life-styles and backgrounds, could
have found each other like this, could have come together like this. A flush suffused her face at the memory
of *how* they had come together—with a wild abandon she
had never even suspected she was capable of until now.
Feeling an uncharacteristic shyness, she slid farther beneath the comforter and pulled it up to her chin.

Innocent! her thoughts continued. How could she have
ever thought him *innocent?* He made love with the same
easy expertise as everything else he did. His body had
played hers like a virtuoso—long, pulsating strokes that
reduced her to nothing more than an instrument for his
pleasure, and her own.

Her snuggling beneath the comforter jostled Matt's
hand where it rested on her hip. It moved upward to cup
her breast. She felt his body quicken like the fluttering of
a bird against her back.

"I didn't know you were awake," she said softly.

"*I* can't believe I fell asleep," he countered. "I meant to stay awake all night so I could enjoy every minute of being here with you."

"You needed your sleep," Elizabeth teased. "You earned it."

"You think so?" She couldn't see his face, but she knew he was smiling. "I'm glad. I never in my life wanted to please a woman as much as I did you last night."

"Matt, last night...what made you change your mind?"

"Well, I did a lot of thinking," he replied slowly, his lips moving softly against the back of her head. "And I finally figured out that I'd have to be crazy to let you go just because I can't keep you forever. You warned me when you first came here that you'd come to do a job and that was all. I know you, Elizabeth—I know the kind of woman you are. It's going to be hard for you to leave after this, isn't it?"

In reply Elizabeth turned her face toward the pillow to press her lips against his broad forearm which rested beneath her neck. His body quickened again.

"But you were willing to take the risk," he continued in a voice softer still. "If you're that strong, how can I be any less? We'll always have this summer. Maybe it'll be enough. But even if it isn't I'll still have had you for a little while, been inside you the way I've wanted to be ever since the day I met you."

He kissed the back of her neck. "Look," he said, pointing out the window. The first pink fingers of the sun were creeping through the gray sky. "We're going to have a beautiful day for our trip home."

Home. She loved the way he said it; she loved the sound of it.

Matt's hand began to outline the fine curves of her body. It skimmed her shoulder and upper arm, dipped low at her waist and rose again at the prominence of her hip. There was more light in the room than there had been last night, and Elizabeth felt alternately modest and proud as he investigated her body with his hands and his eyes.

"Beautiful," he whispered as he turned her over and tangled his fingers in the soft black hair at the base of her smooth belly.

His hand continued upward to lift one full breast in his palm. He held it to his mouth, and his tongue flicked lazily over the tanned top and the soft milky-white flesh of the underside. He ignored the nipple until he had finished with the rest, then took it between his lips and sucked it inside with a greediness that made Elizabeth quiver.

He thrust one knee between her thighs. "Again?" he said. But it wasn't a question.

CHAPTER FIFTEEN

"WELL, I DECLARE! It's so blessed *nice* to see Matthew with a member of the fairer sex on his arm!" Melanie Milton spoke in exclamation points. "And don't you look nice, my dear!" She fell back to inspect Elizabeth with a critical feminine eye. "That red is so becomin' to you!"

Captain Rodney Milton's petite wife was the acknowledged queen of Deception Bay society, having overcome the town's innate resistance to outlanders by virtue of her irresistible Southern hospitality and the sheer force of her effusive personality.

Her perfectly coiffed helmet of blond hair reached only as high as Elizabeth's shoulder as she stood on her toes and kissed the air on either side of Elizabeth's face. Then she reached a little higher and did the same to Matt.

Although she hadn't expected to need it, Elizabeth was glad she had tossed a dress into her suitcase. The simple sheath, short and strapless, with large red poppies screened onto white silk, skimmed the fine lines of her body and was a perfect foil for her dark hair. It bared the smooth, tanned flesh of her shoulders and back, and the shadowed ivory of the valley between her breasts.

It had come in handy when she dined with the president of the Lighthouse Society in San Francisco. He had certainly admired it, at any rate. And when he picked her up this evening, so had Matt, if the pleased surprise that had lit up his face was any indication.

Matt had surprised her, too. All traces of the fisherman were gone. The unruly hair was tamed. The smell of diesel fuel and fish had vanished, and the aftershave had been replaced by a musky cologne.

"*Do* come into the parlor and join the others!" Melanie continued. Her own hostess gown, an aquamarine chiffon the same color as her eye shadow, rustled efficiently as she led the way.

"Rodney is preparin' mint juleps for everyone. Such a refreshin' summer drink, don't you think? You *do* like mint juleps, don't you? I'm sure you do! Everyone does, don't they? If we were back home in Savannah, of course, we'd be out on the veranda enjoyin' the fine summer night, but here . . . well, my dears . . ."

She shrugged eloquently, allowing them to draw their own conclusions from the colorful Chinese lanterns that hung unappreciated in the trees beyond the closed patio doors, and the fire that burned in the hearth.

Matt took Elizabeth's elbow as they followed Melanie's bustling figure into the parlor. Elizabeth liked the unconscious possessiveness of the gesture.

The parlor was intimately lit by a chandelier dimmed to glow rather than shine. Candles sparkled on a buffet loaded with appetizers. Because this gathering was a fund-raiser for the restoration of Deception Head Light, a miniature replica of the lighthouse stood in the place of honor between the crudités and the caviar. Ice cubes clinked gaily in crystal glasses. Laughter as gay as the ice against the crystal rose and fell above the lighthearted hum of conversation.

There were a number of faces that Elizabeth had seen around town at one time or another—the business people, the merchants, the council members who ran the town. Over the heads of the other guests she saw a broad, florid man whom she recognized as the sheriff talking to a distinguished silver-haired gentleman she knew to be the mayor. They nodded to Matt as he and Elizabeth entered the room, and eyed Elizabeth guardedly.

"I feel like Mata Hari or something!" Elizabeth whispered. "How long do you think they're going to keep up this silent treatment?"

He glanced jokingly at his watch. "Oh, not much longer," he quipped. "Probably about as long as it takes Melanie to tell them how much the Lighthouse Society expects to make on the pictorial you're doing for them and what percentage they're going to donate to restoring Deception Head Light!"

Matt wore a navy blue blazer with a silk tie and white linen slacks, and wore them with a careless elegance that belied his occupation. But somehow he looked out of place, with his eyes like a boy's and his gentle smile, and the beard that made him look like something off a China clipper.

The rough Spartan clothes of a fisherman suited him better than the formal blazer, Elizabeth decided, and the sharp, clean lines of the *Chinook Wind* more than Melanie Milton's plush parlor.

Presiding over a wet bar in the corner, Rodney Milton smiled effusively. "Matt. Elizabeth. Glad you could make it!" He looked at Elizabeth approvingly. "I hope you know that you're dashing the hopes of every single woman in Deception Bay tonight, Elizabeth."

"Give Elizabeth her drink, my dear," Melanie directed. "And then I'm going to steal her away and introduce her to our other guests. It isn't often that we have an honest-to-goodness celebrity among us!"

"I'm not a celebrity," Elizabeth protested, laughing as Rodney handed her a frosty glass and Melanie led her away.

"Oh, but you will be, my dear! I'm sure of it! Matt has told us how talented you are. I'm sure once you publish your paintings you'll be quite famous! And so will we. Oh, I know what you're thinking! It's true I'm not a native here, and I don't see quite eye to eye with most of the town on that particular subject! But I love Deception Bay, too—I'm sure I shall miss it terribly when Rodney is transferred to another duty station!"

She stopped at a group of people in the middle of the room and ushered Elizabeth into their midst. "Elizabeth, I'm sure you know Millicent Smith and Sidney Tsung, and let me introduce you to Professor Grover Atkins." Her professional hostess's voice circled the group, indicating the wife of the mayor, the owner of the only Chinese restaurant in town, and a tall, cadaverous-faced man wearing a soft tweed jacket with leather patches at the elbows and hornrimmed glasses.

"Professor Atkins is dean of ancient studies at the university in Ashland, and we're very honored that he drove all the way over here for our little soiree." Having discharged her duty, Melanie flashed Elizabeth a brilliant smile and bustled off.

Professor Atkins took Elizabeth's extended hand limply. "So you're the one who took away my summer cottage."

"Oh, I *am* sorry. The Lighthouse Society made all the arrangements..."

"Don't give it another thought." He made a languid gesture of dismissal with graceful white fingers. "I'm only writing a book. Nothing important, nothing that will shake the world or make me rich and famous. Just an insignificant little book."

Elizabeth recognized his type immediately: a sensitive young man, no longer young but still chronically sensitive.

"For the past several years I've leased the old caretaker's quarters during summer break," he continued. "Sometimes my students come down to assist me with my research, and I allow them to stay there with me." He sighed, shaking his head with gentle irony. "*They* seem to think my work is important. Of course, commercial considerations so often outweigh purely artistic ones that it's no wonder the Lighthouse Society was able to lease it for *you* this summer."

"Well, that *is* too bad," Elizabeth said in a voice she kept carefully neutral.

"What does surprise me is the fact that the mayor— Pardon me, Millicent. I mean no disrespect to your husband. I'm sure it was simply an oversight on his part! As I was saying, when the mayor allowed it to be snatched right out from under his nose like that."

"It wasn't *snatched*, Grover," Millicent said tartly. "After careful consideration, the city council decided it would be in the best interests of everyone to cooperate with the Lighthouse Society on this community service project. I'm sure one summer won't set your book back very much. After all, you've been working on it—how long? Seven years? Eight?"

Professor Atkins sniffed. "It's true that academic dissertations *do* take longer to produce than potboilers."

"What is your book about, Professor?" Elizabeth asked, more to change the subject than because she was really interested.

"Oh," he waved his hand vaguely and rolled his eyes toward the ceiling with patronizing tolerance, "I'm doing my own reinterpretation of the twelfth-century Roman translations of the writings of the poet Lucretius and his influence on early Christianity. Do you—" he paused, giving her a condescending smile "—know him?"

"Lucretius? Do you mean his theory that all things, including man, act according to their own natural laws and aren't in any way influenced by supernatural powers? Never heard of him."

The smile vanished. Those on the faces of Millicent Smith and Sidney Tsung broadened into grins. "Well, if you'll excuse me," Professor Atkins said tightly, "I see someone has just arrived to whom I must speak." He jerked his head stiffly. "Ladies? Mr. Tsung?"

Elizabeth bent her head to take a sip of her julep. Her hair fell forward like a black-lacquered fan, hiding the grin she couldn't quite suppress.

"You handled that very well, my dear," Millicent Smith complimented Elizabeth with a discreet chuckle.

Melanie Milton's Southern drawl, managing to sound both sweet and strident at the same time, swept over the crowd. "'Scuse me, ya'll. 'Scuse me!" She rapped her diamond solitaire smartly against the crystal glass she held in her hand. All eyes turned to her. "I'd like to thank ya'll for comin' tonight. Rodney and I are very pleased to host this fund-raisin' benefit for our grand old lighthouse."

A smattering of applause greeted her words. "You'll be pleased, I'm sure, to know that with the matching funds from Salem, we're very near our goal. Due to the generosity of all you kind, *kind* supporters, and to the donations that have come in from all over the state, the Lighthouse Society estimates that we should be able to purchase Deception Head Light and the quarter acre surrounding it outright by next year!" More applause rippled through the room. "And to that end they have offered us ten percent of their receipts on the sale of their lighthouse pictorial to be released next year!"

A dazzled whisper circulated through the crowd—*ten percent!* The applause that followed was thunderous.

"Thank you, thank you," Melanie said as she held up one soft hand to still the crowd. "Thank you! Just one more thing before I allow ya'll to return to your festivities. With us tonight we have the talented young woman chosen by the Lighthouse Society to immortalize our Light and be its spokeswoman to the rest of the world. Elizabeth, please come up here!"

Elizabeth walked to the fireplace and stood next to Melanie.

"Elizabeth La Salle, ladies and gentlemen."

When the enthusiastic clapping ended, Melanie smiled brightly. "Thank you. Now ya'll please enjoy the music, enjoy the company, and enjoy the fine sense of accomplishment ya'll have surely earned!"

The buzz of conversation resumed. Melanie turned to Elizabeth. "You didn't mind that, did you, dear? It never hurts to remind the old guard where the money's comin' from, now does it?" She squeezed Elizabeth's waist girlishly as if they shared a fascinating secret, then hustled off to find something else that required her attention.

Elizabeth sipped her drink and let her eyes wander around the room. Her glance found Matt. He was deep in conversation with Rodney Milton and several other guests, and he must have said something funny, because Elizabeth saw his down-turned smile become an impish grin and heard laughter circle the group. Especially spirited was the quicksilver laughter of the women.

Women clung to him like limpets, she saw with a stab
of jealousy as she watched him take his leave and make
his way around the room. They detained him with coy
smiles and soft hands on his arm. Matt, however, talked
only as long as courtesy dictated, then pried himself away
to mingle with the next group.

He was quite good at socializing, Elizabeth thought.
He had obviously had a great deal of practice at it. It was
a side of him she had never seen before, and she found it
intriguing.

She wondered about the women in his life. There must
have been a good many. A man didn't become celibate
just because he didn't want any commitments! Especially not a man who looked like Matt, who had his involuntary yet compelling sensuality.

Dashing the hopes of every woman in Deception Bay,
Rodney Milton had said. Elizabeth wondered if Matt had
made love to any of the women who flirted with him tonight. Had any of their soft, clinging hands touched him
in other places, secret places? Done the things to that
long body that she did, the things she had learned would
drive him wild?

A familiar muscle coiled in her stomach. She felt a
flush suffuse her face. The shoulders, neck and arms left
bare by her strapless sheath felt very warm, a heat that
couldn't be accounted for entirely by the crush of people
in the room or by the fire in the hearth. Heat. In heat.
This was what it meant!

When a maid carrying a tray of fresh juleps walked
past, Elizabeth deposited her empty glass on the tray and
picked up another. She rolled the frosty goblet against
her cheek, inhaling the tangy aroma of the mint sprig that
decorated the glass as though they were smelling salts.

Millicent Smith strolled by on the arm of her husband, the distinguished silver-haired mayor. They paused, and the mayor smiled and offered Elizabeth his hand, making some hospitable remark welcoming her to their little community.

She must have made some appropriate response, Elizabeth thought, because Millicent and the mayor nodded graciously and continued on their way. Vaguely it occurred to her that this was a breakthrough in her relationship with the people of Deception Bay. But for the moment that seemed less important than the fact that the room was intolerably close, and Matt, whom she knew was both the cause and the cure for the heat, was much too far away.

I've got to get out of here, she thought frantically. She tucked her small clutch bag tighter beneath her arm and walked quickly out of the room. A few minutes later she was leaning over the vanity in the Miltons' opulent powder room. Her heels sunk into the plush peach carpet, which was the same color as the Mediterranean marble that surrounded the vanity and the swagged draperies that covered the window.

She examined her face in the mirror. Shakily she touched her lips with color and ran a comb through her hair. Jonathan was right, no doubt about it—her hair showed little trace of the sleek, geometric cut she had worn when she arrived in Deception Bay. She wondered if Reginald would banish her from his chair forever if she came home with someone else's scissor marks on her hair.

"Elizabeth?" She looked up, startled. It was Matt's voice, whispering on the other side of the door. He tapped lightly. "Sweetheart?"

She opened the door, and he slid inside, closing it quickly behind him and twisting the lock.

"Matt! What on earth—?"

"Shh." He silenced her with a quick, forceful kiss. Then he turned around and sat on the edge of the tub, feet planted apart, and drew her between his knees. His hands fitted themselves around her buttocks and he grinned up at her engagingly.

"What are you doing here?" Elizabeth tried to object, laughing and at the same time trying to push him away.

"Hush!" He reached over to the sink and turned on the tap. "Don't worry. No one saw me."

"But, Matt, this is crazy! Why—?"

"I was watching you across the room."

"I was watching you, too."

His hand moved up and down the back of her legs, and slowly his fingers inched the hemline of her dress upward. "Nice party," he said conversationally.

"Mmm. Very nice."

"What did you say to Grover? He was talking as though he wanted to run you out of town on a rail." Matt's hand slipped between her legs, and he touched her moist woman's core through the supple mesh of her panty hose.

"Nothing he didn't already know, I'm sure," Elizabeth replied faintly. She moved her legs to accommodate the new direction his hand was taking.

"You'll be happy to know that several people came to your defense. I think Melanie's announcement did the trick."

They weren't really talking about the party or about Grover Atkins, and both of them knew it. They were playing an escalating game of seduction, a game that had begun across a crowded room, and the words were only a tool to disguise the shimmering tension that was building between them. Pulling one of Elizabeth's knees toward him, Matt began to explore the longed-for flesh.

"I think we should leave now," he said, his voice thick.

"But we can't," Elizabeth protested, although her tone suggested she might be willing to be persuaded. "Melanie hasn't even served dinner yet!"

"I'm not hungry. Are you?" Matt stood up, letting her skirt fall back down to her knees. He turned off the gushing water faucet, still holding her tightly, and she could feel the hard bulge of his groin against her stomach.

She hesitated.

"I could whip us up some bacon and eggs later," Matt urged.

It was the *later* that decided her. "Now there's an offer I can't refuse."

Carefully Matt unlocked the door and opened it a crack, looking both ways down the hallway. Seeing no one, he took Elizabeth's hand and pulled her along behind him. They scurried down the hall, away from the sounds of the party and through swinging doors that led into the kitchen. Several pairs of eyes looked up in surprise as the caterer's crew watched them hurry through the room and duck out the back door.

"What was that all about?" one of the maids asked.

"*¿Quién sabe?*" another commented, shrugging without much interest. "Who knows?"

ELIZABETH SAT close to Matt on the front seat of the truck. Her hand rested intimately on the inside of his leg. The muscles of his inner thigh tensed as he pressed the gas pedal, then flexed again as he shifted his foot to the brake when they rounded a curve.

The white line down the center of the road flew up to meet them. In no time at all the truck swerved sharply and came to a halt in the front yard of the caretaker's cottage.

Matt jerked on the handle beside him and pushed open the door, at the same time reaching down to turn off the ignition and the headlights. Instant darkness enveloped the yard.

Elizabeth frowned, looking in the direction of the cottage. "The porch light," she said uncertainly. "I'm sure I left it on."

"Maybe you forgot," Matt said as he slid out of the truck.

"No. No, I don't think so." She slid out behind him and eyed the dark cottage uneasily. "It's something I always do. I hate coming home to a dark house."

"Well, then it must have burned out." He reached into the truck and switched the headlights back on. "You go on in and turn on some lights and then I'll—"

There was no moon, but the headlight beams made a path across the yard and reflected in concentric circles from the windows of the cottage. When Elizabeth reached the porch, she hesitated.

Something felt wrong. She climbed the stairs suspiciously, peering into the blinding glare of the headlights reflected in the windows. She could see nothing.

Key in hand, she reached for the doorknob, and that was when she realized the door was standing open. She fell back, catching her heel in a loose board and nearly losing her balance.

If this were Chicago, she'd know what to do. She'd kick off her shoes and run as fast as her legs would carry her down to the lobby and then tell the superintendent to call 911. But here there was no telephone, no superintendent, no 911, not even any police she was aware of, except the jovial political appointee who was the sheriff.

Acting on her only other alternative, she screamed Matt's name in a voice that came out a panicked whisper. "Matt!" she tried again, backing away from the door and down the steps.

She whirled around to scream again and gasped with fright when she crashed headlong into someone standing directly behind her. It was Matt. In the glare of the headlights her eyes were enormous and washed out by fear to the noncolor of cellophane.

"What's wrong?" he asked. Sensing her panic, he kept his voice instinctively at a whisper.

"Matt, the door," she whispered, terrified fingers clutching at his arm. "The door! It's open! And I know I locked it. I always do!"

Matt's eyes froze on the doorway. He grasped Elizabeth by the arm and stepped in front of her. "You get back in the truck," he said quietly. "If anything happens, get over to Milt's for the sheriff."

"No, Matt," she protested, "don't go in there. Let's both go get the sheriff!"

He shook her hands off his arm and motioned her to be still. Then, slowly, cautiously, he crept up the stairs, keeping his body flattened against the banister, freezing in his tracks whenever a step creaked under his foot.

God, did he think someone might still be in there? Elizabeth wondered as she climbed into the truck and gripped the steering wheel fearfully. He was stalking the house as though he were stalking an animal in the woods. An anguished yearning swept through her for the uncomplicated urban solution to such situations—dial the telephone and wait for the professionals to handle it!

Matt hunkered down and crept around the edge of the porch, keeping out of reach of the headlight beams as he approached the doorway from the side. He raised his head and listened.

Suddenly he leaped forward with a harsh, guttural cry and kicked the door open wide. It slammed with a sickening crack against the doorjamb. The force of his leap carried him to the opposite side of the opening, where he landed in a crouched position and waited intently for some response from inside.

The headlight beams streamed into the house through the doorway. They reached clear across the living room and spotlighted the antique chifforobe that stood against the back wall, but the glaring white lights revealed nothing out of the ordinary. The door slowly swung to a stop, still creaking protestingly on its hinges.

Cautiously Matt got to his feet. He walked up to the door and stepped inside, then flipped the light switch beside the door. "What the—?"

Elizabeth turned off the headlights and clambered out of the truck. She ran awkwardly across the yard, her heels sinking into the ground with each step, and scrambled up the porch to join Matt in the doorway.

His arm barred her way. Looking over his shoulder, she gasped, then expelled the air from her lungs in a single, shocked breath.

CHAPTER SIXTEEN

THE COTTAGE had been vandalized. Savagely. Thoroughly.

Canvases were scattered everywhere, slashed and broken. Paint tubes were twisted and their contents spewed onto the rugs and floor, the smeared paint already beginning to dry around the edges. Pages had been torn from Elizabeth's sketchbooks and crumpled into balls, and everything was smeared with crumbled charcoal.

"Oh, my God," she breathed, staring at the devastation in stunned disbelief. She looked from the carnage that had been her living room to Matt's face, and then back to the living room again.

She lifted his arm out of the way and walked into the house. She looked at the kitchen and saw that the sketches that had been tacked to the cupboards lay in a wrinkled heap on the linoleum floor.

In a state of shock she walked into the living room, stepping into a puddle of paint that she then unwittingly tracked across the wooden floor. She stopped in the middle of the room and surveyed the damage with dismay. She knew she was going to be very angry eventually, but for the moment she was in shock.

Matt, meanwhile, had made his own damage assessment. He grabbed the telephone receiver with barely concealed fury and dialed with short, furious stabs of his finger.

"Milt? Matt. Look, send Tom over to the lighthouse compound. Right away. Yes. Yes, right away." He slammed the receiver down, and he and Elizabeth stared at each other across the ruins of the living room with angry, baffled eyes.

A canvas remnant of Deception Head Light's red-tiled roof was stuck to her foot. She bent to pick it up. Upon the canvas a splotch of hooker green had been imprinted on the red roof by the sole of her shoe. She held the scrap in her hand, looking at it dully.

"No, sweetheart, don't touch anything. Leave it just the way it is for the sheriff." Quickly he crossed the room and took the piece of canvas board from her hand, dropping it back onto the floor, then guided her to the sofa and made her sit. "Is anything missing?" he asked suddenly.

"I don't know," Elizabeth replied. "Let me look in the bedroom...." But she hesitated, unwilling for the moment to face any more carnage.

Matt reached for the bedroom door and threw it open. The room appeared unscathed.

He opened the dresser drawers and, reaching down, rifled through the apparently untouched contents. For an instant his hands clutched convulsively in the silk of Elizabeth's lingerie, and his knuckles turned white. His face contorted—it was the look of impotent fury that had never left his face during the entire eighteen months he spent in Vietnam, and which he hadn't allowed himself to feel since.

It was only for an instant, and then he regained his self-control. His fingers relaxed and the silk slipped through them like a waterfall. He smoothed the fabric and carefully slid the drawer shut.

Crossing to the dresser, he opened the lacquered jewelry box sitting on top. Inside were a few gold chains, a scattering of earrings and the filigree heart he had bought for her at the street fair. There was also about a hundred dollars in bills, which appeared untouched, as well.

"Whatever the motive," Matt said, returning to the living room, "it wasn't robbery."

Just then they heard a siren wailing in the distance. It came closer and closer until the sound seemed to fill the summer night. Shock waves reverberated around the cottage, keeping the air churning even after the shrieking siren had whimpered into silence. Suddenly the yard was full of red and blue flashing lights. One squad car and then another tore through the yard, tires spinning and rear ends fishtailing as they came to a dead stop only inches from the porch.

The sheriff, still in his dinner jacket, got out of one of the cars, leaving the door hanging open, and stomped up the steps. Close on his heels from the other car followed a uniformed deputy who kept fingering the grip of his pistol where it protruded from the holster on his hip.

The sheriff knocked peremptorily on the door and pushed it open. "Ker-r-ist!" he exclaimed, stopping so abruptly in the doorway that the fidgety deputy bumped into him from behind. "What the hell happened here?"

"That's what we'd like to find out," Matt replied tersely. "Tom, you know Elizabeth La Salle?"

"Seen you around town, ma'am." The sheriff nodded at Elizabeth with a gesture that would have been a tip of his hat if he'd been wearing one. "Sorry about this, ma'am. Huey!" he bellowed over his shoulder. "Go get the camera!"

While the antsy deputy's flashbulbs popped all over the
room, the sheriff questioned Elizabeth and Matt, jot-
ting down their statements on a yellow legal pad.

"Well, I'll tell you," he said finally, closing his legal
pad and handing it to the deputy. "It's a damn shame,
but I can pretty well guarantee you that whoever did this
isn't going to be found."

"What do you mean?"

The sheriff looked uncomfortable. He took off his
jacket and handed it to the deputy. Although the fire was
banked and the house was cold, damp semicircles stained
the shirt beneath his armpits.

"Well, ma'am," he began, "I'd be willing to bet it was
kids, maybe high on something. Who knows? Or else
someone just passing through. This place is so isolated,
probably figured there'd be no chance they'd ever get
caught. Huey dusted the place for prints, of course, but
unless the perpetrator or perpetrators already have a rap
sheet, it won't do us any good. And I'd bet dollars to
doughnuts that there's nothing on the records."

"Now wait a minute, Tom!" Matt exclaimed angrily.
"You mean that anyone can just come in here and tear
the place up and no one is going—"

"Hold on, Matt, hold on." The sheriff held up a pla-
cating hand. He ran his finger under his collar, unhook-
ing his clip-on bow tie and handing it to the deputy, then
unbuttoned his collar with a sigh of relief. "I didn't say
that. I'm just giving you my considered opinion. With
nothing of value taken—you *did* say nothing was missing, didn't you, ma'am?—there won't be anything to
trace. You have to understand—"

"But something of value *was* taken!" Elizabeth had
been studying the shambles on the floor. Suddenly she
turned to the sheriff. "Several paintings are missing. I'm

sure of it! Some of the completed ones—one of Deception Head Light and the one I just finished of Heceta Head."

"Are you sure?" the sheriff asked. "You mean that in all this mess you can tell that a couple of pictures aren't here?" His voice sounded doubtful.

"Yes," Elizabeth responded firmly. "I can pretty well piece together what's here, and I'm telling you, two of the big canvases are gone!" She looked at the sheriff hopefully. "Will that help?"

"Are they worth anything?"

Elizabeth shrugged unhappily. "Not yet."

"Well, tell you what. You come down to my office tomorrow and give Huey here a complete description of what all's missing and we'll see what we can do."

"Tom," Matt said carefully, "what do you think of the possibility that this was done by someone in town? You know, someone who doesn't like outsiders?"

"We got a fair number of those," the sheriff conceded, "But whether any of them would go so far as to pull a stunt like this, well, I just don't know." He stroked the stubble on his chin thoughtfully. "We'll keep it mind, Matt. We surely will, and I'll put some extra patrols out here, too, ma'am, just to be on the safe side. But I doubt you need to worry. I think it's likely that the perp or perps are a long way from here now, or else home in bed praying their folks don't find out!" He threw an irritated glance at his deputy, who was encumbered with all the investigative paraphernalia and the sheriff's dinner jacket, as well. "If you're finished, Huey," he growled, "let's roll."

Turning once more to Elizabeth and Matt, giving them another tip of his nonexistent hat, he bid them goodnight. Then, gesturing toward the door in a brusque jerk of his head, he summoned his overloaded deputy and preceded him out.

Now that the crisis was over, the numbness began to wear off, and suddenly Elizabeth was angry. More than angry. She felt violated. She began to walk around the living room, haphazardly picking up pieces of canvas and wood and hurling them into the fireplace.

"This has never," she exclaimed, launching a splintered bit of wood at the hearth, "happened to me before!" Another fragment of wood sailed across the room. "Never!"

She scooped up several scraps of canvas board and pitched them furiously onto the banked embers. Her voice quavered. "All my life I've lived right in the middle of Chicago, and nothing like this has ever happened to me before!"

As quickly as it started, the temper tantrum was over. She stopped short, a corner of canvas board still clutched in her hand, and stared at Matt with large, frightened eyes. The shock and anger, combined with the chill that was on the room, hit her all at once, and suddenly she began to shiver uncontrollably.

Matt took off his blazer and draped it around her shoulders. "Bad things can happen anywhere," he said soothingly. "I'm just so goddamn sorry that it had to happen here."

He nuzzled her neck as he wrapped his arms around her from behind and buttoned the coat's single button. The blue blazer swallowed her completely.

Elizabeth tried to smile through her chattering teeth. "I n-never s-seem to be d-d-dressed for the w-weather around h-here, d-do I?" She sat on the edge of the sofa, the jacket hugged tightly around her body.

"Let me poke up the fire, and you'll feel a lot better." Matt rolled up the sleeves of his pleated dress shirt. She watched him add kindling and two small logs to the fire. Almost immediately the kindling caught fire. The scorched scraps of canvas burst into flame with tiny showers of sparks.

Then Matt walked into the kitchen, and Elizabeth heard him dialing the telephone. "Tran," she heard him say. "Look, pardner, I've got a problem. I'm not going to be able to make my charters tomorrow. I've got that bunch from Portland in the morning, and a boatload of singles later on. Will you go by early and see if Jory can get someone to cover for me?"

There was a pause. "I'll tell you later. No. No! I'm sure you could use the money, but—"

Listening to the one-sided conversation, Elizabeth could tell that the boy was being difficult. Matt paced a few steps then, turned on his heel and paced back again. "No, Tran. I know you can do the job, but you're not licensed, so you're not insured—"

He switched the receiver from one ear to the other and raked an agitated hand through his hair. "Listen, damn it! Just tell Jory I can't make it. He'll know what to do. If you want to go along with one of the other guides, that's fine with me, but the *Chinook Wind*'s not to go out. Got that? I'll be home tomorrow."

He hung up the receiver with a curt gesture that in anyone else would have been a slam, but by the time he returned to the living room his face was calm. From the floor he scooped up several crumpled sheets of paper and brought them to Elizabeth.

"Look," he said, smoothing them out carefully so as not to smear the chalk further, "some of these are salvageable. At least you can get some idea what they were supposed to look like.''

Elizabeth took the wrinkled sheets from him and laid them on the coffee table. "Matt, I know how busy you are." She tried to affect a confidence she was far from feeling. "You don't need to stay. You heard what the sheriff said—whoever did this is miles away from here by now."

"Probably," Matt reiterated in a no-nonsense voice. "He said *probably.* There's no way I would leave you alone tonight."

"What about Tran?"

"He'll be fine. During the school year, he stays by himself whenever I have overnighters." Matt smiled wryly. "And he resents it, too. Doesn't know why I won't let him skip school and come along."

"Well, as long as you're sure," Elizabeth said dubiously, but more than willing to be convinced.

"I'm sure. He's just not your average sixteen-year-old, you know. After the life he's lived, how could he be?"

Elizabeth reached up and took his hands, pulling him down to sit beside her on the sofa. "I'm awfully glad you can stay," she said softly. Her voice fell seductively. "And not only because of the vandals, either." Her eyes confirmed the suggestive invitation that was in her voice as she leaned toward him to touch his lips with her own.

"So am I," he said in the instant before their lips met.

"So am I," he said again, his mouth whispering directly into her ear this time as his cheek pressed against hers, his beard grazing her neck agreeably.

Elizabeth felt his hands slip beneath the jacket that was still draped around her body. The button gave way, and the jacket slid off her shoulders as he pulled her against him.

Everything—the ruined living room, the sheriff and his jittery deputy, Tran, everything—was forgotten in the fever that picked up right where it had left off in the front seat of the truck. With one sure twist of his body Matt stretched her across his lap. The fire was warm on her bared back.

Half sitting, half reclining on his knees, her arms around his neck, she clung to him. She was falling and falling and falling, and it was only her arms around his neck and his big hand at the small of her back that kept her anchored.

He lifted her with one hand under her buttocks so that her breasts were available to his questing lips. Beneath the silk of her strapless dress her nipples hardened against the moist pursuit of his tongue. He buried his head in the shadowed valley of her cleavage, and her arms held him there, filling him with her own hot hunger.

Then he released her and pulled her across his lap again. She felt the jutting ferocity of him against her hip, and once again she was falling and falling and falling with Matt's hard masculinity her only point of reference. She arched her back, and her body was as taut as a bow. When she felt his mouth on the elongated white column of her throat, a sound escaped her lips, more expressive and more explicit than any words could ever have been.

With another twist of his body he turned over and slid her knees beneath him, and suddenly he was on top of her, his hard body pinning her to the sofa. He moved his hand urgently between the two of them, struggling to free himself from the confines of his trousers. She heard the silken swish of her panty hose as he pulled them unceremoniously down her legs and disposed of them with a decisive sweep of his arm, and then she felt him raise her skirt. She felt his hand between her legs, and his fingers parted the soft flesh of her inner thighs. Her hips rose up to meet him.

Her breath came in quick, shallow gasps, and the soft cries she made were unconscious and instinctive, their only purpose to let him know that she was ready to be taken.

Supporting himself on his forearms, Matt settled himself between her thighs, his knees urging them farther apart. One of her legs dropped over the edge of the sofa, and she braced her toes on the floor. With a harsh, triumphant cry he entered her, burying himself to the hilt. With a cry of joy and of surrender, she welcomed him.

MATT LAY on the sofa with his head in Elizabeth's lap. She was teasing the hair on his chest, letting it curl around her finger in tiny whorls. With her forefinger she stroked the flat brown nipple, so different from her own and yet sensitive, too, in its own way.

Her eyes traveled down the length of his body—tanned and covered with the same crisp golden hair as his chest, all except the narrow white band of flesh that covered his hips. There the hair was softer and darker. Her eyes stopped at his pendulous masculinity, no longer fierce but soft and vulnerable. She reached down his long body to cradle him gently.

His eyes flickered open, and she smiled into them. "I sure know how to get your attention," she teased.

"Always," he said. He reached up and cupped her chin with his palm, then began to move his thumb lightly across her lips.

The last traces of the conventional wisdom of singles bars deserted Elizabeth. *Don't commit yourself first.*

Keep them guessing. "I love you, Matthew McCullough," she whispered against the tender pressure of his thumb.

"I love you, too."

CHAPTER SEVENTEEN

"WAITING FOR MATT?" Celebration asked. Her voice was cheerful as she upturned Elizabeth's coffee cup.

It had taken weeks of seeing Matt and Elizabeth together before Celebration was able to pronounce his name without a catch in her voice, but she had bounced back with the resilience of youth. Now she had come to regard Elizabeth as a confidante, somewhere between a big sister and a best friend.

"I heard you had some trouble down at the lighthouse last week."

"I'm afraid so." Elizabeth had mentioned it to no one, and neither, she was sure, had Matt. Yet the entire town seemed to know. She wondered wryly if they also knew that she had spent every night of the past week at Matt's cabin up on the old Greensprings Highway.

He had insisted, and Elizabeth felt threatened enough by the vandalism not to put up more than token resistance. She had packed up her art supplies and some clothing and agreed to allow Matt to move her into his small bedroom while he bunked with Tran in his even smaller one.

Matt had told Tran that Elizabeth was coming to stay with them for a while, but apparently the boy had decided to make plans of his own. When Matt pulled into the driveway and began unloading Elizabeth's bags, Tran met them at the door, looking surly and carrying his old army jacket slung across one shoulder.

"I told Leon Redwing you wasn't goin' out the rest of the week," he announced without preamble. "And he says he's got a charter goin' down to Catalina. He wants to know if I can go."

Matt put down the bags he was carrying and looked at him. "Well, pardner," he replied slowly, "I was kind of hoping we could spend a little time together, the three of us. Maybe take Elizabeth around to see the sights."

"Leon says he'll pay me a hundred dollars for the week," Tran persisted sullenly.

Matt looked unhappy. "If it's what you want to do—" he began.

"Does that mean I can go?" Tran demanded.

"Sure, pardner, I guess so," Matt agreed, a defeated tone in his voice. "Go ahead."

Tran pulled his baseball cap from the back pocket of his jeans and settled it firmly on his head, then ran down the steps two at a time. He mounted the bicycle that was propped against the porch and pedaled out of the driveway.

"Tran!" Matt called.

The boy skidded to a stop and looked over his shoulder. "Yeah?"

"Be careful, son." He watched Tran until the boy disappeared around the bend in the road, then picked up the two suitcases and turned to Elizabeth. "Well, looks like we've got the place to ourselves." From the crooked smile on his face she couldn't tell whether he was sorry or glad.

The A-frame cabin was set well back from the highway, its split-log exterior hardly distinguishable from the tall pines that surrounded it. It was very rustic on the outside, but the interior was refreshingly modern. There were hardwood floors with area rugs scattered here and there and box-pleated ivory draperies over a large picture window that looked out onto the foothills of the Cascades. There was a fireplace, but there was also central heat, indicated by a thermostat on one paneled wall.

The furniture was the sort a man would choose for himself—massive, comfortable and plain. No fussy little tables to trip up big feet, no knickknacks that would only gather dust. There were a few woodsy prints on the walls and a bearskin, including head and vicious-looking teeth, on the floor in front of the fireplace.

Over the next week they were like castaways on their own private, deserted island. There was nothing to mark the passage of time except the regular progression of days and nights. They made love, slept, then woke to make love again. Between times they concocted meals from whatever they could find in Matt's larder—barbecue and beans, venison burgers, peanut butter and jelly sandwiches, cookies and milk.

They hiked through the woods and rode Matt's horses down to the beach and into the foothills. His big Appaloosas weren't the demoralized specimens that Elizabeth used to rent by the hour to ride through the forest preserves in Chicago, and her mount, a spirited mare named Carousel, kept her on her toes.

Elizabeth learned that Matt's reserve didn't extend to all things, for he was a bold and uninhibited lover, and he made Jonathan's slick urbanity seem almost decadent by comparison.

Sometimes his audacity took her by surprise. City born and bred, where every square inch of land had its own collection of broken glass, rusty nails or dog piles, Elizabeth was understandably dubious when, during a ride through the woods one afternoon, Matt stopped under an

ancient pine, tied the horses to a nearby sapling and began to make love to her.

Once she was nearly naked, dappled by the few sunbeams that found their way through the trees, she had to
admit that the bed of pine needles was as soft and clean
as any mattress. Still, the lack of privacy made her uneasy.

Matt had dismissed her protests with a laugh as im-
portunate as his hands. "We haven't seen another soul
for days!" he said gruffly. He stripped off his Pendleton
and spread it on top of the pine needles, then brought
Elizabeth down first to her knees and then to the ground.
"We're as alone here as if we were Adam and Eve."

That was certainly true. It was also true that the feath-
ery breeze on parts of her body that had never seen the
sun excited her beyond belief. The sounds of their mat-
ing seemed an intrinsic part of the natural world around
them. Once, during a moment of supreme ecstasy, Elizabeth opened her eyes and saw framed in the blue circle
of sky a lone gull, snowy white, wheeling slowly in the
sunshine.

The Garden of Eden—it was a perfect analogy, she'd
thought afterward, as they lay exhausted on the soft bed
of pine needles without even a fig leaf to cover them.
Remembering, she could almost smell the musky scent of
their lovemaking blended with the earthiness of the
pines—and then it was dispelled by the strong odor of
coffee as Celebration filled her cup.

"Does he have any idea who did it?"

"I'm sorry?" Elizabeth looked at the girl blankly.

"I said," Celebration repeated, "does the sheriff have
any idea who might've broken into your place?"

"Oh, yes. Well, he's still—" What had Tom said when
she talked to him this morning? "Pursuing all leads."

Five days had passed, and the sheriff's investigation had turned up nothing. In a way, Elizabeth found that comforting. It suggested that his original theory had probably been correct and that those responsible for the vandalism were indeed long gone.

"Ha! That means he rounded up all the usual suspects and they all had alibis, and now he doesn't know what to do next!"

Elizabeth couldn't help laughing. Celebration's shrewd observation correlated with her own. "What 'usual suspects'? I wouldn't have guessed there was much of a criminal element in Deception Bay."

"Oh, you know. The druggies who hang around outside the doughnut shop. A few of the junior high school kids. Otis Lee—he's always getting some tourist to buy him beer. Then he gets drunk and passes out in the street and the sheriff locks him up and calls his folks. You know, like that—the kids who're just plain troublemakers."

The face of one such troublemaker flashed across Elizabeth's mind. "Like Tran McCullough, you mean?" she asked thoughtlessly.

"Tran?" The girl looked puzzled. "Not Tran. He's a weird kid, all right, but he never gets into trouble. He just runs away."

"Runs away?"

"All the time." Celebration slid into the seat opposite Elizabeth and set the coffeepot down on the table. Her voice fell confidentially. "Sheriff's had to track him down, oh, ten, twelve times, I guess. He usually ends up in San Francisco, but once they found him in Portland, and the last time, I heard he was over in Medford."

"What's his problem?"

"Well, he tells the kids at school that he needs money and figures he can earn more in a city than he could ever make here."

"Why does he need so much money? He doesn't spend it on clothes, that's for sure! And I know he drives Matt's truck..."

"Who knows?" Celebration shrugged. "He's weird, like I said. I've known him since he came here, and he's always been a little weird. I guess it make sense, considering what he's been through. But still, the kids at school tried to be nice to him, knowing the kind of life he must have had and all, and he just wasn't having any."

"Maybe he doesn't want anyone feeling sorry for him." Elizabeth felt a sneaking sympathy for the boy. "Maybe he wants someone to like him for himself, not for what he's been through."

It crossed her mind that she, too, had tried to be his friend because she felt sorry for him and because he was Matt's son—reasons that had nothing to do with Tran himself. What was the boy like beneath that abrasive exterior? Did anybody really know?

Celebration shrugged again. "Could be. I don't know. All I know is he's pretty much of loner. He doesn't like anyone, and no one likes him much, either. Course, soon it won't matter, anyway."

"What do you mean?"

"Well, it's just that he'll be of age soon, is all. No one's going to be looking too hard for him the next time he disappears, and they won't be able to make him come back even if they *do* find him."

"Well, that's too bad."

"I guess I understand him in a way," Celebration went on. "Bright lights, big city. I'd like to see some of that myself.'' Her face was eager and inquisitive. ''What's it like living in a place like Chicago?''

''It's exciting. Things are happening there.'' A wave of nostalgia washed over Elizabeth. But when it was gone, she realized that it left no lingering residue of homesickness. Chicago and her life there seemed very far away. ''And it's beautiful in its own way. Completely different from here, of course. The skyline along Lakeshore Drive looks like a billion tiny stars at night. And the buildings are so tall they really do seem to scrape the sky...'' She stopped, looking at Celebration curiously. She wondered if the girl had ever seen a skyscraper.

''I'd sure like to go there someday,'' Celebration said dreamily.

''Why don't you? Oh, maybe not Chicago necessarily, but you've got Portland just north of you and San Francisco south—''

''Oh, no!'' Celebration looked at her, distressed. How much she looked like her mother, with Hannah's wide blue eyes! ''I wouldn't want to go that far away! I was thinking of maybe Medford. My grandmother lives there....''

''Oh. Yes. Well, I'm sure that's a very interesting city, too.''

Celebration didn't really want to change her life-style, Elizabeth realized, amused. She just wanted to spread her wings a little, sow a few wild oats. But when she was finished she wanted to come back to Deception Bay, like the salmon in the ocean, heading upriver when the chinook began to blow!

''Here comes Matt,'' Celebration interrupted her daydreaming to announce. He had parked his truck at the curb and was feeding the meter. She looked mischievously across the table. "So...when are you and Matt going to tie the knot?"

Elizabeth sputtered her coffee. So the whole town *did* know! "What on earth makes you think we're going to get married?" she asked in a strangled voice.

"Well, you don't have to get married, actually. But Matt needs someone. Look at him."

She did. "He looks just fine to me." He looked more than fine. He looked fantastic. Although he had left the cabin that morning wearing his customary black turtle-neck and pea jacket, the day had turned warm; now he had shed the cold-weather gear in favor of a plaid Pendleton, unbuttoned down the front, with only a T-shirt underneath. The sleeves were rolled up past his elbows and the shirttail was tucked into his low-slung jeans.

"Well, after all," Celebration said, "it must be hard for someone his age to meet women...."

Elizabeth almost sputtered her coffee again.

"And where's he going to make contacts in a little town like this?" Celebration gazed at her with Hannah's artless look, which Elizabeth suddenly suspected wasn't artless at all. "I mean," she continued, "once you're out of school, where do you go to meet people, anyway?"

The plate glass doors at the front of the diner swung open, and Matt came in. He walked past the lunch counter to the booth at the rear, where his arrival put an end to Celebration's discourse on his impending senility.

Celebration slid out of the booth. "This stuff's cold," she judged as she lifted the glass coffeepot and tested its temperature against her hand. "Let me go get you some fresh."

"And the blue plate special," Matt told her with a smile as she walked away. When the girl was gone, he took her place in the booth. He must have just come from the boat, because he still smelled of fresh sea air and diesel fuel, with the familiar underlying hint of fish and cologne. It was a smell Elizabeth suspected she would always associate with him. Even years later. Even in her dreams.

"Hi, sweetheart," he said. He reached across the table and clasped her hand. His thumb rubbed lovingly back and forth across her knuckles. "Jory said you were looking for me."

"Have some lunch first," Elizabeth told him with a smile. "I don't want to argue on an empty stomach."

His eyebrows shot up. "Are we going to argue?"

Celebration returned with a steaming pot of coffee and Matt's blue plate special—poached salmon decorated with lemon wedges and a parsley sprig. "What do we have to argue about?" Matt repeated when she was gone.

"Matt, you have to go back to work. No, wait, listen to me," she insisted as he opened his mouth to object. "I was talking to Jory this morning, and he told me you canceled two overnight trips last week and you're canceling another one tonight."

"I'll find someone to cover for me," Matt said. "It's only a matter of time."

"That's not what Jory says. He says everyone is completely booked for the rest of the summer, and it'll be a fluke—a cold day in hell is the way he phrased it—before you'll find someone who's got time to do your job for you."

"Jory talks too much," Matt muttered ungraciously.

Elizabeth almost smiled. That seemed to be Matt's response to anyone who showed concern for him.

He was a very private person and probably had been even before Vietnam forced him farther inside himself. But Jory, in his own inarticulate way, *was* concerned; that was why he had cornered Elizabeth when she set up her easel behind his bait shop this morning and transmitted that concern to her in a few, succinct hisses.

Will also "talked too much," but he loved Matt, too. And so did she.

"Jory's right, though. This is your peak season. I know that. And you've got to make a living. Let's face it, people reserve you a year in a advance, often even earlier. If you let them down, they're not going to come back next year. They'll find someone else."

"Let them. Look, Elizabeth, I love you, damn it! I'm not going to leave you isolated out there at the lighthouse compound, at the mercy of anyone who's in the mood for wreaking a little havoc! The next time you might even *be* there!"

"Matt, listen to me. The sheriff thinks it was just a drifter passing through. You know that. And yet here we are disrupting our entire lives over someone who's probably getting stoned on the beach in Mendocino and forgotten all about it by now."

"We can't take the chance," Matt said stubbornly,

"We can't *not* take the chance. I'll be gone in another few weeks, but you're life will still be here. . . ."

She remembered when she had spoken those words before. It was when she had come aboard the *Chinook Wind* for the first time, and Matt had told her that the townspeople didn't want her in Deception Bay. It had been simple statement of fact then; now the words dangled in the air between them like a hangman's noose.

Matt shook his head firmly. "Whatever time we have left, I'm going to spend it with you." He smiled. It was the forced, down-turned smile, the one she thought she'd never see on his face again, at least not directed toward her.

"That's what I want, too. But how do you think I'll feel when I go back to Chicago, knowing that you sacrificed everything you've built in the past ten years because of me? I couldn't handle that. Besides—" her voice fell lower "—I'm running out of time. If I'm going to make up for the time I lost, I'm going to have to get back to work."

It was a lie, of course, but she willed it to be convincing. Matt didn't interfere with her painting. Rather, in a way that seemed very natural and very right, he had become an integral part of it.

"If the lighthouse people like your stuff," Matt suggested carefully, "maybe you won't have to leave at all."

That possibility had crossed Elizabeth's mind more often than she cared to admit. But not returning to Chicago was unthinkable. She had a life there, and she loved it. That that life had recently become empty and unrewarding didn't change the fact that she was a city dweller, born and raised. The city was in her blood. Her family was there, her friends. Her roots were there.

But, of course, her parents wintered in Arizona now. She seldom saw anyone except the people with whom she worked. And when was the last time she had bought a season's ticket to the opera? A long time ago. And why not? Because there was no parking downtown, the taxi drivers were a surly and unpredictable lot, and it was dangerous to walk the streets after dark anyway.

"Matt, that's an awfully big if, but even if the lighthouse people *do* give me the contract, I'll have to go back to Chicago, anyway, at least for a little while. Jonathan's not going to let me off the hook that easily."

"Damn Jonathan! And the damn the lighthouse people, too! You had the courage to come all the way out here in the first place, sweetheart. Don't back off now."

"It's not that simple."

"Of course it is. Stay."

"How can I stay, Matt?" she asked quietly. "Tran doesn't like me, you know that. He'll never accept me, and you'd never desert him—I would never ask you to. Being the kind of man who would take on a responsibility like that is one of the reasons I love you. But it does make things impossible for us."

"Tran will be gone in a few years...." Matt began tentatively.

"But they're going to be important years, busy years, for you and for him. And I wouldn't be able to help you. I'd only be in the way. I'd feel like a ... like a ... *vulture,* just waiting around biding my time until he's gone. You'd grow to hate me, Matt, and it wouldn't accomplish what you started out to do for Tran, anyway. He needs you. And it's very clear that he doesn't need me." She tried to look cheerful through the lackluster smile that twisted her lips. "Besides, we're talking about your job, not mine. You've got to start taking your overnighters again. You can't be letting your people down."

"Elizabeth ..." he said desperately.

She could tell by the cornered look in his eye that he was about to capitulate. "Come on, Matt. I'll be fine." She pressed her advantage. "And we'll still have all the other nights together, you know...."

"All right, sweetheart," he said finally. "We'll do it your way." He looked like a man going to a hanging. His own. "But you *will* call Tran, do you hear, if there's anything you need? At the very least he'll always know how to reach me."

Elizabeth smiled and nodded, all the time telling herself that there was no way she would put herself in the unenviable position of needing help from Tran. If the chips were ever really down, she doubted she would be able to rely on him.

THE IRON DOOR squeaked on its hinges. Elizabeth's nostrils were assailed by the damp, earthy odor she remembered from her first foray inside the lighthouse.

She had the uneasy feeling that the lighthouse had been waiting for her. Maybe it had wondered why she took so long to come back. Or maybe it just wondered if *anyone* would come back. Ever.

She propped the door open with a rock. Sunlight streamed in and disappeared into the dark at the bottom of the staircase. The old lighthouse looked exactly the same as the first time she had seen it except for the footprints she had left then, and even those were already coated with a fine layer of dust.

How long would the traces of her footprints be visible? she wondered. They were already crisscrossed with mouse tracks. Eventually they would disappear under a shroud of dust and there would be no trace of her left— it would be as though she'd never existed at all.

She shivered. She heard Gran's voice say, "Someone just walked over my grave." Absurd, of course. It was only a place where people had once lived and worked and now didn't. Hadn't she already determined that on her first visit?

She got a grip on her flashlight and on herself, tucked the sketchbook under her arm and began to climb the stairs. Once at the top, she lifted the dead bolt and pulled. The door opened a little easier than before, but not much. This time she kept the flashlight firmly in hand.

When she slipped out the narrow opening, a flock of gulls took off from the rail with indignant shrieks. Sunlight touched their wing tips with gold.

Far out to sea a collection of fishing boats trolled for salmon. The day was so clear that Elizabeth could see their downriggers arching over the sides of the boats. This time she knew Matt wasn't among them. He had taken his overnighters farther out, deep-sea fishing for tuna.

Elizabeth sat down with her back against the tower and propped her sketchbook on her knees. The wind made drawing difficult, but she persisted. This clear, sunny afternoon, she knew, might be her only chance to capture the view from Deception Head Light in fair weather.

When she looked up, half a dozen pages later, it was to note that the light was fading. It wasn't yet evening, since it stayed light until nearly nine o'clock this far north, but when the wind died down and the fog bank rolled in, the light went fast.

Elizabeth completed her last drawing, a lone boat looking small and lost against the horizon. Then she closed her pad and zipped it inside her suede jacket. She shivered when the cold air hit her body. Remembering her first foray up to the lantern gallery, she had dressed more warmly this time, but nothing was impervious to the damp chill of a coastal night.

She turned up her collar, then reached for the door and pushed on the handle. Anticipating its opening, she took a step forward and thudded hard against the heavy iron.

She looked blankly at the door. The wind must have blown it closed, she thought; in the next instant she realized that was illogical, for the wind would have blown it open, not closed.

She leaned her shoulder against it and pushed, expecting the door to creak open. It didn't. She leaned harder and pushed again. Nothing. She jerked the handle a few times. Fear began to churn in the pit of her stomach.

Then she stood back and rammed her shoulder against the door with all the strength in her body.

It didn't budge. Suddenly she broke out in a cold sweat. It was locked. Someone had thrown the dead bolt!

She shook the handle as panic threatened to overwhelm her, and she began pounding on the door. "Let me in!" she shouted. "I know someone's in there! Let me in!" Her voice cracked precariously. "Let me in! I know you're in there!" The words took on an edge of hysteria. "Please! Please let me in! Please!"

There was no sound from the other side of the door. There wasn't even a sense that anyone was there. She flattened herself against it, beginning to sob. Her eyes darted around the balcony in a frantic, futile search for an escape she already realized was nonexistent.

A gull soared past, his wing tips almost touching her in the gathering dusk. With a little shriek she shrank further against the cold iron. It was only a sea gull, she told herself frenziedly, but it was enormous, and close up, its beady eye looked malevolent.

She circled around to the back of the tower and tried to make out the slanted gray roofs of the town. They were very far away. The highway was hidden among the gnarled trees, and no one ever traveled it unless they were coming to the lighthouse. With sinking heart she recalled the many long days she had spent in the caretaker's cottage with only the gulls and the raccoons for company.

She ran to the front again. The lone fishing boat was working its way toward the harbor. Frantically she tore the jacket off her shoulders, not even noticing the sketchbook as it tumbled off the balcony, and began waving it in the air.

It was red. They'd see it, even in the fading light. How could they *not* see it? But the boat made its way around Deception Head and disappeared from sight. Maybe they saw. Of course, and they'd be sending someone any minute now.

But the minutes dragged by, and gradually she had to accept the fact that no one was coming. She put her jacket back on, but she couldn't think beyond that. The blood rushed past her ears, pounding in her temples, carrying adrenaline to every cell in her body—an automatic but worthless response, since she could neither fight nor flee.

It was getting dark. Elizabeth paced back and forth like an animal in a cage, peering first over one side of the balcony and then over the other, studying the merciless landscape with hope born of desperation.

Suddenly her eyes riveted on the beach. A figure was approaching out of the mist just at the base of the headland. She peered closer, almost doubting what she saw, then felt her knees go weak with relief. It was Tran! He seemed to have materialized out of nowhere.

"Tran!" she screamed. "Tran!" She struggled out of her jacket and began to wave it frantically.

He didn't even pause.

"Tran!" she screamed over and over again. "Tran! Tran! Tran!"

He kept walking.

"Tran!" she shrieked, and the adrenaline turned out to be of some value, after all, because her voice ripped out of her throat like a thunderhead and caught Tran's attention.

He stopped and then turned. His hands were shoved into the pockets of his ratty jacket and his shoulders were hunched up to his ears. His light brown hair lay in dank strings across his forehead, and in the fading light Elizabeth could just barely make out his features. But he saw her. She knew he did. He looked right at her, then he turned his back and walked away.

Elizabeth stared at him in astonishment. Her mind struggled to comprehend what was happening. He was walking down the beach, away from the town, away from the lighthouse, away from her. He was leaving her there. "Tran!" she screamed, pounding her fists on the railing with helpless fury.

Then, as she watched in stunned disbelief, the boy vanished. He simply fell from sight, as quickly and as completely as if he had dropped off the face of the earth.

My God, what had happened to him? Had he fallen? Was he hurt?

Whatever it was, Elizabeth suddenly knew she was horrifyingly, terrifyingly alone.

Night fell, and with it the temperature. Elizabeth paced back and forth on the back side of the balcony, where the tower offered some slight protection from the chilling breeze. *Keep moving,* she urged her frozen body. *Keep walking. If you stop... don't go to sleep... keep moving. Someone will come eventually. There'll be boats out tomorrow, and if it's not too foggy, you might be able to attract their attention. And Matt will come... tomorrow night or the day after when he gets back from his overnight expedition for tuna.*

The moon rose, a thin silver disc almost obliterated by the fog, and it made grotesque shadows among the twisted trees. Elizabeth's teeth were chattering so hard that her jaw clenched like a vise, closing on her tongue so that she tasted blood. *Keep moving...*

Her limbs became numb. They felt warm and she was running on the beach and her name was Chrissy and she wore tiny gold earrings. No, her name was Lizzie and just ahead her parents waited for her with outstretched arms. She laughed happily, but when she reached out to them, suddenly it was the lighthouse that waited, and its arms were bleached white bones.

Another face floated just beyond her consciousness, a craggy, bearded, smiling face that she almost but not quite recognized. She reached up to touch it, but her numb legs gave out beneath her, and she fell to the stony floor. She huddled there, knees drawn up to her chest like a fetus, cradled in bony, bleached-out arms.

MINUTES OR HOURS or days later Elizabeth became aware of lights. There were sounds of banging and thumping and curses uttered in loud, excited voices. There was a noise like iron against iron and then strong arms swept her up from the cold stone.

There were more shouted epithets that seemed to be coming from a long way off. The arms that held her were shaking her, and someone was calling her name.

"Jesus Ker-r-rist!" another voice exclaimed.

And then the first voice yelled, "Get out of my way!"

The wind rushed through her damp hair as the arms gripped her roughly and carried her away. Elizabeth tried to open her eyes, but they seemed to be extremely heavy. She tried again and hazily focused on a face that was looking down at her. It was the same craggy, bearded face she had seen earlier. This time she recognized it.

"Matt," she whispered in a voice that was as defenseless as a child's. "I thought you were fishing."

Tears glistened in the green eyes above her, and they hung on sun-bleached yellow lashes for an instant before they fell to her icy cheek. "The fishing was lousy," he said.

CHAPTER EIGHTEEN

FOR THE NEXT TWELVE HOURS, Elizabeth drifted in and out of a sleep so deep that it seemed drugged.

She didn't remember Matt undressing her or slipping a nightshirt over her numb body. She didn't remember him putting her down on the sofa in front of the fireplace, nor the blankets he tucked around her, nor his endless, brisk chafing of her hands and feet.

All she knew was that every time she surfaced from the depths of her groggy slumber, he was there. She sipped soup and warm tea from a spoon that he held to her lips. Then she turned over and drifted off again.

Her sleep was dreamless for the most part, but once she woke and didn't remember where she was. A bearded blond giant with a strange down-turned smile and gentle eyes was sitting on the edge of the sofa. She looked at him blankly, as though she didn't quite recognize him. Then it all came back to her, and she stared at him with wide, frightened eyes.

"Easy, easy," he said with a reassuring smile. "You're safe now. Just lie still."

"How did you find me?" she asked. Her voice was very faint.

"Tran," he replied gently. "He told Tom and Tom called me."

"Tran," she said in a voice that was barely audible. "I didn't think he...saw me." Something in the back of her mind told her that she had misjudged the boy, and she was deeply ashamed.

"He didn't know it was you. He thought he saw *someone* out on the lantern balcony. But the minute Tom called I knew it couldn't be anyone else."

Elizabeth shuddered. She burrowed deeper into the sofa, her body curling around Matt as she brought her legs up behind him and rested her cheek on his knee. "It felt as if I was out there all night," she whispered.

"You nearly were," Matt replied tersely. "It was almost dawn when we found you."

Elizabeth looked at him, confused. "But...you said Tran told you...." Her befuddled mind was missing something. She paused uncertainly, then tried again. "If *Tran* told you, what took you so long?" She tried to struggle upright but found that she was still very weak.

"Shh, sweetheart," he cautioned, gently pressing her shoulders back into the sofa. "Don't get yourself so worked up. It didn't take us any time at all. The sheriff was there in half an hour and I beat him by ten minutes."

The terrible apprehension that had consumed him during that wild ride down the foggy mountain still showed plainly in his eyes. "You've had a tough time," he said. "But it's over now. Just rest. We can talk later."

Something was wrong, but Elizabeth couldn't determine quite what it was. She had seen Tran before dark...Matt had found her at dawn... The time frame didn't add up, but for the present she was too groggy to figure it out. She drifted back into oblivion.

Hours later she awoke and saw that night had fallen. She pushed her hair out of her eyes and looked at her watch. Ten o'clock. *What day?* She sat up shakily and glanced around the room.

In the hearth a small fire burned steadily. Matt was asleep in one of the rocking chairs, a book propped open on his knees. The floor lamp behind the chair cast a pool of light over his shoulder and onto the pages. His face looked drawn and tired, with two deep ridges carved into his forehead, and the fine lines engraved around his eyes looked more pronounced.

Elizabeth struggled to her feet, surprised at the weakness in her knees. Bending down, she kissed Matt lightly on top of his head, then made her unsteady way into the bathroom. She leaned over the sink. Her eyes were slightly swollen, with dark smudges beneath the lower lids. Her skin felt crusted with sweat.

In a few minutes a hot shower was bringing her back to life. The old pipes shuddered as the water trickled erratically. She shampooed her hair and rinsed it, luxuriating in the feel of the bubbles sliding down her body. She shampooed a second time.

There was a knock on the bathroom door, and she heard Matt's voice. "Can I come in?"

"Sure."

Through the opaque shower curtain she saw the door open. She could barely discern the indistinct shape of Matt's body as he entered, although she could make out the blurred colors of his plaid shirt and the darker blur of his jeans.

The oval of his face was turned in her direction. She knew she was nothing more than a flesh-colored shadow behind the curtain, as blurred to him as he was to her. Still, with her arms raised above her head and her hands full of shampoo, she felt his eyes watching her. It seemed as physical as a touch.

"You aren't supposed to be up," he admonished her through the curtain. "Doctor's orders."

"Didn't they teach you in medical school that when a woman looks better she feels better?" Elizabeth retorted. "Anyway, I'm finished. The hot water's gone." She turned off the water and reached for the towel she had left on the back of the toilet.

"Let me do that," Matt said. He pulled back the shower curtain and held the towel spread open in his hands. When Elizabeth stepped out of the tub, he wrapped her in the towel and began to pat her dry. She stood naked, dripping on the bath mat, while he squeezed the water out of the ends of her hair, then patted the towel over the rest of her body.

Beneath the towel his big hands caressed her breasts, lifting each one so that it plumped softly in his palms. The friction of his fingers through the rough terry cloth made her nipple tighten. He dried her smooth belly and lingered for a breathtaking moment between her legs, then moved the towel over her buttocks and hips, finally arriving back at her shoulders again.

When he finished, her skin was still damp from the humidity in the tiny bathroom. Her black hair gleamed like patent leather under the light. Matt reached for the kimono behind the door and held it while Elizabeth slipped her arms into the sleeves. Then he folded the lapels across her chest and tied the sash at her waist.

"Put on your slippers and come sit by the fireplace," he commanded. "We've just beaten hypothermia. We don't want to try for pneumonia."

While Elizabeth fluffed her damp hair in front of the fire, Matt busied himself in the kitchen. Soon he came into the living room carrying a tin beer tray on which steamed a bowl of chicken soup with crumbled crackers floating on top, and a cup of hot, sweet tea. "Soup compliments of Hannah," Matt announced. "Everyone in town's been worried about you."

Suddenly Elizabeth was ravenous, and she made quick work of the soup and crackers. When she was finished, Matt made her lie down on the sofa again and piled blankets on top of her. He sat on the edge and leaned over her, propping one elbow against the cushioned back.

"Sweetheart," he began carefully, "I hate to have to bring this up, but Tom wants you to come downtown and give him a statement as soon as you're up to it. The sooner the better, he said."

"Yes, of course." Her voice, although still weak, was firm and decisive. "I'll do everything I can."

"Do you remember anything that happened out there?"

"Not much." She frowned, trying to concentrate on any detail that might prove helpful. It all came back—the numbing cold, the paralyzing fear, the helpless vulnerability.

"I'd been out on the balcony sketching since I left you at the diner. When it started to get dark, I tried to go back inside, and . . . the door was bolted."

"You didn't hear anything? See anything?"

"No. Just Tran. There was a fishing boat, but he didn't see me. I tried to stay warm. I knew I should keep moving, but I guess I must have fallen asleep. That's all I know. Oh, Matt, what do you think is going on?"

"What Tom figures is that someone wants to persuade you to leave town. Have you been aware of anyone who's been especially unfriendly?"

"Not really. Oh, there was some hostility at first, I know, but lately everything's been fine. Or so I thought."

"Well, Tom has some theories but no clues. There must have been footprints in the lighthouse, but after he and I tracked through them, there wasn't much left. Huey did the best he could, and he dusted the door handle and the banisters for prints, but there again I'm afraid we messed up the evidence pretty badly. One thing's certain, though.

"What's that?"

"You're not staying out here by yourself anymore. Not until we get this thing cleared up."

"You won't get any argument out of me," Elizabeth said fervently. "I'll look for a place in town."

"That won't be necessary. You have to stay here to work. And I'm going to stay here with you."

"Matt, you can't! You can't be with me every minute. And what about Tran?"

"I know Tran will understand when I tell him what's happened."

"Well, as a matter of fact, I'm going to be needing a place in town, anyway."

"What do you mean?"

"Well, you know, I had a lot of time to think while I was locked out there on the gallery, and do you know what bothered me the most?"

Matt raised a quizzical eyebrow.

"That nothing I've done in my life is really... *important.* I've spent my entire professional life trying to convince people to buy things they don't want and don't need and probably can't afford, anyway. Oh, I've made a lot of money, but it's not enough. Not anymore." She hesitated, then plunged recklessly ahead. "I'm going to sell my interest in La Salle and La Salle to Jonathan. I'm going to paint."

Matt looked surprised. "You've heard from the lighthouse people then?"

"No. That vandalism set me back so far that I don't have enough work finished even to submit to them. They've agreed to extend my deadline, and I'm grateful for that, but it doesn't matter. Whether they hire me or not, I've decided that I won't be going back to Chicago. At least not for any longer than it takes to arrange for the sale of La Salle and La Salle."

Her eyes searched his face uneasily. His expression was indecipherable.

"You're not going back . . . ?" he repeated.

"Well, no," she said, watching his eyes for some clue to what he was feeling. "But that doesn't mean I'll stay in Deception Bay, of course," she added nervously. "I mean, I can go anywhere, can't I? I'll go wherever the lighthouse people send me. And if they don't give me the assignment, well, what I realize from my interest in La Salle and La Salle will keep me going for a while."

Matt had had nothing to do with her decision, of course. It had been arrived at logically and unemotionally . . . *dear, God, why didn't he say something?*

Her voice rushed on to fill the void. "It'll keep me going for *quite* a while, as a matter of fact. And I'll have a steady income while I'm getting established. Wherever I decide to go. Yes." She knew she was babbling. *Stop!* Her voice ground to a halt. "I thought you'd be pleased," she whispered.

"Pleased?" he growled, his voice suddenly rough, as though his throat were filled with gravel. "*Pleased? I* didn't know how I was going to get through the rest of my life without you. Counting the days until September has been like waiting to have a leg amputated, or an arm. I couldn't even imagine how it would be afterward. I figured I'd wait till it was over and see what was left.

"These past few nights, spending them with you, turning over in the night and finding you there...it's been the best thing that's ever happened to me. I love you, Elizabeth. I want to marry you. It's the only thing that makes any sense. But—"

He raked an agitated hand through his hair, and his eyes were filled with frustration. "I can't. I have nothing to offer you! A cabin in the woods, a secondhand cabin cruiser that's barely paid for! I can't ask you to share a life like that!"

"Didn't you hear what I just said?" Elizabeth replied. "I don't need anything. Just you."

"And I can't ask you to take on Tran," he continued as if she hadn't spoken. "He's not your responsibility." The pain in his voice was the agony of a man caught on the horns of a dilemma. "He'd turn on the both of us. And then he'd hightail it off to San Francisco. Those are his only two reactions—fight or flight. There's no in-between with him."

"Let's don't talk about Tran now," she said urgently. The boy didn't belong between herself and Matt, not ever, but most especially not at this particular moment, when passion was overtaking her body like a narcotic.

Following the line of her jaw with one forefinger, Matt allowed himself to be distracted and dropped the lightest of kisses on her cheek. "We'll work it out," he promised. "There has to be a way and we'll find it."

He looked so confident that Elizabeth chose to believe him. A wave of desire coursed through her body and washed away any last, lingering questions for which she had no answers. She reached up with both hands to cup his face, then pulled him down and kissed him fiercely. To prove her point she kissed him again.

Carrying her proof further, she coaxed his mouth open then let her tongue slip inside. He allowed her to explore, and whatever doubts he was experiencing dissolved in the hot wetness between them. Her tongue retreated and his followed, taking possession of her mouth, filling her with himself in much the same way he would take possession of her body and fill it to overflowing with himself.

The blankets were heavy and cumbersome, and Elizabeth wriggled out from under them, letting them slip unnoticed to the floor. Only her robe covered her now, and the lapels fell open, revealing a white curve of breast.

Matt slipped to one knee beside the sofa. She clasped his hands and drew them to her mouth, pressing her lips into the roughened palms, one at a time, while the tip of her tongue traced the lines.

They had once been the hands of a physician, she mused—smoother and whiter, manicured perhaps, and sure and skilled and capable. Now they were working hands, hard and brown and callused, but every bit as sure and every bit as competent. Her lips caressed each finger, and her eyes met his over the knotted knuckles.

He dropped another kiss on the corner of her mouth, then moved to cover it completely.

The kiss was just a beginning, she knew. In a moment his mouth would fall to the curve of her exposed breast, and he would trail covetous lips across the fullness of the flesh to the swollen nipple, and take it between his teeth in a gentle, soothing bite. His hand would skim the line of her hip and glide beneath the robe, probing to where her feminine core waited in an agony of pleasure for his touch. Elizabeth's eyes fluttered closed.

In the next second they snapped open. She stiffened in Matt's arms. "Matt!" she gasped, struggling to push herself upright. "Someone's out there!"

He leaped to his feet. Before she could utter another word he was out the door. She heard his footsteps pounding on the wooden porch, then she heard a loud thud and the sound of scuffling in the grass. A few unintelligible exclamations followed, and then silence.

It all happened so fast that Elizabeth hardly had time to grasp what was going on. She had seen a face at the window, not clearly, just the fleeing impression of eyes peering in through the dark.

Odd eyes, narrow. Pointed. The image that flashed across her mind was that of a fox. She rose from the sofa, tightening the robe around her body and jerking the sash into a knot. With her heart in her throat she stared at the open door.

I'll count to five, she thought, *and if Matt isn't back in here by the time I finish, I'll call the sheriff.* One. She stood rooted to the spot. Two. Beyond the porch the dark looked black and forbidding. Three. Noises like the frenzied grunts of animals in combat made her clap her hands to her ears. Four. Footsteps on the porch—heavy and plodding, accompanied by unidentifiable scuffling sounds. Five.

Matt appeared in the doorway. His shirt was torn and smeared with grass stains. The knees of his jeans were also stained. By his side, held there by Matt's hand on the scruff of his neck, was Tran. He twisted furiously this way and that in a futile attempt to free himself.

Matt dragged him through the doorway and kicked the door shut behind them. He shook the boy until his bones rattled. Elizabeth's eyes traveled from Tran to Matt and then back to Tran again, who now stared sullenly at the floor as he hung from Matt's hand as limp as a rag doll.

Matt's grip on the back of Tran's neck tightened, and he yanked the boy around to face him. "Are you responsible for what's been happening around here?"

"Yeah," Tran snarled defiantly.

"Tran," Elizabeth whispered. "Why?"

"No one wanted you to come here, not even my father. But you came, anyway, and you changed everything."

"I don't understand, Tran. What did I change?"

"Everything," the boy muttered, then fixed his eyes once more on the floor and wouldn't speak again.

"Go home, Tran," Matt ordered in a voice filled with barely concealed rage. "Go home and wait for me there. You've got a lot of explaining to do."

When he felt Matt's grasp loosen, Tran jerked himself free and scuttled to the door. At the doorway he paused and looked straight at Elizabeth, just as he had the night before when she stood, trapped, on the lantern gallery. At closer proximity she realized with a shock that his face held, not anger, not hate, but a bone-chilling fear. Then he turned and disappeared into the night.

Matt walked over to the door and shut it. He turned toward Elizabeth. His downcast eyes refused to meet hers. Indeed, his whole demeanor signaled defeat. Crossing to the fireplace, he propped the heels of his hands on the mantel and hung his head, gazing down at the fire in the hearth as if he hoped to read in its flames an answer to his problem.

"He could have killed you," he said dully, eyes still fixed on the fire.

"But he didn't," Elizabeth pointed out sensibly. She wanted to go to him, to wrap her arms around him and assure him that everything would be all right. But she couldn't. She realized there was no way she could possibly make this situation any better.

The silence in the room was amplified by a myriad of insignificant sounds—the crackling of the fire, the wind beneath the eaves, a howling in the distance that could have been a dog or a coyote, the rustling of silk as Elizabeth, suddenly chilled, wrapped her robe more tightly around herself and reknotted the sash.

"I'm sorry, Elizabeth. I don't know what to say to you. I don't know what to do with him." He sighed, a deep ragged expulsion of air that demonstrated his feelings of total inadequacy. "I'm just about at the end of my rope. I thought the worst was behind us, but it looks like it's starting all over again."

He let his hands fall from the mantel and thrust them into his pockets, and Elizabeth could see that they were balled impotently into fists. His shoulders slumped dejectedly. He looked old. "I'd thought...well, I'd *hoped* that things might be different between the two of you, but I can see he's never going to let that happen."

"Maybe it's just me," Elizabeth said carefully. "He doesn't like me, you know."

"It's not really you. His first reaction to any new situation is to run, and if that doesn't work, he'll turn and fight with all the savagery of a mad dog. That's the only thing he knows. It's what's gotten him this far. I'm afraid he's going to spend all his life never being able to trust anyone. And that's no kind of life at all."

"Surely he trusts you, Matt."

He shook his head. "Only to a point. I feel as though he's testing me, always testing me, to see how far he can go. Or maybe to see how far I'll *let* him go. And most of the time I can't tell whether I've passed or failed."

"I'm not sure I understand what you mean."

"A lot of things. Like school. He told me last week that he isn't going back in the fall—says he wants to work on the boat full-time. I figured I might as well go along with him—he wasn't attending classes, anyway. But what did he *really* want from me? Freedom? Or limits? I can't tell. I can't make him see that school is what he should be doing now, that it'll pay off in the long run."

His mouth twisted ruefully. "How can you blame a kid like Tran for not trusting in 'the long run'?"

"But he works for you, doesn't he?" Elizabeth interrupted. "Surely you can just refuse to let him help out on the boats unless he does his schoolwork."

"He works for me. And for Jory. And he sweeps up at the drugstore, nights. There's also the fish stand. And then he has a contract with a fish market in Portland to run fresh salmon up there twice a week. That's where he was going the night he almost ran you down. I told him not to go. I told him the weather was too bad...."

"What does he do with all that money?" Elizabeth asked. A terrible suspicion crept up on her—drugs. What else could possibly drive a person like that? That would explain his surly manner, his reputation as a loner, his furtive skulking around town in that ratty, oversized army jacket....

Matt looked at her bleakly, shoving his clenched hands deeper into his pockets. "He wants to get his mother out of Vietnam."

"*What?*" Elizabeth asked. Her expression registered total bewilderment. "But I thought you said no one knows who his mother is."

"No one does. But he's convinced himself that she's alive. Somewhere. And he wants to go back and find her and bring her out."

"Oh, no," Elizabeth breathed.

"Yeah, I know. It's some fantasy that kept him going all those years when he was knocked around half of Southeast Asia."

Matt paced in front of the fireplace with long, deliberate strides. Back and forth, back and forth. There seemed to be an anger building up in him that he was scarcely able to contain.

He paced the length of the hearth once more and then swiveled around ferociously, and blazing in his face Elizabeth saw all the wrath, all the fury, all the indignation that he had banked inside himself for fifteen long years.

She hardly recognized in this stranger's face the kind and gentle man she had loved enough to take inside her. *And I thought he was incapable of anger!* she thought incredulously.

"All I know is that I can't give up on him," Matt exclaimed in a voice that struggled to break loose into a savage, primal roar. "I *can't . . . let . . . him . . . lose!*"

Each word was punctuated by the violent pounding of one fist into the palm of the other hand. "If he loses—if I *let* him lose—then what was that whole ugly, stinking war all about? If *he* loses, we all lose. You understand, don't you? You see why I can't just give up?"

"I understand," she said. But she didn't. Not entirely. It had all happened too fast. There was only one coherent thought in her mind: that Matt had been wrong, that there was no way they could ever work this out. The thing was impossible. It had been from the start.

Fool! she cried inwardly. The word provided a harsh counterpoint to the sound of the breaking of her heart. *Fool!*

Affecting a calmness she didn't feel, she walked into the kitchen and poured herself a cup of the lukewarm tea that was left in the china pot. She held the cup in both hands and sipped slowly, lowering her eyes to gaze into the cup as if she were trying to read the tea leaves. *I'm stalling,* she realized abruptly, and forced herself to meet Matt's eyes.

"Maybe you'd better go to him now," she suggested gently.

"Yeah, I guess I'd better." His shoulders sagged as if all the air had been let out of his chest. He wiped one hand across his face and released a ragged breath with a short, explosive sigh. After a moment, he straightened, then crossed to where Elizabeth stood beside the kitchen counter and took the cup away from her. "I love you," he said, clasping her hands tightly between his.

"I love you, too," she replied with the same fragile gentleness. She disengaged her hands and moved them up to touch his face.

The crisp, springy texture of his beard was achingly familiar to her touch. The ache traveled from her fingers to her throat, which tightened, trapping a sob. Her face cramped into a counterfeit smile that made the corners of her mouth hurt.

She felt as though she were looking at him from some great distance. She felt—the thought astonished her!— almost as though she were saying goodbye.

She let her hands fall heavily to her sides.

"I don't know when I'll be back," Matt said, "but it'll be as soon as I can."

"Just do what you have to do, Matt. I'll be here when you're finished."

Giving her a smile that devastated her with its gratitude, Matt turned and hurried out the door. It closed behind him with dull finality.

Elizabeth poked up the fire and then sank down in the rocking chair, pulling the old quilt around her knees. She moved very slowly and deliberately, as if something in her would break if she made any sudden moves.

How could she have allowed herself to fall in love with Matt? How could she have imagined they could ever have any kind of future with this damaged bit of humanity, this sad relic from someone else's war, always between them? The thought that this sullen manchild—this almost-man—could be a force to be reckoned with in her life appalled her.

Babies, yes. Children, of course. But *this!* The timing was all wrong, for one thing. The boy hated her, for another. Matt had said it himself—*he could have killed her!* And she...well, she had tried her best to win him over, and he had spurned her overtures again and again. His whole life had been a tragedy, but what could she do? What more was expected of her?

Slowly she rocked back and forth, feeling as brittle as ice and every bit as cold.

CHAPTER NINETEEN

ALTHOUGH SHE wasn't asleep, Elizabeth's mind was wandering far from its moorings, and the shrilling of the telephone brought her back to reality. *Wandering from its moorings.* Matt's phrase. It meant unanchored, drifting, lost. It also meant daydreaming. Both definitions applied to what she'd been doing for the past several hours while the fire slowly died and a damp chill settled over the cottage.

The irritating ring jolted her again. She let the afghan slide from her knees as she got up to answer the telephone.

"Elizabeth, it's me," Matt said, as if she wouldn't recognize his voice even in her sleep. "I'm sorry, but it looks as if I'm going to be delayed."

His voice was exceptionally quiet, which immediately told Elizabeth that something was wrong. "What is it, Matt?"

"Well, it's Tran." He paused. "As a matter of fact, he's run away. I've got the sheriffs from two counties out looking for him, but no luck so far."

"Matt, let me come," she said impulsively. "I'll wait with you."

"I'd like that."

WHY AM I DOING THIS? she asked herself more than once during the thirty-minute drive. Lights from occasional

oncoming traffic glared in the windshield, then shot past
and disappeared behind her.

The misery in Matt's voice had pained her. *Tran's
probably halfway to San Francisco by now,* she thought
as she veered off the highway onto the deserted
Greensprings Road. *Or Portland, or wherever it is he's
decided to go this time.*

Gravel pelted the underside of the station wagon. It
sounded like rain. *It's not my problem,* she argued with
herself as the small stones crunched beneath her tires. *I'm
not involved. I'm just going to wait with Matt, help him
through this thing, that's all. He needs me, and when this
particular crisis is over... what? What?* She pressed
harder on the gas pedal, and the gravel flew.

The split-log exterior of the cabin was invisible at night
through the trees, but it would have been hard to miss in
any case—all the windows were ablaze with lights, and
several squad cars were parked haphazardly in the front
yard. Their doors hung wide open, and the voice of a
dispatcher bleated periodically over the radios, splitting
the quiet forest with static. Flashing lights made mania-
cal patterns of red and blue on the trees.

Elizabeth pulled her station wagon to a halt behind the
squad cars and walked past them to the front steps. Unnoticed, she entered the house. Tran's army jacket hung
from a hook in the hallway. Directly in front of her was
the kitchen, and framed in the lighted doorway sat Matt.
He was slumped over the table. His head was propped on
one hand and his ubiquitous coffee mug was clutched
precariously in the other.

His big yellow dog sprawled under his chair. The dog's
tail thumped once or twice to acknowledge the arrival of
a newcomer, but he seemed to lack the heart for a more
enthusiastic greeting. With nose between his paws and

tongue lolling on the floor, he looked as disconsolate as his master.

Voices drifted from the kitchen as Elizabeth drew closer—one blustering and pompous that she knew to be the sheriff's, the other a dull monotone. Matt.

Halfway down the hall, she hesitated. Something elusive lurked in her memory, just beyond her ability to recall. Where had she heard these voices together before? They sounded familiar—the sheriff's loud, and Matt's...? But, no, Matt's had been different the last time....

Huey, the sheriff's nervous deputy, walked past the lighted doorway, muttering something unintelligible into a walkie-talkie. "Get out of my way," she heard the sheriff growl as the hapless deputy stumbled over a crack in the linoleum, almost dropping his walkie-talkie in the process.

In a flash it came to her. The lighthouse! Of course! That was where she had heard these voices together before—the sheriff's loud and bombastic, and Matt shouting words she wouldn't have guessed he even knew as he held her in strong, warm arms and hurtled into the spiraling darkness.

And in the same instant she knew without a shadow of a doubt where Tran had gone. She stopped and grabbed his jacket from the hook on the wall, then retraced her steps and slipped quietly out the door.

THE PATH LEADING DOWN to the beach was steep, and dark on this moonless night. Even with her flashlight Elizabeth kept stumbling over the uneven terrain. She picked her way carefully among the flotsam washed up by the tide—seaweed, driftwood, an occasional plastic bottle—until she came to the spot where she had seen Tran drop from sight the night before.

Her flashlight beam shone across the basalt wall and its honeycomb of caves. Some were no more than shallow dimples on the surface, while others tunneled deep into the rock.

For a moment Elizabeth was dismayed. She knew Tran had to be here somewhere, but how would she ever find him? There was no use in calling his name; it was unlikely he would answer. Moving the beam of light up and down in a gridlike pattern, she methodically began to inspect the cliff.

Suddenly she heard a noise—not even a noise, just the suggestion of a sound, really, above the pounding surf—and then she heard it again. She turned her flashlight in the direction of the noise with the accuracy of a homing beacon. Sure enough, the beam reflected off the metal handlebars of a bicycle propped against an outcropping of rock.

As she moved closer, the beam of her flashlight revealed the entrance to a cave. Elizabeth crept forward and shone the flashlight inside. The interior was dark and shadowy, but the flashlight illuminated jagged, damp walls and a packed sand floor. It also illuminated two large oil paintings leaning against one of the walls—the canvases that had been stolen from her cottage the night of the vandalism.

And at the back of the cave, sitting on the hard ground, it illuminated Tran. His knees were drawn beneath his chin and his arms were wrapped around his legs. His face was buried in his hands. She aimed the flashlight directly at him.

"Tran?" she said cautiously. He didn't look up. She stooped and crawled through the entrance of the cave.

"Tran?" she said again. When he still didn't answer she crouched and forced herself to move through the shadows to the back of the cave. He was crying as if his heart were breaking. The noises she had heard, she realized, were the sound of his muffled sobs.

She looked down at him uncertainly. His narrow shoulders were shaking. The sound of his desolate weeping echoed hollowly through the cave. Not sure what else to do, she crouched lower and sat beside him on the cold ground. Tentatively she draped the jacket over his shivering body.

When his sobs showed no sign of slowing down, she put a hesitant hand on his trembling back. His shoulder blades felt like the fragile bones of a bird.

She patted his shoulder awkwardly. How small he was. How thin! She patted him again. Then, somehow not so awkwardly anymore, she wrapped one arm around his trembling shoulders. Suddenly, in a way she could neither understand nor explain, his face was buried in her lap.

Harsh, ugly sobs racked his slight body, and in a broken voice interspersed with sobs, he poured out all the anger, all the bitterness, all the horror, all the fear of his short life.

Elizabeth heard only half of what he said and understood even less, but it was enough to make her whole body recoil with revulsion—life on the razor's edge in the streets of Saigon, the cruelty of the refugee camps, the indifferent brutality, the starvation, the abuse. The images his words evoked made her want to turn away in horror, but instead she hugged him tighter. Something only partly understood within herself made her realize that, if he had had the courage to live it, she must at least have the courage to listen.

She put both arms around Tran and rested her cheek on his hair, instinctively rocking him back and forth the way Matt had rocked her on the *Chinook Wind* the day of the storm. Her tears mingled with his. Maybe he had never been held like this before, she speculated, overwhelmed with pity that cut through her soul like a knife. Never rocked. He was a tough nut, Matt had said, and she realized from the torrential outpouring of tears that it was possible Tran had never even cried before.

"And so I tried to make you go away," he concluded in his slightly halting English as his sobs subsided to hiccups. "When I saw you go up in the lighthouse that first time, I snuck in and took your flashlight. I broke into your house to scare you. And then I followed you to the lighthouse yesterday and locked you out on the gallery. But I became afraid you might die, so I called the sheriff. Nobody wanted you here," he hiccuped. "Things would change if you stayed. Everyone said so. You would bring more people, and Deception Bay wouldn't be nice anymore. And everything *did* change. I could see."

"What changed, Tran?" Elizabeth asked gently.

"My father changed, not like the way he was before you came—always so quiet. And he didn't want to fish anymore. He wanted to spend all the time with you. Drawing *pictures!*" He tried to snarl the word like an epithet, but it came out more of a sob. "You made him more happy than me, and I was afraid he was going to send me back to Dong Khoi Camp, where I am *bui doi*, the dust of the street."

Everything Tran said made perfect sense. He was just trying to survive. He thought he was losing Matt's love, and he fought for it in the only way he knew how. How could he be blamed for trying to hold on to the only safe harbor he had known in his short life?

"Now my father hates me. Everyone hates me." He sobbed again. "I do not belong here. I am only *bui doi*."

"Your father doesn't hate you, Tran," Elizabeth said with quiet assurance. "He's terribly worried about you. And I think we'd better be getting back to let him know you're all right."

She felt him withdraw. "No," he insisted adamantly. "They will put me in jail. Or send me back to Dong Khoi Camp." He shuddered involuntarily. "If I go back to Dong Khoi Camp, I die," he added in a voice of absolute certainty.

"Tran, listen to me. No one hates you. I'm not mad at you, and if I'm not, why should anyone else be? Your father will understand. I promise you."

"That day on the boat... the day I threw the water on you..." Tran faltered. "You said you wanted to be my friend."

She heard doubt and hope struggling in his voice as he clutched at the only straw available to him. "I *am* your friend, Tran," she said firmly.

"Will you tell my father that...you aren't mad at me? He'll listen to you."

Elizabeth blinked away tears in the dark. "Of course I will."

As she picked up the flashlight, its beam fell on the paintings leaning against the far wall. "Tran," she said curiously, "why did you bring these paintings here? Why didn't you destroy them with the others?" Elizabeth couldn't see his face in the darkness, but she felt a tremor pass through his thin body. "Don't be afraid, Tran. I'm not mad. I would like to know, that's all."

"I was going to cut them," he admitted in a frightened voice. "Like the rest. But I couldn't—not after I knew you saw the ghosts."

"The ghosts? What do you mean?"

Instead of replying, Tran scrambled to his feet and walked to the spot where the canvases were propped against the rough wall. Mystified, Elizabeth followed.

"There," he said, pointing. "And there."

She directed her flashlight at each canvas in turn as he pointed. Her forehead furrowed as she studied them, and suddenly she felt her breath catch in her throat. A chill ran up her spine, and it had nothing to do with the dampness in the cave.

The first was a painting of Deception Head Lighthouse with a storm coming on. The surf churned, throwing itself madly against the rocky headland, and the foaming surf *did* coil back on itself and suggest, ever so slightly, the shape of a broad-beamed surfboat. In the stern was a curl of spume that could conceivably resemble the body of a man—a headless man.

The wandering ghost of Evan McClure. Elizabeth's eyes widened.

The other canvas was of Heceta Head Lighthouse. There was a sunbeam slanting across the highway behind the tower, but now that Elizabeth looked at it again, the shaft of light almost took the form of a woman, old and plump and footless, dressed in turn-of-the-century clothes and floating a few feet off the ground between the lighthouse and the caretaker's quarters.

Old Rue, searching in vain for her lost child.

Elizabeth shivered. In the glare of the flashlight Tran's eyes were fixed solemnly on her.

I don't believe in ghosts, she started to say, but something stopped her. She hadn't seen ghosts in the paintings before, that was certain, but Tran had, and looking through his eyes, suddenly she could see them, too.

Maybe that's all ghosts are, she thought, *just a differ ent perspective, a new way of looking at old, familia things.* She was seeing her paintings in a whole new light and then it dawned on her that she was seeing man things in a whole new light.

Tran, for one. Behind his sullen facade she suddenl glimpsed a child who had never had a childhood, a bo whose desperate survival skills weren't valid in the worl in which he now found himself, a bitter survivor clingin to life because it was intrinsically precious, but not be cause he, himself, had ever seen any proof of that pre ciousness.

Possibly it was too late for him, Elizabeth thought Possibly his hard outer shell might be so tough that n one would ever be able to breach it, but suddenly sh understood why Matt had to try.

She thought about Tran's mother and the intolerabl gamble she had had to take. She had chosen life for he son, and she had passed her courage on to him, becaus he had obviously opted for life, too, every time he ha been faced with the choice.

A face floated before Elizabeth's eyes, indistinct an featureless, not much more than a blurred female ve sion of Tran's. Another ghost, of a sort. And in her ow mind she was aware of a dimly articulated sense of si terhood with the unknown woman who had been h mother.

She dropped her arm around Tran's shoulders. "Com on," she said gently. "Let's go home."

THE POLICE CARS were gone when Elizabeth pulled int the yard, but the house was still blazing with lights. Th front door stood wide open, admitting a steady draft c cold night air into the house. Beneath her hand Eliza beth could feel Tran quaking as they mounted the stairs and slipped inside.

Matt was slumped at the table. He didn't appear to have moved since she'd left. His elbows were folded across his chest, and his chin was buried in the collar of his woolen shirt. Smoke spiraled upward from the cigarette that he held immobile between two fingers. A large ashtray on the table was overflowing with cigarette butts, and as Elizabeth led Tran toward the kitchen, Matt reached over and stubbed out another one.

He hadn't heard the car pull up. He hadn't heard footsteps in the hall. So when the yellow dog beneath his chair began to whine deep in his throat, Matt just reached down with one hand and scratched his ear. "Good fella," he said automatically.

The dog's tail began to thump, then he hauled himself to his feet and trotted over to where Tran and Elizabeth stood in the doorway.

"Hi ya, Beau. How're ya doin', big guy?" Tran said softly. The dog nosed him happily, and Tran dropped to one knee, cuffing the big yellow head between his hands. Stalling, Elizabeth thought, instinctively recognizing the ruse from her own behavioral repertoire.

"Tran!" Matt leaped to his feet, and the chair on which he had been sitting keeled over with a thud.

Tran looked up with a guarded expression on his face. He released his hold on the dog's neck and stood, hanging his head guiltily.

"Where have you been? Do you know I have half the state out looking for you?" He gripped Tran's shoulders and held him out at arm's length, scowling at him, then dragged him forward in a savage embrace. "Do you have any idea how many threats I had to make to get them even to *look* for you this time?"

He held Tran at arm's length again, glaring at him with fierce and furious eyes, and shook him so roughly that the boy winced. Tran jerked away, his face as ambiguous as Matt's as he threw himself through a door that opened off the kitchen and slammed it behind him.

"Matt..."

"I'm sorry, Elizabeth." Matt righted the overturned chair and fell heavily into it. "I don't know what gets into me where that kid is concerned...." He propped his elbows on the table and dropped his head into his hands, gingerly massaging his tired, bloodshot eyes with the heels of his palms. Everything about his body language screamed frustration and defeat.

"You love him," Elizabeth said simply.

"A lot of good it's doing either one of us," he muttered.

"He loves you, too."

Matt looked at her incredulously. "Is *that* what you call it?"

"He doesn't know how to show it, Matt. He's never seen it in his whole life, and he doesn't recognize it now. He tried to drive me away because he thought I was taking you away from him. He's afraid you're going to send him back to the refugee camp."

"*What?*"

"He thinks the whole thing—you, this town, everything—is going to be snatched away from him at any moment, and he's not going to let himself care. He's afraid to let himself be happy."

She crossed the few feet of flooring between herself and Matt and stopped directly in front of him. "He's a little like his father that way."

Matt looked dubious. "How do you know so much about Tran?" he demanded.

"He told me," Elizabeth said simply. "I guess he finally had to tell *someone,* and I was there."

For the space of a heartbeat Matt's drawn face and weary eyes still looked doubtful. Elizabeth took his face between her hands and lifted it up so that he had to meet her eyes. "Have you ever actually said—come right out and *told* him—that you love him?"

Slowly and ponderously Matt pushed himself to his feet. He walked to the door Tran had slammed shut, hit it abruptly with the back of his hand and then pushed it open.

The open doorway framed Tran sitting cross-legged on the bed. He was counting his money. From where she stood in the kitchen Elizabeth could see piles of greenbacks, obviously arranged according to denomination— a large stack of singles, smaller stacks of fives, ten, twenties, and fifties. There were even a couple of one-hundred-dollar bills.

Tran looked up warily as Matt entered, and kept dealing dollars onto the stacks from the thick wad of bills he held in his hands.

"Put the money down, Tran," Matt said quietly.

Tran stared at him insolently.

"Put the money down," Matt repeated. "I want to talk to you."

Tran threw the wad onto the bedspread and stood, slouching on one hip as he eyed Matt defiantly. Because it was obvious that he wasn't going to take a step in Matt's direction, Matt went to him instead. He propped his big hands on Tran's narrow shoulders and bent down to his level, looking him straight in the eye.

"Listen to me, Tran," he said, and his voice was very firm. "I will never send you back. Never. Do you hear me? Never."

The boy lowered his eyes, staring sullenly at the floor.

"There is nothing in this world you could do that would make me send you back. Do you understand what I'm saying? Nothing!" His voice fell brokenly. "I love you, Tran."

For a long moment Tran's body was stiff, and Elizabeth was afraid he wasn't going to respond. Then, through the veil of tears that misted her eyes, she saw his hands move. They inched hesitantly upward, paused for a moment suspended in space, and then slowly, uncertainly, wrapped themselves around Matt in an awkward embrace.

Matt pulled him into a fierce hug. He put his cheek against the boy's head and squeezed his eyes shut, and after a moment Elizabeth saw tears falling into Tran's russet hair. "I love you, son," he whispered hoarsely.

CHAPTER TWENTY

THE NEXT MORNING, curled up on a rocking chair on the porch, Elizabeth waited for Matt to come. It was another gray morning, but the wind swept sharply across the headland, and she knew it would blow the clouds away by noon.

She had just started on her second cup of coffee when Matt's old blue truck pulled into the yard. Tran was with him. Smiling, she ran down into the yard to greet them.

A chastened Tran dragged his baseball cap off his head and shoved it into his back pocket. He looked very humble. Clasping his hands together, fingers spread wide in the traditional Asian kowtow, he bowed his head in several quick nods.

"My father told me to find out what you need done," he mumbled, keeping his eyes lowered. Beside him Matt's big hand rested reassuringly on the boy's thin shoulder.

Elizabeth considered his request thoughtfully. "Well, I do have some chores around here. The grass...um, it should be cut, I think. Yes, and my car could certainly do with a wash. Is that enough?"

"I will do it every week," Tran promised.

"I think I've seen an old hand mower out back in the shed," Elizabeth told him.

He bowed his head again. "My father also says— please tell me the cost of the damage I did, so I can repay you."

"Oh, no, Tran, that won't be necessary."

"It *is* necessary," he asserted solemnly, his head bobbing like a jack-in-the-box. His glance shifted obliquely toward Matt, and Matt smiled his approval.

"Good job, pardner," he said under his breath. "Go to it."

Tran sagged visibly with relief. He pulled his baseball cap out of his pocket and settled it firmly back on his head. Then he turned and took the porch steps two at a time.

When he disappeared around the corner, Matt and Elizabeth put their arms around each other and strolled leisurely into the house.

"I telephoned Jonathan this morning. I told him I wanted him to buy me out."

"And?"

She smiled at the memory of Jonathan's outraged sputterings. "Well, at first he thought I was just getting even with him for trying to make me come back. Then he decided I was trying to force him to renegotiate our partnership agreement. 'Hold him up' was the way he put it. Finally he realized I meant it, and he was livid. Threatened to sue me for breach of contract and a few other things."

"Will he do that?"

"I don't know. I don't care. When I offered to take payments instead of a lump sum, he calmed down a bit. He said he'd get the attorney on it right away."

At the top of the steps Matt stopped and looked down at her with questioning eyes. "You're sure you really want to do this? You aren't afraid you'll regret it later?"

Elizabeth laughed gaily. "I haven't been so sure of anything in my entire life! Regret it? I've never felt so free!"

They were standing just inside the door. Matt turned and shut it behind them. He threw the dead bolt with one decisive twist of his fingers, then leaned against the door and pulled Elizabeth close. "I don't know how to thank you..." he began.

"What on earth for?"

"For being what you are. For loving me. For giving me back my son." He reached down and cupped her face in both his hands, tilting it up so that he looked directly into her eyes. "And something else," he said. His eyes searched hers for a long moment. "I've decided to go back to medicine."

Anticipating her reaction, his arms were ready to catch her when she jumped up and threw herself happily into them. He chuckled as he wrapped them around her waist and clasped her tightly.

"Oh, Matt," she cried into his neck, "I'm so happy for you!"

"You were right, you know," he confessed into her ear as his big arms held her suspended a foot off the floor. "What you said up at Will's that night—giving it up *was* the harder choice. Now all of sudden I feel like a whole person again, for the first time in nearly fifteen years."

He set her back down on the floor and smoothed her tousled hair away from her face. "When you were so willing to start all over again," he said quietly, "I realized I couldn't do any less. You not only gave me back my son—you gave me back my life. And now the only way I want to live it is with you."

He paused for a moment, framing the words with solemnity. "Will you marry me, Elizabeth?"

She drank in his rugged face, his calm eyes, his slight down-turned smile. A great feeling of humility and gratitude washed over her. How often was someone offered

a second chance at love and at life? She told herself tha
if she was very, very lucky, Matt would never, ever have
to know about the hours she had spent rocking in fron
of the dying fire last night, desperately seeking a way out
In her heart she determined, right there and then, to de
vote the rest of her life to making sure he never even sus
pected.

"Yes, Matthew McCullough. Yes, I'll marry you."

Matt's eyes darkened provocatively. Somewhere in the
vicinity of her stomach the secret muscle coiled with
piercing sweetness.

He slipped one arm under her knees and swept her up
into his arms. "Let me love you? Now?" But it wasn'
really a question.

"But Tran...?"

"He'll be out there for hours." Matt's voice was gruff
"Kid won't stop till he's through." He carried her into the
bedroom and kicked the door shut behind them.

The room was dim, with ashen sunlight filtering
through the drawn window shade. Matt carried Eliza
beth across the room to the bed, where he let her legs slide
to the floor.

Keeping his mouth fastened to hers, he began to un
button the red cable-knit cardigan that she wore. His
fingers were slow and unhurried, becoming only a little
more urgent when they reached for the top of her jeans
Deftly he unzipped them and pulled them off.

At the same time Elizabeth went to work on his shirt
When it was unbuttoned, she untucked it from his jeans
and pushed it free, then caught his T-shirt in her hands
and pulled it over his head. The first contact of her sen
sitized breasts against his chest made her back arch with
the need to get closer.

He began to push her down onto the bed.

"No, wait," she said huskily. "I want to undress you, too." She turned him around so that the backs of his knees were pressed against the edge of the bed. Then she made him sit down and pushed him so that he was lying flat on his back. Kneeling, she pulled off his boots and the crew socks that he wore with them.

Her hands slid along his bare feet planted wide apart on the floor. They were softer than his work-roughened hands, she marveled. Then she loosened his jeans and tugged them and his briefs out from under him. Stripping them down his legs, she tossed them out of the way.

She looked up at the great, jutting thrust of him. Moving forward, she brushed hungry, teasing lips on the inside of his knees. She moved farther forward, kissing his inner thighs, then closer still and heard his involuntary groans of pleasure. It was a gift, she thought, a gift for everything he had given her. And she knew it was the sweetest debt she'd ever have to pay.

His whole body was as taut as a bow, and his fingers clenched in her hair. His breathing was rapid and shallow. "I can't take much more of that," he warned hoarsely, so she slid up his body and lowered herself onto him.

Her cries blended with his as she felt him all the way up. Halfway off the bed and half on, he supported them both on his powerful legs, and the climax, when it came, awed them both with its intensity.

'I FIGURE it's going to take a year of Continuing Medical Education for me to reactivate my license," Matt said later.

They were sitting at the kitchen table, drinking Matt's thick black coffee. He had made it while she was dress-

ing, and not even in Elizabeth's percolator could he bre
it any way but strong.

The curtains fluttered at the open window like gauz
blue flags. The wind had swept away the clouds, and th
sun glinted off the tip of Deception Head Light like ne
brass.

"I thought maybe I'd get an apartment in Portlan
while I go to the State Sciences Institute. We could ge
married next summer and—"

"I wouldn't want to wait that long," Elizabeth de
murred quietly.

"It's going to be a pretty grueling year. I won't hav
much free time. That's no way to begin a marriage."

"What are you going to do about Tran while you're i
school?" she interrupted. "He'll never be happy in a
apartment in Portland. You know that."

"Well, I haven't thought the whole thing through ye
My entire family lives up there. I think one of them migl
be willing to add him to their brood for a little while."

"But he's not really a kid, is he? Not after the life he
lived. You said so yourself. How do you think he'll mai
age, being treated like one at this point?"

Matt shook his head, "He's not the most flexible pe
son in the world, that's true."

"It sounds as though he's just barely gotten adjuste
to Deception Bay. He feels that he belongs someplace fe
the first time in his life. If you move him now and the
move him again a year from now, he may never put dow
any roots."

"I don't see what else I can do," Matt began, then h
caught the twinkle in her eye. "Unless, by any chanc
you have an alternative in mind?"

"As a matter of fact I do." She reached across the ta
ble and took his hand. The words rushed out almost d

their own volition. She didn't know where they were coming from, but they made perfect sense.

"I want to marry you. Now. And I want to make a home for us—for all three of us—in your cabin. I could paint. Tran could fish. Maybe we could convince him to go back to school. And you ... you could come home on the weekends." She smiled, both persuasion and promise evident in the clear gray depths of her eyes. "After all, you can't study every minute."

Matt pulled back the fluttering curtain. "Tran!" he bellowed over the sudden catch in his voice. "Tran, come in here!"

Elizabeth looked past his shoulder through the open window. Tran's head appeared over the slope of the bluff. Matt's son. *Her* son. The small blond figment of her imagination faded forever, replaced by the reality of a thin, silent, russet-haired boy who needed her.

Tran dropped the handle of the lawn mower and loped across the yard. He stomped his feet on the porch to shake off the grass and sand, then came inside. "What?" he asked unceremoniously.

Matt dropped a hand on his shoulder. "Tran, I've asked Elizabeth to marry me...."

Tran's eyes instantly became wary. "So?" he asked with a look that implied it was no concern of his.

"And she said yes."

Tran looked from one to the other. His face was impassive. "So?" he asked again in a surly voice.

It wasn't going to be easy, Elizabeth thought as she studied his reaction. Maybe it would never get any easier. But it was going to be done. She was going to do everything in her power to make sure that this one boy, this one child at least, didn't lose. For Tran's sake, and Matt's, and for her own; and also for the sense of allegiance she felt toward the unknown, long-dead sister who had been his mother.

"I'd like to be your mother, Tran," she said.

As he digested this bit of information, the machinations of his mind showed plainly in Tran's face. Doubt. Suspicion. Distrust. And at last the barest glimmer of hope.

"But... I already have a mother," he said haltingly.

"I know that, Tran. And she must have been a very brave woman. She must have loved you very much. I would never try to take her place."

Conflicting loyalties struggled in his face. "But... then... what should I call you?" he asked finally.

Elizabeth looked thoughtful for a moment, then inspiration dawned. She smiled. "Why don't you call me... Lizzie?"

The wind was high. The sea off Deception Head was turbulent as always, the breakers crashing against the headland in their eternal, immutable pattern.

Matt's arm was around Elizabeth's shoulders, strong and supportive. His calm green eyes shone downward, encompassing both Tran and herself. She could feel his warmth beside her, a fact of life as immutable as the sea and the rocky headland, and the old lighthouse that overlooked them both.

She reached out for Tran and drew him into the charmed circle of their embrace.

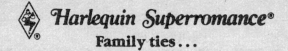

Harlequin Superromance®
Family ties...

SEVENTH HEAVEN
In the introduction to the Osborne family trilogy,
Kate Osborne finds her destiny with Police
Commissioner Donovan Cade.

Available in December

ON CLOUD NINE
Juliet Osborne's old-fashioned values are tested when
she meets jazz musician Ross Stafford, the object of
her younger sister's affections. Can Juliet only achieve
her heart's desire at the cost of her integrity?

Available in January

SWINGING ON A STAR
Meridee is Kate's oldest daughter, but very much her
own person. Determined to climb the corporate
ladder, she has never had time for love. But her life is
turned upside down when Zeb Farrell storms into
town determined to eliminate jobs in her company—
her sister's among them! Meridee is prepared to do
battle, but for once she's met her match.

Available in February

HARLEQUIN
PROUDLY PRESENTS
A DAZZLING NEW CONCEPT IN ROMANCE FICTION

One small town—twelve terrific love stories

Welcome to Tyler, Wisconsin—a town full of people
you'll enjoy getting to know, memorable friends and
unforgettable lovers, and a long-buried secret that
lurks beneath its serene surface....

JOIN US FOR A YEAR IN THE LIFE OF
TYLER

Each book set in Tyler is a self-contained love story;
together, the twelve novels stitch the fabric of a
community.

LOSE YOUR HEART TO TYLER!

The excitement begins in March 1992, with
WHIRLWIND, by Nancy Martin. When lively, brash
Liza Baron arrives home unexpectedly, she moves
into the old family lodge, where the silent and
mysterious Cliff Forrester has been living in seclusion
for years....

WATCH FOR ALL TWELVE BOOKS
OF THE TYLER SERIES
Available wherever Harlequin books are sold

Janet Dailey
Americana

A romantic tour of America through fifty favorite
Harlequin Presents novels, each one set in a different
state, and researched by Janet and her husband, Bill.
A journey of a lifetime in one cherished collection.

Don't miss the romantic stories set in these states:

Available wherever
Harlequin books are sold.

■ H A R L E Q U I N ®

A Calendar of Romance

Be a part of American Romance's year-long celebration of love
and the holidays of 1992. Celebrate those special times each
month with your favorite authors.

Next month, live out a St. Patrick's Day fantasy in

MARCH

S	M	T	W	T	F	S
1	2	3	4	5	6	7
8	9	10	11	12	13	14
15	16	17			20	21
22	23					
29						

**#429 FLANNERY'S
RAINBOW
by Julie Kistler**

Read all the books in *A Calendar of Romance*, coming to you one
per month, all year, only in American Romance.

HARLEQUIN Temptation®

Rebels & Rogues

All men are not created equal. Some are rough around the edges. Tough-minded but tenderhearted. Incredibly sexy. The tempting fulfillment of every woman's fantasy.

When it's time to fight for what they believe in, to win that special woman, our Rebels and Rogues are heroes at heart.

Cameron: He came on a mission from light-years away... then a flesh-and-blood female changed everything.

THE OUTSIDER by *Barbara Delinsky*.
Temptation #385, March 1992.

Jake: He was a rebel with a cause... but a beautiful woman threatened it all.

THE WOLF by *Madeline Harper*.
Temptation #389, April 1992.

At Temptation, 1992 is the Year of Rebels and Rogues. Look for twelve exciting stories, one each month, about bold and courageous men.

Don't miss upcoming books by your favorite authors, including Candace Schuler, JoAnn Ross and Janice Kaiser.

AVAILABLE WHEREVER HARLEQUIN BOOKS ARE SOLD.
RR-3

my VALENTINE 1992

Celebrate the most romantic day of the year with
MY VALENTINE 1992—a sexy new collection of four
romantic stories written by our famous Temptation
authors:

GINA WILKINS
KRISTINE ROLOFSON
JOANN ROSS
VICKI LEWIS THOMPSON

My Valentine 1992—an exquisite escape into a romantic
and sensuous world.

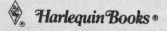

◆ **Harlequin Books** ®

VAL-92-R